BATTLING
THE
BLUESTOCKING

PARADIGM
PRESS

MARTHA KEYES

To Micah and Jonah
Thank you for your "help" typing some of the words in this book. May you receive credit for any stubborn typos, but more importantly, may you support your future spouses as heartily as Phineas supports Sarah and your dad supports me.

Chapter One

PHINEAS

BIRCHLEIGH HALL, AUGUST 1819

"Why not Bettencourt *Hall* or Bettencourt *Manor*? That is all I am asking."

I hardly paid my brother Valentine's comment any heed as, one by one, I placed the stack of books beside me into the traveling trunk, crossing off each title from my penciled list.

"Bettencourt Court is so … repetitive. So inelegant. It begs whether the family will be receptive to your tutoring, Phin. I cannot think highly of the mind of a man who would choose such a name to represent his family's legacy."

My brow furrowed as I reached the end of the list, one title glaring back at me, still uncrossed. "I doubt the Earl of Bettencourt cares much for your opinion." My gaze scoured the neat line of books filling the trunk in search of the missing one. I was certain, though, I had brought the book with me from home.

I glanced at Valentine. He stretched out in the chair beside the bed, legs crossing leisurely in front of him while he flipped through the pages of the precise book I was searching for.

I had stayed with my sister, Diana, and her husband, Marmaduke, for the last two days—ever since they had sent me word of the sudden situation Duke, as we called him, had discovered for me. Valentine and his wife, Rebecca, had joined yesterday.

I rose from my knees, walked over, and took the book unceremoniously from Valentine. He made no attempt to stop me, which was as I had expected, for I had never seen a book in his hands unless it was being wielded as a weapon.

"Is the earl not in possession of a library?" Valentine asked as I set the book in its place and crossed it off the list. There was such satisfaction in crossing off the final item from a list— almost as much as there was in the way the books fit perfectly into my trunk.

"Not having been to Bettencourt Court, I couldn't say."

"Phineas…" Valentine's brow cocked as he watched me in amusement.

I busied myself with closing the trunk.

When I forbore responding, he continued, "You would never take a tutoring position at an estate without first making certain of the quality of its library."

I secured the latch, then went over to the bell cord next to Valentine and gave it a firm tug. "Duke assured me it has a fine one." My brother-in-law had gone to no small trouble to secure the position for me. It was so ideal as to be nearly miraculous— not that I put much stock in talk of miracles; everything had an explanation if one had the determination to understand it.

Miracle or not, though, I could not have asked for a better situation: firstly, tutor to the son of a wealthy earl at an estate not far from my family—whatever Valentine thought of the name of that estate; secondly, acting curate to the local vicar, who, if reports were to be believed, would soon advance to another position in the church, making me the most obvious replacement.

Valentine rose from his chair and looked at the collection in the trunk. "Then why the preoccupation with taking so many of your own books? You will break the backs of the servants unfortunate enough to be saddled with that trunk."

Perhaps I *was* taking too many, but the thought of finding myself without my most prized works was not one I could stomach.

When the servants appeared, Valentine's words proved nearly true. Both of us were obliged to help the footmen carry the trunk down the stairs, then out to the waiting carriage.

Valentine wiped at his brow with his forearm and loosened his cravat once it was secured in place. It was a fine Kentish August day, which was to say a very warm one. "Remind me to absent myself the next time you move," Valentine said.

"He doesn't mean that." Rebecca descended the steps energetically, despite her growing stomach. Behind her, Duke and Diana held the hand of their toddling daughter. Charlotte struggled against their protective hold, undeterred by the dangers posed by the uneven stone steps before her.

"Oh, but I do mean it," Valentine said, receiving his wife in his arms.

"Is that everything?" Duke asked me.

I looked at the other list I had made, detailing the relatively short catalog of things I needed to take with me. "Yes," I said firmly. My lists might seem unnecessary to some, but they made me confident I was not forgetting anything, and I was in dire need of confidence just now.

Charlotte attempted to break free from her parents once the steps had been navigated. Her apparent destination was the horses, one of which was pawing at the gravel.

Diana let out a sound of frustration as she tried to wrangle her daughter. "She is determined to be the death of both herself and me."

Duke gathered Charlotte into his arms. "It is anyone's guess where she inherited such a characteristic."

Diana shot her husband a look. "*I* have always been the picture of well-considered decisions, as my brothers can attest to." She looked at Valentine, who took the opportunity to inspect his nails rather than confirm. Her gaze flicked to me.

"I should be going," I said, avoiding her just as Valentine had done. "Bettencourt Court is a matter of twenty-two miles, and at a rate of six miles per hour, that puts me there"—I glanced at my pocket watch—"just shy of four o'clock."

"Well," Diana said in a voice saturated with offense, "so much for loyalty to family." She took Charlotte from Duke's arms. "Come, love. It seems we are unappreciated in present company."

"Not at all." Valentine came over and put out his arms for Charlotte. She readily leaned toward him, leaving her mother without a second thought. "I very much appreciate Charlotte."

"Traitor," Diana hissed at her daughter, though the kiss she planted on her capped head belied the insult. "Well, Phineas. I suppose this is goodbye for now. We shall visit one of these Sundays to hear one of your sermons, so it shan't be too long before we see you again."

"Speak for yourself," Valentine said, tickling Charlotte mercilessly.

"We shall certainly be attending one of your sermons," Rebecca said. "Though he will never admit it, Valentine missed you terribly while you were at Cambridge."

Valentine ignored this comment, busy as he was turning Charlotte upside down, but I happened to believe it. Thanks to Diana, I knew it was Valentine who insisted on coming to visit in order to see me before I left for my new position. I was not one for sentimentality myself, so it didn't bother me he would refuse to acknowledge such a thing.

"Oh," Rebecca said suddenly, "I had nearly forgotten! We have a parting gift. One moment." She went up the stairs and disappeared into the house while my family took turns embracing me.

For the most part, I looked with anticipation on this new venture in life. I was confident in my abilities and qualifications. But every now and then, nerves would creep in. It was no small thing to live in the house of an earl—or to teach a future earl. My father was a respected admiral, but I was only a third son.

Rebecca returned moments later, a set of books in hand and a servant following behind carrying even more.

"Good heavens, Becca," Valentine said. "The last thing in the world Phineas needs is more books."

"You only say that because you don't wish to give them up." She turned to me. "Valentine and I enjoyed these, and we thought you would, as well."

"Correction," said Valentine, returning Charlotte to Diana. "Rebecca enjoyed them. I was subjected to her reading them aloud each night, the sound of which put me to sleep with astounding reliability."

Rebecca cocked an eyebrow and shook her head subtly.

"In any case," Valentine continued, "you will find plenty of examples for what *not* to do as a vicar within those pages."

"Thank you," I said sincerely, curious what sort of books they might be to contain such information and eager to acquaint myself with them. There was no feeling comparable to opening a new book, its contents a mystery. And if there was anything to guide me in this new venture, I was anxious to know of it.

As my trunk of books was already closed and strapped to the top of the carriage, I instructed the books be set inside on the seats. That way, I could peruse them on the journey.

It wasn't long before final farewells were said and Birchleigh

Hall slipped away from view, the carriage rumbling along the road to Bettencourt Court.

Impatient for a distraction from my growing nerves, I picked up one of the books on the seat across from me, choosing the one with a paper protruding from its pages. I let it fall open in my hands where the note sat. I unfolded it, adjusted my glasses, and read:

Dear Phineas,

May these books provide a different sort of enjoyment and learning to you, for many of life's most precious truths, including those about love, are only to be found in fiction.

Your loving sister-in-law,

Rebecca (Valentine insists I not include his name here, but I assure you, he enjoyed the books every bit as much as I did.)

My brows pulled together, and, turning the page, I read the title.

Sense and Sensibility: A Novel in three volumes by A Lady

I eyed the abundance of books gifted to me with wariness. These were not treatises on how to operate as an effective man of the cloth. They were novels, the lot of them.

The first word of the title couldn't but intrigue me, for I valued sense highly. But sensibility... that was a weakness I avoided.

I put a thumb to the pages, a flicker of anticipation warring with the certainty that Rebecca was mistaken in her assessment of their value. Truth was of utmost interest to me; truths about *love*, though... well, I had long since given up the search for those.

I shut the cover.

I would need to see that these were moved to my book trunk at one of the inns along the way. The last thing I needed was for

Lord Bettencourt to worry I would be exposing his son—or myself—to the reading of frivolous novels.

Chapter Two

PHINEAS

ettencourt Court. It rose before the carriage, looming larger with every passing second, its columned, symmetrical façade attesting to its relatively recent construction. The stone on the shorter wings that flanked the central bulk of the estate was cleaner, implying they might be an even more recent addition.

I removed my spectacles and pulled a small cloth from the pocket of my waistcoat, rubbing the lenses, then replacing them on my nose. This was to be my new home for the foreseeable future, and it was far grander even than I had imagined.

Surely, Lord Bettencourt could have had his pick of tutors. It was only thanks to Duke's acquaintance with the earl and his efforts on my behalf that I had been offered the position. That meant I needed to prove myself quickly and irrefutably.

Watching the servants—five of them—take away the dreaded book trunk with sour glances at me did not inspire confidence I would be welcome, but there was nothing to be done about that now.

I was met at the door by the butler, Hughes, a man on the shady side of fifty, who looked over me with all the practice of a seasoned servant. As he informed me his lordship was awaiting my arrival in the study, I was left to assume he found my appearance acceptable enough to be presented.

The entry hall of Bettencourt Court was made to impress—or, in my case, intimidate—with checkered stone floors, sage green walls, fine Persian rugs, and a fireplace with an elaborate mantel. Plasterwork more intricate than I had ever before seen dominated the areas above my head, decorating the ceiling, the foot-tall crown molding, and the space above each of the four doors that led off the hall.

Hughes led me past the cantilever staircase, which seemed to float effortlessly in the air, then through a door on the left. A window-lined corridor greeted us, and my gaze strayed to the views the tall glass afforded of the area behind Bettencourt Court: a long stretch of grass and, farther still, lawns where sheep grazed serenely amongst the trees.

Hughes stopped outside one of the doors and glanced at me as though warning me not to follow him. Pulling open the door, he stepped just out of sight. I reminded myself that the man inside held my entire future in his hands, and taking in a breath and straightening my shoulders, I tried to channel the easy confidence and undeniable leadership I had always admired in my older brother, Theo.

Hughes emerged a moment later and opened the door for me to pass through.

Lord Bettencourt was seated behind a grand mahogany desk, but he rose to his feet upon my entrance. He was younger than I had expected—in his late forties, perhaps—with a large but straight nose, hair teetering between blond and gray, and a kind enough countenance.

"Mr. Donovan," he said, his gaze traveling over me in curiosity. "How good to meet you. Your brother-in-law has spoken so very highly of you, I have been anxious for this moment. Do have a seat." He gestured to the chair opposite his desk.

I sat on the edge of the seat. "I must thank you, too, my lord, for the opportunity you have given me to—"

He waved away my gratitude as he sat down. "None of that, if you please. I have employed you for a specific task, and I would not have done so if I did not trust Mr. Russell's opinion of your abilities. I should warn you, perhaps, that my son, George—Lord Danneville to you—has already had two tutors since our return to the country."

I nodded slowly, my unease increasing. Had Duke known this and decided against telling me? Or was he as ignorant of the fact as I had been? "I see…"

"Unfortunately, George was not making the progress I had hoped for under their tutelage, but I hope this will change at your hands." He smiled, apparently unaware of the threat his words implied.

I gave a nod. "I am confident that, given time to understand his needs, Lord Danneville and I will manage to find the success you wish for, Lord Bettencourt."

"I am happy to hear you say so," he said. "I would like for you to meet him now. He is just in the library, unless he has escaped, which is entirely possible. Shall we?" He didn't wait for a response; I doubted he was accustomed to *having* to wait for such a thing. He could phrase orders like questions with the assurance they would be obeyed.

As for my part, the word *library* stirred an insatiable curiosity in me, equal, in fact, to my anxiousness to meet my charge. Duke was a trustworthy man by all accounts, but there was no saying whether he and I shared the same ideas of what a truly robust library would comprise.

Lord Bettencourt led the way toward the entry hall. "Mr. Vickers is also looking forward to making your acquaintance, though you can be sure I made it clear to him that your priority is here at Bettencourt Court."

"Mr. Vickers?" I asked, though there was only one person he could possibly be referring to.

"The vicar," he clarified.

Vicar Vickers. Of course. How else would the man who served the parish surrounding Bettencourt Court be named?

"You will meet with him the day after tomorrow at the vicarage, where he will make known to you what to expect of your curacy." He stopped before a door on the right, which stood ajar, pushing it open as I held my breath.

The library.

It was amazing how quickly and reliably four solid walls could transport one—or offer the prospect of future transportation—and the library at Bettencourt Court provided that prospect in spades. A rectangular room, its walls were floor-to-ceiling mahogany shelves of books, uninterrupted in their beauty save for a fireplace, a door on either side of the room, and two large windows.

I glanced with a hint of regret at the sources of light, imagining what books might have filled the shelves in their place. But they were necessary evils. Years of clandestine assignations with books in dim light had taught me that the dark significantly reduced my reading endurance, giving me headaches and making my eyes itch.

I let my gaze scour the nearest shelves, hoping to glimpse a few titles. I was nearly certain I could see Plautus—or perhaps it was Propertius.

"Mr. Donovan?"

I whipped my head around to Lord Bettencourt, who was looking at me with a mixture of expectation and concern.

I straightened, my neck warming behind my cravat. There would be plenty of time to inspect these shelves later, but I would have no such opportunity if I failed to impress the earl now. I moved my gaze to the less interesting parts of the library—the barren, nearly bookless center, where there was a slowly spinning globe, a desk with a large, open atlas, and a sofa. My gaze stopped, noting for the first time the young boy sitting there, arms folded across his chest, a mulish expression on his face.

"George, I would like you to meet your new tutor, Mr. Phineas Donovan. Mr. Donovan, this is my son, Lord Danneville."

I made a bow I thought appropriate for a ten-year-old viscount, but I must have done it ill, for his expression remained unaltered.

"Very good," said the earl, apparently pleased with the introduction. "I shall leave the two of you to become acquainted. You may begin lessons in earnest tomorrow."

And then he left.

Chapter Three

SARAH

I stretched my neck to see past the stack of books in my arms as I took the wide stairs. I kept a selection of books in my room—well, rather more than a selection, for there were two bookcases of them—but this particular assortment would be required in the library for some time now. George's geographical knowledge was woefully deficient. Of course, I could say the same of a great number of other topics, but I thought I might have the most success if I started with this one.

"Would you like help with your burden, my lady?" the footman asked as I reached the bottom.

"Books are a blessing, not a burden, Collins. And thank you, but no." I was quite content with the load I carried, for it meant the time had come in earnest: I would be taking over my brother's education. It wasn't clear how much time I would have before other parts of my plan fell into place, but I meant to take advantage of every moment I had with him. Father would be unable to deny that I was the most fitting, the most qualified tutor, for I would succeed where all others had failed. He wouldn't be able to avoid acknowledging the value of my intellectual pursuits.

The heavy door to the library was closed, and I sighed with annoyance. Both arms were occupied, so I had no choice but to kick the door to signal my need to enter. I glanced behind me before doing so to ensure Father was nowhere in sight.

"Open the door, George. I promise I shall only make you do half an hour more." I paused. "A quarter of an hour, then."

The door opened, and I took a step back at the unfamiliar man before me. Blond hair a sandier variety than mine, wiry spectacles framing blue eyes, and a colorless expression stared back at me. The man's eyes lingered on my face long enough for me to feel the need to clear my throat.

He blinked, and his eyes shot to the books in my arms. "Forgive me," he said hurriedly. "Allow me…"

He slipped his arms under the stack, but as mine already occupied the space, his hands slid over mine in a way that made me startle.

"Forgive me," he repeated, retracting and repositioning his hands under the stack.

"I do not require assistance," I said, pulling away from him. His hands were already gripping the bottom, though, and my movement caused him to stumble toward me, sending the books bumping into my chest and stomach, creating a sort of book sandwich as our bodies caged them between us.

My determination not to accept his help warred with my distaste for a level of proximity which allowed me to see that his lashes were not sandy, but closer to the color of tar.

The latter inclination emerged victorious, and I released my hold on the books.

So did he.

They tumbled to the ground, smashing my toes, one after the other. A few choice curses flew from my tongue, as much on account of the possible damage to the books as for the pain shooting through my feet.

Face filling with the heat of exasperation, I dropped to my knees. And so did he.

Our heads met in a jarring collision of skulls.

"Forgive me," the man said, one hand on his own head, the other on mine.

I slid my hand to my newest injury, displacing his. "We are fast approaching seventy times seven, sir."

His gaze came up, the hint of a smile pulling up at one corner of his mouth, as though he found unexpected humor in my response. It was charming and terribly out of place, for if ever there was a situation without humor, it was this one: toes and head throbbing, my precious books scattered about the floor, and my temper in precisely the sort of state I tried to prevent it ever reaching. Women of intellect had a difficult enough time being taken seriously by our male counterparts without being discounted due to rapid shifts in mood.

The stranger and I worked to gather up the fallen books, he with a growing stack in his arms, I with one in mine. His gaze tripped to the ones in my arms every few seconds, his bespectacled eyes surveying the titles, judging them. Judging *me*, it almost seemed.

We tussled for a moment over the last book, but he seemed to think better of trying to win, for he let me take it. I rose to my feet, one arm cradling the books, the other brushing at my disordered hair. "At the risk of sounding impolite, sir, *who in heaven's name are you?*"

He followed me up to his feet. "Forgi—" He stopped himself, apparently remembering my annoyance with his constant requests for forgiveness.

"He's my new tutor." George sat on the couch, watching the scene play out with an amused smile on his face, but his arms crossed in a petulant way that made him look half his age. "Gullivan's his name."

"Donovan," the man corrected. "Phineas Donovan."

I hardly heard him, too focused on what George had first said. "Tutor?"

Mr. Donovan gave a curt nod.

I stared for a moment, my chest rising and falling more deeply with each passing second. *This* man, a tutor? He looked more like a frequenter of Jackson's boxing club. Certainly, he had spectacles, and that gave him a sort of *air* of intelligence, I supposed, but I wasn't foolish enough to focus solely on those. He was young, broad-shouldered, handsome-faced—

I pinched my lips together. It was impossible that he was George's new tutor. *I* was George's new tutor.

I spun on my heel and, half of my books in arm, half still in Mr. Donovan's, I left the room.

Hurt and frustration battled within me as I stalked through the house. Neither emotion was ideal, but of the two, I preferred the latter. How could Father do this? How could he not have even *told* me of it? I took in deep, calming breaths as I approached the study, but there was simply not enough time for them to take the desired effect.

Father was poring over account books with the steward.

"You hired a new tutor?"

Both men looked up. Father met my gaze for a moment, sighed, then nodded at Mr. Wright, who made his way over to where I was near the door, bowed, and saw himself out.

"Sarah," Father said, sitting with a sigh. "We have discussed this. George needs a—"

"He does *not* need a man, Father. He needs an education, and I am more than qualified to provide him with one."

"Hardly more qualified than Mr. Donovan."

I smiled humorlessly. "That child of a man in the library, you mean?"

Father smiled slightly. "He is three years your senior, Sarah."

"That may be, but as he cannot even form a coherent

16

sentence, I tend to doubt his ability to educate the son of an earl."

"If he could not form such a sentence, I can only think it a result of you pestering him. He comes highly recommended."

I tried to keep my tone even. Father would tire of me the moment I gave my anger full rein, but my hands shook, as though the emotion my voice lacked was being stored there instead. "Just as the last two tutors came highly recommended, and look at what became of them. How can you truly prefer to pay the exorbitant sum you have offered George's tutors when I would do a better job at no cost at all to you?"

His lips pinched together. "You have other things you should be focusing on, Sarah."

Marriage. He meant I should focus on marriage. But I had other plans—ones that did not require me to be dictated to by a man or become his chattel. No, I would follow in the footsteps of Lady Hester Stanhope, making a name for myself and receiving recognition for my ideas and intellect, just as she had done—and was still doing.

I could hardly tell Father of those aspirations, though. Lady Hester might be the daughter of an earl, just as I was, but I was under no illusion that Father would approve of her adventures and undertakings. Neither could I tell him of the letter I had sent to his cousin two days ago in pursuit of my hopes. I shuddered to think of his reaction. Cousin Arthur would receive that letter shortly, and my fingers shook with mixed anticipation and anxiety at the thought.

Mother came up behind me, soft-footed and elegant enough to have entered the room undetected. She threaded her arm through mine. "Come, Sarah," she said softly. "Your father is not finished with Mr. Wright, and it is not polite to interrupt. You and I can discuss things together privately."

The fact that Father had already returned his attention to the account book made me wish to refuse. But Mother was much more reasonable than Father, and her comment on my interruption held a veiled reminder to me: Father was intent I display the accomplishments worthy of an earl's daughter, including, but certainly not limited to, politeness. Failing to meet those expectations made him less likely to pay heed to my arguments and wishes.

I forced myself to take a deep breath, declined to send a look of displeasure at the top of Father's balding head, and allowed Mother to pull me from the room.

"He should have told me," I said once Mr. Wright had closed the door to the study behind him. "He knows very well I have been wishing to tutor George myself. Did I not teach him to read? To write?" Father would never understand what a wrestle even those things had been, for George was not easily taught.

"It happened very quickly, as I understand it. He saw Mr. Russell just a few days ago. Before that, I believe he was truly considering allowing you to undertake things."

I clenched my eyes shut in frustration. I had been so close. If not for this Mr. Donovan, it would be me in the library with George right now. He would be making progress and doing so without the stinging remarks of tutors who would never understand him.

Mother opened the door to the breakfast room, leading us through it and into the parlor. "You know, my dear, if you showed more interest in marrying, I think he would be more apt to consider your proposal seriously." She pressed my hand with hers. "We want you to be happy, Sarah, and for your future to be secure."

"For the earldom's future to be secure," I corrected her. Father did not wish for me to be a drain on the estate's resources.

"That too, of course, and it is only natural. But it does not mean he has no thought for your happiness. The goals are not mutually exclusive. If we knew what sort of man took your fancy, we might help you find just such a gentleman."

"Perhaps if I knew, I would tell you." I was not at all certain that was true, though. I had little interest in marrying or in encouraging my parents to *help* me toward that end. Marriage was a secondary option to the one I was pursuing, and I very much hoped it would not prove necessary.

"Well," Mother said, "you are not one to let things go unknown, are you? I am certain with some observation and investigation, you could solve that question to your satisfaction."

Mother was both wise and intelligent, and she understood me in a way Father did not. She knew I could not resist anything framed as a problem to be solved.

She faced me, her eyes surveying me, her hand still holding one of mine. "You wish for freedom, Sarah, and the fact of the matter, little though you may relish it, is that in this world, a woman's greatest freedom can only be achieved through marriage."

"Or widowhood."

Mother chuckled softly. "Yes, but the route to that destination necessarily passes *through* marriage." Her soft eyes twinkled a bit. "And you may find it difficult to persuade a man to marry you if he knows you are hoping for his demise."

"He needn't know it." Just as Mother and Father didn't need to know I was not seriously considering marriage. Not yet.

She cocked a brow.

I sighed. "Very well. If you think it will appease Father, I will try to determine what... *takes my fancy* in a gentleman, as you put it." It was prudent to have a secondary plan in place in case mine failed. And perhaps if I came to my parents with an impossible list of qualities, they would be indefinitely engaged in the search while I saw to George's education. But that would mean getting rid of Mr. Donovan first. "In the meantime, though, I fully intend to ensure the quality of the education Mr. Donovan is providing for George."

"Good heavens. What does that mean?"

"Only that I will be spending a great deal of time in the library."

"Sarah…"

"I shan't interfere. I shall only observe."

She regarded me with incredulity.

"Unless there is good reason for my intervention," I conceded.

And I trusted there would be. George could be maddening to those who did not understand him—his refusal to focus, his tendency toward mischief. And being new, Mr. Donovan would undoubtedly suffer at least a few pranks at his student's hands.

Mother smiled, touching a hand to my coiffure. "It makes me happy that you care for your brother so much, Sarah."

"For his education," I corrected, smiling teasingly. "I cannot be having a dunce for a brother."

Mother laughed softly, but she saw through me. I *did* want to ensure George could discuss and debate with the best of his peers as he matured and took on the title one day. But I also cared deeply that he be treated with kindness, that he be protected from the people who might mock the difficulty learning presented him.

"As long as you do not neglect your other tasks," Mother said.

I suppressed a sigh. "I shall entertain and socialize and sew and practice at the pianoforte as I always do."

She held my gaze, understanding passing between us. She would ensure Father made no fuss over my supervision of George's tutelage. That was how it had always been. She had ensured I was allowed ample time and material for reading, provided I satisfied Father's wish that I excel in all the areas women of breeding were expected to. Books in exchange for accomplishments.

While I had resented all the lessons in dancing, sewing, singing, and the like at the time—they had merely been obstacles between me and the things I truly cared about—I was glad for them now. It had equipped me in the perfect way to follow in the footsteps of Lady Hester. It was the combination of social graces and intellect which had allowed her, as an unmarried woman and the daughter of an earl, to take on the role of hostess for the prime minister. If she could do such a thing, why could I not do the same for Cousin Arthur? She had made a name for herself, become respected for her own mind, and maintained her independence. And all without marriage. What better future could I hope for?

Until I could secure such a position with the help of Cousin Arthur, though, I would set my mind to what was currently within my power: George's education. Mr. Donovan would buckle under the pressure of educating my brother, just as the other tutors had, and the sooner that happened, the sooner order could be restored and true progress could be made.

Chapter Four

PHINEAS

As tutor in the house of an earl, I occupied neither the world of my employers nor the world of their servants. I inhabited the strange and perplexing space in between.

It suited me well. While I wished to be liked by my employers and their servants, I preferred to be liked *passively* —the sort of mild affection that might cause one to smile serenely at the thought of a person and forget them the next moment. I could spend hours discussing Dryden and Dante, but navigating the waters of polite conversation was a different matter entirely. I inevitably came away from those encounters rehearsing all the ways I had misspoken or given unintentional offense.

To my relief, neither Lord Bettencourt nor his wife—a very amiable woman with a ready smile and a soothing voice— invited me to dine with the family. My relief was acute, for it allowed me to take both refuge and dinner in the solitude of my bedchamber.

The most pressing matter, of course, was to decide what the topic of study would be with Lord Danneville on the morrow.

My encounter with him had not been fruitful. In fact, I had struggled to get more than a word from him in response to any of my questions, until the entrance and baffling exit of that intriguing, mysterious woman. I could only assume she was a relative of Lord Bettencourt's—a niece, perhaps, making a summer visit.

I had been distracted after her abrupt departure, left to wonder what I had done to annoy her, for it was clear I *had*. Of course, dropping a stack of books on her feet and then knocking my head into hers had certainly not helped matters, but based on the way she had looked at me, her dislike of me had started before that.

A perusal of the books she had left in my arms—an excellent collection of geographical studies, including one I had never seen on the Rattanakosin Kingdom—had nearly sent me after her.

Unfortunately, my interest in the books had provided an opportunity for Lord Danneville's escape. I had been unable to find him thereafter, as reluctant to scour an unfamiliar house as I was to admit to Lord Bettencourt I had lost his son after no longer than fifteen minutes in his company.

I knelt before the trunks the servants had brought to my bedchamber, hesitating for a moment between the one with my clothing and the one full of books, then selecting the latter. Naturally.

To my knowledge, I had never been disliked by a woman. This was not a feat I claimed with any measure of pompousness. It was merely that a prerequisite to being disliked was being noticed, and I generally failed even at that. My brother Theo had always been the strapping officer, rising through the ranks with ease; Valentine had been the rogue, fomenting gossip and turning heads with his brooding intrigue; Diana could have commanded her own fleet if circumstance had allowed it.

All of them had married within two years of one other. And

I... well, I was the forgotten Donovan. People rarely spoke of marriage and me within the same sentence, for I was married to books, to the pursuit of knowledge, and I was content with that. For the most part.

I had studied the works of Petronius, Ovid, and Catullus, but the subject of women remained shrouded in mystery. In a way, such works were like the geographical maps the young, anonymous woman had brought to the library—representations of someone *else's* knowledge of something. They were indisputably useful for certain purposes, but frankly nothing like lived experience.

I had learned that during my interminable time in the Navy. To know the location and borders of the Aegean Sea was nothing at all like navigating its waters. It was precisely why I had left the Navy as soon as my father had permitted it. I preferred intellect to experience. Intellect allowed for order; experience was chaos.

I opened the trunk lid, and the books Rebecca had given me stared back. *Sense and Sensibility, Pride and Prejudice, Emma, Mansfield Park, Northanger Abbey, Persuasion.*

I pulled Rebecca's note from its place again.

Many of life's most precious truths, including those about love, can only be found in fiction.

It was an intriguing idea, but I was supremely skeptical.

My brow furrowed as I stared at the titles. I reached for the first one, drawn again to it by that first word in its title: *sense.* I had never read a novel, but the way people spoke of them made it clear that sense was precisely what they lacked.

But people had often said things I had found from my own study to be false. And surely, I owed it to Rebecca to at least make a quick perusal of her generous gift.

T he closing of a door somewhere in the vicinity brought my head up in the middle of a paragraph. I winced and put a hand to my neck, which had bowed over to the point that my nose had been mere inches from the pages of the book on my lap.

My bedchamber was nearly dark, something which must have happened so gradually I had not noticed. The quality of the light told me it was nigh on nine o'clock.

Good gracious. I snapped the book shut.

I had been reading for quite some time. And not just reading —reading a *novel*. For more than two hours.

Not that it mattered so greatly to me whether Miss Lucy Steele's confidences about Mr. Ferrars were to be trusted. I frowned. But, then, how else would she be in possession of a miniature of him? Surely, that meant *something*. But what, then, was one left to think of Mr. Ferrars?

My brow furrowed deeper. Here I had come to trust the cur. And poor Miss Dashwood…

I tapped a finger on the cover, then opened the book determinedly. Only the depraved stopped in the middle of a chapter. This was a matter of principle; it had nothing to do with wanting to read more. I would finish the chapter honorably, then set my mind to tomorrow's lessons.

I stood by the desk in the library while Lord Danneville sat across from me, fiddling with the model ship before him. In the northeast corner of the room, the young woman from yesterday's unfortunate encounter sat reading in a chair. At least I had not given her such a distaste for me that she could not bear to be in the same room.

Lady Sarah Danneville was her name, as I had discovered

from one of the maids this morning. She was *not*, however, a niece of the earl's; she was his daughter. Duke had conveniently failed to mention the existence of any other children in Lord Bettencourt's family. Not that her existence changed anything; it was merely a fact, but like any fact, I preferred to know it rather than be ignorant.

Unlike the fact of her existence, though, her presence in the library I found... unhelpful. Perhaps it was the way the morning sun pouring through the window fell on her silvery blonde hair. The way it reflected the light might feasibly blind a man. Or it might have been the fact that, despite her gaze remaining on the book she held, her lips turned up in a smile every now and then, making me wonder whether she was finding humor in her book or in my unsuccessful attempts to converse with her brother.

I had not prepared a lesson for the young viscount last night. It was not because I had stayed up until past midnight to finish *Sense and Sensibility*. That would be grossly irresponsible, though I *had* stayed up to finish all three of its volumes.

No, it was because I realized it would be most sensible for me to first gain an understanding of what Lord Danneville had already been taught before launching into any course of study. It wouldn't do to waste time preparing lessons that might be unnecessary.

I took off my glasses and cleaned the lenses with my cloth. They weren't dirty, but I was nervous. Lady Sarah made me anxious, listening to every word I uttered to her brother. It sapped all the confidence with which I had imbued myself before coming downstairs earlier.

"Have you studied Homer or Virgil yet?" I asked the young viscount.

"Who?"

I set the cloth on the table and put my glasses on to inspect Lord Danneville's expression. I wasn't certain whether he had simply not heard me or if he was unfamiliar with the names. I sincerely hoped it was the former. At age ten, he should certainly know at least *those* names.

"*Whom,*" I said, determined Lady Sarah should know I was not ignorant of proper grammar. "Homer and Virgil are the objects of the verb *to study,* so the question should take the accusative case. But returning to my question: have you studied Homer or Virgil yet?" I repeated it more clearly this time.

"Never heard of them." Lord Danneville touched a finger to one of the ship cannons, looked up at me, and made the noise of an explosion as he held my gaze.

Charming.

And there was that smile again from Lady Sarah.

I focused my gaze on the cover of the book she held. I could just see the title, and it made me frown. *Ajax* was not a humorous play—not unless one was deranged.

Lord Danneville rose suddenly. "I need the privy."

I didn't believe him; he was bored and using any excuse to leave. The beginnings of panic crept into my stomach. My tutelage was off to an unfortunate start. But I could hardly refuse him the privy, and he didn't give me the opportunity to do so. He merely left the library.

Like his father, he was accustomed to doing as he pleased. And he did not please to listen to me.

Lady Sarah still smiled to herself—a silent but persistent mocking. It was in my best interests to make a friend of her—to try to undo the damage of our first encounter.

"Enjoying your reading of Sophocles?" I asked.

Her gaze flicked up, followed by her chin. "Immensely." Her gaze returned to the page.

"Is it your first time?"

One corner of her mouth tugged upward, though her eyes never wavered from the book. "Fourth."

My brows went up. The beautiful daughter of an earl—for she *was* undeniably beautiful—who had read *Ajax* four times?

Experience told me not to believe such a thing. "And what is your opinion of it?"

She gave a little sigh and closed the book, leaving a finger to guard her place. The expression she leveled at me told me she understood my question held an implicit challenge. "A masterful study in the character of a hero, of course."

An entirely defensible opinion, surely, but not one that would require a close reading. "That hero being…"

She looked like I might belong at Bedlam. "Ajax. The eponymous hero."

My brow furrowed. "Hm."

"What other hero do you imagine there could *be* in the play?" she said, nettled.

"Odysseus, of course."

"Odysseus?" She might as well have spat the word. Indeed, the way she brushed her finger at the side of her mouth made me wonder if she *had* spat.

"Yes," I responded evenly.

She stood, keeping her eyes on me as she took slow steps in my direction. "Odysseus, who had less claim to Achilles's armor than Ajax and was awarded it only due to Athena's meddling? Odysseus, who pretended lunacy rather than muster the bravery to retrieve Helen of Troy after her abduction? Odysseus, who only offered *reluctantly* to fight Hector, where Ajax volunteered willingly and then defeated him? You think *he* is the hero of this play?"

Well, when she put it like that…

Her points were undeniably valid, and beyond that, they effectively demonstrated that her knowledge of Greek classics went well beyond *Ajax*. I had a sudden, fleeting fear that I was not the better read between the two of us.

But to concede would be an unforgivable admission of intellectual weakness in the man employed as a tutor to her brother. It was out of the question. It was also unnecessary. If there was anything I had learned at Cambridge, it was that a sharp intellect should be able to argue a position other than the one he personally espoused.

I took a slight step back, for Lady Sarah was now but two feet from me, and maintaining a safe distance from things I did not understand was the only way I knew of to ensure my safety.

"Certainly Odysseus had his failings," I conceded. "But in Sophocles's *Ajax*, I maintain he is still the hero more worthy of emulation. Despite Ajax's firm intention to murder him, Odysseus argues for a proper burial when Ajax takes his own life. It is only thanks to Odysseus that Ajax's body is not left for the vultures. And yet, despite how instrumental he was in ensuring said burial, he agrees to absent himself out of respect for Ajax, his rival."

"None of that would have happened if the armor had gone to Ajax in the first place, as it should have."

My heart beat a little more quickly at the excitement of debate. It was a novel feeling, for though I had enjoyed such activities at Cambridge, never had my opponent been quite so captivating—or feminine. It added an element of difficulty to my task, for I was not accustomed to long conversations with women. "Or perhaps it only appeared that way. Perhaps it was all a test to show Odysseus as the more meritorious of the two."

Her nostrils flared.

Good heavens. Never had I known anyone—much less a woman, who must be three or four years my junior—to be so invested in Greek literature.

Book still in hand, she folded her arms across her chest. "The only reason you can point to Odysseus as the better hero is because he lived well after Ajax, long enough to do a few distinguishing things."

I couldn't stop an incredulous laugh. "The entire *Odyssey* falling under the description of *a few distinguishing things?*"

She lifted a careless shoulder. "An unnecessarily long journey for which the success required a great deal of good fortune."

I shut my jaw, which had been hanging open. "Odysseus showed the strength of his mind, his ability to persuade, his even keel time and again. Ajax, on the other hand, was so beset by his own arrogance that he was easily duped by Athena."

Her lips pressed tightly together as she stared at me, her blue eyes bright and as piercing as Ajax's fatal sword. When her voice came, it was soft but trembling. "Well, just to make you aware, Mr. Donovan, the most recent rules of English grammar give preference to the use of the *objective case* rather than the *accusative case*."

The shift in subject made me blink. But only for a moment. "You refer to Murray's work?"

She nodded.

"I have a copy of *English Grammar* in my bedchamber, which I will of course utilize, but as I assume Lord Danneville's education thus far has focused on a Latin-based approach to English, I thought it best to speak of the accusative case until we can discuss the merits of Murray's assertions."

"Does this mean my lessons are over for the day?"

Our heads whirled around to find Lord Danneville a few feet away, staring at us with curiosity from his place beside the desk. I hadn't even noted his return from the privy.

"No," both Lady Sarah and I said in concert.

We glanced at one another.

"Do not let us keep you from your reading, my lady," I said. "It looks as though you have yet to reach the best parts of *Ajax*. Perhaps you will see things differently this time."

She smiled without warmth. "I sincerely doubt that."

My heart thumping, I turned toward Lord Danneville, uncomfortably aware that, while I had perhaps experienced moderate success in persuading Lady Sarah of my qualification for the position of tutor, I had in no way endeared myself to her. I was not one for passionate argument, but her persistence, her obvious understanding of the subject, and the knowledge that my future was at stake had elicited that reaction in me.

I took a seat at the desk, determined to focus on my charge, who was playing with the model ship again.

My fingers trembling, I pulled the spectacles from my face and reached instinctively for the cloth in my pocket. It was not there, though. It was sitting where I had left it—on the table. I was making all manner of thoughtless decisions today.

Taking it up, I rubbed the cloth on the lenses. If I continued to clean them with this much frequency, they would soon be rubbed away entirely.

I perched the frames in place and blinked. Everything was blurry, unfocused. I blinked again, but nothing changed. It was worse than if I had not been wearing them at all.

I removed them again and extended them away from me to a distance where my eyesight wasn't quite so poor. The glass was not clear, as it should have been. Instead, there was a film of some sort, shiny, swirling. It almost looked like oil.

A little sniggering drew my attention to Lord Danneville, who immediately covered his laughter with an unconvincing cough.

Observing him for a moment, I brought the cloth to my nose and sniffed. The unmistakable smell of lamp oil met my nostrils. The viscount must have taken the cloth on his expedition to the "privy" and dipped it in oil.

My heart began to trip and hasten, my forehead to sweat. It was not the first time I had been the victim of such a trick. My spectacles had been hidden, heated, painted—in short, anything my fellow sailors had concocted in order to amuse themselves. My father had done nothing to stop the tricks, for he had been of the opinion that such ribaldry amongst the ranks had the effect of naturally showing who was most resilient.

I had quickly observed that any reaction from me aggravated the bullying. So, I had instead forced myself to take the bullying in stride, ignoring it as well as I could. Such tricks had never ceased to affect me, to make me feel like a stranger and an oddity, but with practice, I managed to conceal it. They primarily became an annoyance due to the time it required to undo whatever mischief had been done, for it cut into the precious study time permitted me.

"Clever," I said, taking the cloth and putting it to the wire frame. "And timely, too. The hinges have been needing a bit of lubrication. If you had truly been trying to wreak havoc, some melted tallow on the lenses might have been used to better effect. Oil wipes away without too much trouble."

Lord Danneville was far enough from me, I could see the intrigued tilt of his lips even without my spectacles. "Tallow! By Jove, that would have been funny! And malodorous, too!" His brow furrowed. "Though, I could not have put melted tallow on the cloth without it hardening before I returned to the library, could I? I would have needed to put it directly onto the spectacles."

I nodded, pleased with his analytical approach to playing pranks.

His head tilted to the side as he regarded me. "Do you always wear your spectacles? I thought most people only wore them while reading."

"I prefer to wear them always, for I am rarely long without reading, and to take them off means to risk misplacing them"—I raised a brow—"or someone making mischief with them."

Lord Danneville smiled guiltily.

Surely, that counted as a measure of success. He was much more likely to agree to learn from me if he did not hate or disdain me.

It seemed, though, that in eliciting a smile from Lord Danneville, I had extinguished the one on Lady Sarah's lips. Or perhaps she was finally realizing a smile had no place on a person studying *Ajax*.

Chapter Five

SARAH

I t was not my proudest moment, certainly, but as there was no doubt in my mind that Mr. Donovan would eventually go the way of the other tutors, planting an idea or two in George's mind had simply been my way of speeding up the process. Once Mr. Donovan departed, George could settle into my tutelage, and as for Mr. Donovan... well, it was good for him, too, for he would waste less time at Bettencourt Court in the state of frustration inevitable for someone trying to force George to learn what he had decided against learning.

I had not told George to prank Mr. Donovan, though. Not in so many words, at least. I had merely pointed out how frustrating it must be for those who wore spectacles to lose or damage them. And when I had shortly thereafter mentioned the recent delivery of oil for the few lamps we had at Bettencourt Court... well, it had only been a matter of time before George's mind had jumped to the inevitable conclusion.

He was so very predictable. Or perhaps reliable was the better word.

Mr. Donovan, on the other hand, was nothing of the sort. I had anticipated he would react with aggravation to the prank when it became clear who was responsible; George was terrible at hiding his culpability. It was a harmless trick, but men's pride was so easily piqued, in my experience. I had hoped he might seek Father to report on George's behavior, as that was what the other tutors had done. Nothing was more likely to antagonize Father, for, while he himself had no patience at all with George's antics, he had even less for those who came expecting *him* to address them. Part of the generous wage he offered was for the management of George's difficult personality.

But Mr. Donovan had responded with a maddening amount of patience. Indeed, he had used the oil to lubricate the hinges of his spectacles.

As for our discussion of *Ajax*... I gripped the book more firmly in my hands, shifting uncomfortably in my chair as I stole a furtive glance at Mr. Donovan. He had put aside his oily glasses, leaving his profile looking bare. Some might admire the color of his hair, describing it as a light caramel. Personally, I would have described it as burnt sugar, rather, and burning sugar was a sad waste of a perfectly good thing. There was nothing admirable about it.

I returned my gaze to my book, still disappointed with myself for the interaction. I prided myself on my ability to discuss the classics. Indeed, I was anxious for anyone who might be willing to do so with me, but I had become frustratingly flustered with Mr. Donovan when he had offered such an opportunity.

It was more than the fact that he had pointed out the weaknesses in my opinions. In my life, Mr. Donovan was the embodiment of Odysseus, and I was Ajax. Father had given him the position that should have belonged to me, and that meant I could not admit the validity of any of his arguments without an implicit admission that he was more deserving than I to teach George.

It was insufferable. Mr. Donovan was insufferable.

I took the small, empty notebook that sat beside me and set it atop the pages of *Ajax*, opening it to where the small pencil sat, awaiting use. I hadn't truly intended to set my mind to the issue of what I would want in a husband, but now that Mother had attuned me to it, I had an idea or two, at least.

Not insufferable, I wrote on the first page. I stared in dissatisfaction at the double negative. Crossing it off firmly, beside it I wrote *sufferable*. It was a much more apt adjective, for that was the best I could hope for from a marriage—something I could at least bear suffering through.

Which reminded me...

Old, I added. The older, the better, for it would mean less time before I left the desert of marriage and entered the oasis of widowhood.

I thought for another moment, then wrote *Ajax, not Odysseus*. My discussion with Mr. Donovan had resulted in a number of emotions—excitement, frustration, not to mention a general discomposure on my part. It would be better to find a husband who did not inspire me with any emotions.

I closed the pencil inside the notebook and set it aside again, content that I had a start to the list. Of course, ideally, I would never even need the list, but it was best to be prepared.

Now I could again put my mind to the far more important task of reading Sophocles.

I had not read more than two sentences when my brow furrowed and I sent a sidelong glance at the notebook. In my disputations with Mr. Donovan, I had cast myself as Ajax and he as Odysseus. In this notebook, though, I had implied I wished for a *husband* who would be like Ajax. So, was I Ajax? Or was this hypothetical husband of mine Ajax? The metaphor was becoming quite muddled.

Nevermind that. The mark of a truly good metaphor was that it could be interpreted in more than one way.

"Are the pages stuck together?"

I brought my head up and found Mr. Donovan's gaze on me.

"It has been some time since you turned a page," he explained. "I merely wondered if the pages had perhaps become stuck. Unfortunately, some printers do not allow the ink to dry long enough before laying the pages atop each other, resulting in their adhering together. I have my own copy of *Ajax* in my bedchamber and would be more than happy to lend it to you if you wish."

My face pulsed with heat. I had been staring at the same page for some time now, too distracted to read—distracted thinking, at least in part, of Mr. Donovan.

I smiled as best I could. "The pages turn quite satisfactorily, I thank you. I simply prefer a close reading of the text."

His eyes glinted appreciatively at my answer. "I quite agree. That explains the notes you are taking."

I stared at him for a moment, then followed his gaze to the notebook beside me. I snatched it up, as though he might suddenly come over and peruse it himself. "Yes. Copious notes."

He smiled slightly, and I wished he would put his glasses back on. His face looked so… aggravatingly naked without the metal frames.

"I would be interested to see how your notes compare to mine," he said.

I gripped the notebook more tightly, determined that he should never so much as touch it. Not that he would understand what I had written. "I am afraid you wouldn't be able to read my shorthand, and certainly not without your spectacles."

"If you held it two feet from my face, I could. My sight is at its worst up close. But you, for instance, I can see quite well, down to the lace trim on the neckline of your dress."

Instinctively, I brought a hand up to my chest, my fingers toying with the trim, which was, as he had said, lace.

His eyes widened slightly, as though he realized the impropriety of his remark. He cleared his throat. "As for shorthand, I am well-acquainted with it, so that would present no issue."

I dropped my hand to the notebook again, grasping it securely. "I have my own particular shorthand, so I'm afraid the issue remains."

He gave a little nod, his gaze flitting to my white-knuckled hold. "I did not mean to pry, my lady," he said, his voice calm. "Forgive me." He turned to George, leaving me feeling simultaneously relieved he had abandoned the subject and amazed at the calm he exuded.

But my brother had the tenacity and the wherewithal to break men even more even-keeled than Mr. Donovan. George would do anything rather than let it be seen he struggled to learn the way he was expected to. It was why he behaved so abominably at times—to distract from his weaknesses and protect his pride.

As I observed Mr. Donovan over the next hour—making such a close study of *Ajax* that I only managed to turn a single page in that time—I couldn't help but note the frown in his brow deepen or how he waved away the pesky fly buzzing around his head with more and more annoyance.

I smiled and returned my gaze to my book. Perhaps he was not so collected as he at first appeared. George would make quick enough work of sending him packing. And with my help, it would happen all the sooner.

"This is disgusting!" George's lips turned down at the sides. He held his nose with one hand, making his pronouncement nasal as well as loud as he took a step closer to the barrel of spoiled vegetables at the back of the estate.

"Shh!" I glanced at the nearest window, which led to the

kitchen. "Just a few more, and we will be done." If we were discovered by any of the kitchen servants, word would inevitably travel to Father, and I had no desire to explain myself. Catching flies was not on the list of accomplishments he wished for me to lay claim to.

When I had first asked George if he wished to trap flies, he had jumped up from the breakfast table with the force of a cannon explosion, only to immediately still, narrowing his eyes at me, as though he suspected me of laying a trap for *him*. When I had insisted the only things I wished to catch were insects, he had enthusiastically agreed. He had a talent for catching stray flies in the house. It was quite impressive, in fact, for he had made a practice of snatching them out of the air with his small hand.

His enthusiasm had expired quickly near the stench of the kitchen compost, though. I couldn't blame him; it was truly nauseating. Catching one pesky fly in the drawing room was a different matter than seeking ten of them in the place to which they naturally gravitated. I hoped our zeal would return once we could move to the next part of the plan.

George took in a deep breath through his mouth, released his nose, and smacked a cupped hand atop the pile, cringing.

"Well done!" I said, forgetting my revulsion for one victorious moment.

With a level of care foreign to every other part of his life, George slowly closed his hand around the fly and brought it over to me. "If you tell Father of this, Sarah, I shall—"

"I shan't do that, silly," I said, lifting the jar lid as he released the fly into it.

He glanced at me warily, as though he wasn't sure whether to believe me. "I thought you would do anything to keep me from Harrow."

I pinched my lips together. George had been eavesdropping when I had said such a thing to Father, and ever since, I had been working to regain his trust of me. It was his greatest ambition to attend the school, while I was determined to prevent it. His attendance at Harrow would be a disaster.

He watched with a frown as I hurried to replace the lid.

"George," I said, meeting his gaze squarely, "just because I don't think Harrow is the best choice for you does not mean I have forgotten our agreement." I raised my brows and put out my pinky.

He looked at it for a moment, then offered his own with a small, resigned sigh belied by the ghost of a smile on his lips. With our pinkies hooked together, George met my gaze, and we nodded in unison.

My heart twinged a bit at the realization that he would soon outgrow this silly gesture. It was a remnant of a time when George had been three and I fourteen. I had been charged with watching over him while Nurse had been ill one morning, but my interest in Moore's *Utopia* had distracted me for long enough that he had sneaked into the kitchen and eaten the majority of Cook's rising dough.

He had been sick to his stomach, but his tears had not been for discomfort but rather for fear that I should tell Father. I had promised not to, sealing my assurance with a pinky—a gesture we employed whenever we meant to remind ourselves that our loyalties lay with each other.

"Isn't that enough?" he asked, tipping his head to watch the flies in the jar. "There are eight of them there already."

I put a hand on his shoulder. "Would you like to finish and study your maps, then?"

He hurried to shake his head. "I shall catch fifty!"

I laughed softly. "Ten will do well enough."

"Ha!" George cried out as he cupped his hand over another fly.

I opened the jar and watched the ninth fly join its fellows. George might easily catch twenty of them before Mr. Donovan returned from the vicarage, but I would settle for the ten we had agreed upon.

It was hypocritical of me to encourage my brother in these antics when his penchant for mischief was one of the reasons I was determined he should not attend Harrow. But compared to the dangerous devilry he would undoubtedly get mixed up in there, this was harmless.

Though, hopefully not so harmless that it wouldn't chip at Phineas Donovan's resolve to continue in his position here at Bettencourt Court.

Chapter Six

PHINEAS

The walk to the vicarage followed a pleasant path shaded on either side by tall bushes, some of which were overgrown enough that I had to turn to the side to pass by them.

The fresh air and solitude gave me an opportunity to set my mind to what I had learned since arriving at Bettencourt Court two days ago.

Lord Danneville was not, as I had hoped, the star pupil who would gaze at me with doe-eyed hunger as I enumerated the merits of iambic and anapest verse. He was easily distractible and supremely disinterested.

Until, that was, I engaged him on a topic of interest to him or asked him to do something with his hands. It was a foreign thing to me, for I had always preferred reading and listening to lectures over anything of a practical nature. It was why my time in the Navy had been so painful and long. Everything there had been practical.

But if I wished to remain at Bettencourt Court—and I did—I would have to adapt myself to do what would elicit success in my tutoring efforts. Particularly as Lady Sarah seemed to have an eye—or two—on me.

She seemed oddly inclined to resent me, though I could find no reason for it. But I intended to discover it, for it could mean the difference between keeping my position and losing it. It was a shame she had taken me in dislike, for I would have enjoyed discussing literature together. And that notebook of hers—I knew a curiosity to see what sort of things she noted as she studied. But she had made it abundantly clear that she had no intention of sharing her insights.

The vicarage sat just east of the church, and I stopped when the lane afforded me a view of both buildings. The vicarage was a fine, two-story building of orange brick, with five windows facing the road and two chimneys on the roof, from one of which furled a plume of smoke. The house looked as though it would have ample space for my books, at least.

As for the church, it was smaller than the one in my home parish. There was no tapered steeple but rather a crenulated tower covered in ivy.

It was a strange thing to stare at one building and then the other. If things went as I hoped, I might well spend the rest of my life going between them.

"Mr. Donovan? Is that you?" A man in a wide-brimmed hat hailed me from the front door of the vicarage.

I gave a smiling nod and resumed my walk as he made his way toward the front gate, lifting the metal latch and opening it. He was a man of perhaps sixty years, and in one arm, he carried a cat. From the number of white hairs on his coat, this was a common practice of his. He greeted me again and, prattling away about what he had been doing before my arrival, led me to the door of the vicarage.

Despite my having said nothing but an initial, polite greeting, Mr. Vickers had no shortage of things to say. The world was a strange place, surely, where people like him carried on entire conversations without the contribution of anyone else, but people like me could struggle to find anything to say. Such differing personalities might have been thought to complement and balance one another, making us quick friends, but for the fact that the constant flow of talk exhausted me. Had it not been for his kindness and my interest in learning what my curacy would entail, I might have cried off with some excuse.

Mr. Vickers was unmarried, but he employed a woman from the village to see to the cooking and cleaning, and it was she who served us tea in the small sitting room. All the while, the cat sat on Mr. Vickers's lap, staring at me through slowly blinking eyes.

"It is well that you arrived this week," said Mr. Vickers, petting the cat with one hand and sipping from his tea with the other, "for it gives me enough time to show you how to go on here before I make my way to Dunley on Monday. Dunley is the other parish I have charge over, you know, but the curate I have been employing there has received a living of his own, so I must go about the business of finding a new one." The cat slipped from his lap onto the floor, stretching one hind leg and then the other. "That, of course, means you will be in charge of the services and any parish needs while I am away for a fortnight."

"Oh," I said, blinking. I hadn't anticipated my curacy would require much of my time, for my responsibilities with Lord Danneville required a great deal of it already. And then there was the time I hoped to devote to my own interests.

"Lord Bettencourt is aware of the situation," Mr. Vickers said, anticipating my dilemma, "so you needn't worry yourself over that."

The cat made its way to me, brushing against my legs and leaving tufts of white hair on my pantaloons. I cringed inwardly while Mr. Vickers smiled at the feline as though each hair was a charming deposit I should treasure. If that was indeed the case, he was a very wealthy man.

The cat turned its soulful eyes to me and let out an astoundingly loud mew.

"Chester likes you," Mr. Vickers said, interpreting.

"Does he?" It was all I could find to reply. The bright eyes were striking, but I could find no evidence of *like* there. In fact, they were disconcerting. Threatening, one might even surmise.

Chester held my gaze firmly, mewing again.

"Yes, but he is very fickle, you know. He comes and goes as he pleases, no matter what incentive I provide him to stay." Mr. Vickers reached his teacup toward Chester, offering its contents to the cat as I watched with wide eyes. The cat turned its head ever so slightly toward the cup, then returned its gaze to me and mewed. Mr. Vickers set the cup on the floor. "Just in case he changes his mind. He loves to be caressed and cosseted."

Mr. Vickers turned his gaze to me, smiling serenely—and expectantly, which made two sets of watchful, expectant eyes.

Setting aside my inclination to keep well out of reach of the animal, I politely reached a hand to its head. The cat responded with inordinate enthusiasm, lodging its head into my palm and moving its body so I was forced to pet it.

"I cherish his company when he is here," Mr. Vickers said with a hint of nostalgia, "but once he has had his fill of the insects and rodents, nothing can keep him."

This was followed by a lengthy recounting of various tales of Chester's escapades in the garden. The cat's subsequent departure from the room couldn't help but make me wonder if its temperament tended to be more similar to mine—disinclined toward polite conversation. Unlike the cat, though, I could not slip out as soon as I pleased.

I listened to the vicar, trying not to let my eyes and mind wander too frequently to explore the bits of the vicarage within my sight. The sitting room was too small to fit more than one bookcase, but surely the home possessed some sort of library, however limited it might be.

Finally, to my relief, Mr. Vickers suggested a quick tour of the church.

It was as small as its exterior had given me to expect, but it was well-kept—the floors swept, the prayer books in good condition, and a few vases of flowers brightening the otherwise dim interior. I tried to imagine myself standing at the lectern, delivering a sermon to the likes of Lord and Lady Bettencourt or Lady Sarah. It made me shift and wriggle a bit, for I was not accustomed to public speaking. Thankfully, that part of the curacy and the—if all went well—vicaracy would only consume a relatively small amount of my time.

Mr. Vickers invited me to the vicarage afterward, but I made my excuses, anxious for even the surly, unwilling Lord Danneville and the antagonistic Lady Sarah after so much time with the garrulous vicar.

I let out a slow breath through rounded lips as I started down the lane toward Bettencourt Court, reminding myself it was normal to feel overwhelmed with the future. Everything about my life was new and different right now. In time, I would become accustomed to the reality of the life I had gone to Cambridge with the intention of securing.

I jumped as a creature sailed through the bushes to my right and landed on the road before me.

"Chester," I said, half-relieved, half-nervous.

He stalked over to me and threaded his body through my legs, forcing me to remain still for fear of tripping over him.

"Go on," I said, shooing him toward the vicarage and continuing on my way to prevent him from leaving any more hair on me.

But obedience was not a strength he possessed, for he

continued to follow me. *Stalk* might be a better descriptor, though stalking was generally done quietly; Chester's mewing was constant and piercing. The only thing less pleasant was the way I found myself looking over my shoulder in between mews, as though the eerie silence might be due to his intent to pounce on me.

When I reached the servant entrance to Bettencourt Court, he was still behind me, meowing more insistently than ever. He tried to join me when I opened the door, and I only managed to stop him by wedging my body between the door and the jamb, shuffling my feet in an effort to avoid his slipping through the smallest of holes, as I knew cats to be capable of.

His mewing easily permeated the barrier of the closed door, providing anyone in the vicinity with a stirring and tragic performance.

"Shh," I said in aggravation through the closed door. I might have spared my breath.

Hoping that, with time, he would surrender to the futility of his efforts, I turned away and took the stairs toward my bedchamber. It behooved me to change my clothing, which was now generously cloaked in white cat hair. Then I could go in search of Lord Danneville to begin our lessons for the day.

Far from having to search for the young viscount, I found him in the corridor of my bedchamber, playing with a spinning top on the edge of the wooden floor uncovered by the long rug.

Instead of running away as I had expected he might do, he smiled at me, looking almost pleased.

"If you will only excuse me while I change," I said, "I shall be ready to start in a trice."

He nodded, looking serene as ever, and I wondered if perhaps his reticence and opposition since my arrival had merely been a result of temporary ill humor.

Feeling hopeful, I stepped into my bedchamber and made my way for the armoire that contained my clothing, sighing at the way Chester's muted but persistent auditory accompaniment continued in my mind like a musical tune one couldn't escape. Only now, it was joined by a constant humming. I had heard it said that there was a fine line separating intelligence and madness; perhaps the relentless sound on my walk home had tipped me over that boundary.

As I secured the braces on a new pair of pantaloons, the volume of the mewing increased. I paused, frowning more deeply as I noted the sound was coming from the direction of the windows, one of which was ajar. One of the servants must have opened it during my absence.

Inordinately relieved to know I was *not* on the brink of a mental decline, I walked over, readjusting the brace straps to a comfortable position on my shoulders. I peered through the partially open window to where Chester sat below, crying for heaven only knew what, as though Mr. Vickers had not offered his own cup of tea to the creature half an hour ago.

I shushed him—an unfortunate decision, for it alerted him to my presence, where before, he had merely been mewing at the unkind universe. He fixed his unsettling gaze on me and mewed louder than ever.

I pulled the window shut and secured the latch, dampening his pathetic cries. The buzzing, however, persisted.

Hand on the latch, I listened, hoping to solve the mystery of its origin. My gaze caught on the curtain, where a fly landed. I narrowed my eyes at it, wondering if there was any way this was the same insect which had pestered me all afternoon yesterday. Or perhaps it was a new one, come through the open window. It was truly astounding how insects could find their way into a home through the smallest of openings, yet one might open every window and door in an effort to shoo them out with no success at all.

I watched the fly for a moment, tilting my head as I observed its stillness—and the continued buzzing in the room. Flies only buzzed when their wings were in use, and this one's wings were entirely stationary.

Keeping an eye on the insect, I turned slowly, surveying the bedchamber. My eyes widened as they caught sight of the erratic movements of a handful of other flies at various points in the room.

What in the world?

I counted them as well as I could, given their constantly shifting positions. As far as I could tell, there were eight or nine of them.

One fly making its way through a window slightly ajar was credible, if somewhat improbable. Nine of them, however...

A soft but distinct snickering met my ears, and my gaze flew to the door, which, like the window had been, was ajar, despite the fact that, like the window, I had shut it. Lord Danneville's head disappeared from view, and the laughter stopped.

I sighed. The mystery was solved, at least.

Lord Danneville was the mastermind behind the gathering of flies in my bedchamber, and he was having a laugh at my expense. I didn't grudge him that. It was a clever trick he had succeeded at, and it meant he must have observed my irritation with the one in the library yesterday. Observation was a prerequisite for a great mind, and I was pleased to know he possessed that skill, even if it was not currently being used for the purposes I might prefer. Beyond that, though, I was curious to know the methods the viscount had employed to lure so many flies.

It was becoming more and more apparent why my predecessors had not lasted at Bettencourt Court. Lord Danneville wanted no tutor, and he was finding every method possible to communicate that. I took no personal offense at the tricks he was playing, though. I saw them for what they were: a challenge.

Well, he had underestimated me if he thought I could be

ousted and my future prospects abandoned for a few child's tricks.

Rather than chastising him for his behavior or betraying any frustration with his antics, I would use this as an opportunity to defeat him at his own game, and, if I was careful, teach him a thing or two without his even realizing it.

Chapter Seven

SARAH

George snickered in the corridor, and I pursed my lips from my position in the bedchamber beside Mr. Donovan's to conceal the smile trying to creep through. I envied George his place and wished I could witness what precisely he had found to laugh at. An image of Mr. Donovan swatting at flies as they flew repeatedly past his head assailed me, and I nearly abandoned the pretense of looking for a book.

But the thought of being caught and my involvement in the trick made known overcame my curiosity, and I settled for staying with an ear to the door with the hopes of hearing any sound that might be loud and obliging enough to travel to me. Mr. Donovan did not seem the type of person to speak loudly, but his subdued personality was precisely why the flies had been necessary.

The other two tutors had been ousted with a fair amount of ease. Between George's refusal to cooperate with their teaching, the pranks he had played on them, and Father's unwillingness to hear his son disparaged, they had been eager to leave Bettencourt Court. Phineas Donovan might be of a disposition less easily ruffled, but everyone had a point at which their civility became taxed beyond bearing.

The door flew open, smacking me in the head. Stunned, I stepped aside as George ran through, joining me in the bedchamber and giving the door a shove so that it nearly closed.

"What are you doing?" I hissed, holding a hand to the throbbing place on my forehead.

George put a finger to his lips, flattening himself against the wall.

Stifling a few well-chosen epithets, I listened. The sound of Mr. Donovan's firm footsteps coming closer met my ears, and my heart sprang to action.

He was coming to catch us in our crime, and I didn't know whether to feel victorious to have upset him or disappointed it had only required two small tricks to do so. Part of me had looked forward to the continued challenge of rousing his temper.

But this was much better. Perhaps—just perhaps—Father would see that employing anyone but me as a tutor for George was simply unsustainable.

But the footsteps came and went, retreating down the corridor.

George let out a whooshing breath of relief, his lips curling up into a mischievous smile. That smile was precisely why he could not be allowed to go to Harrow. He would learn nothing and be sent home with astounding rapidity for wreaking havoc with his peers.

"You are undeservedly lucky," I said.

"It is not luck," he said. "It is quickness. Besides, better try my luck than hide away like a coward, missing all the fun!"

"You call it cowardice; I call it good sense." I frowned, trying to decide whether it was safe to look out into the corridor. "Where is he going, I wonder?"

George shrugged. "To tell one of the servants to catch the flies, I suppose."

I opened the door enough to peek my head out. There was no sign of Mr. Donovan, though. "He might have summoned one with the bell pull if that was his intention." He occupied the room previously used by my own governess. She had been well-loved by my parents and, after a few weeks at the estate, had begun to dine with us each night, almost like a member of the family. If Mr. Donovan was ever invited to do such a thing, it would be the seal on his acceptance at Bettencourt Court. I was determined that should not happen.

"Did he open the windows?" I asked of no one in particular. Perhaps he was trusting the flies would find their way out by the time he returned. If that was his game, he would be disappointed. Flies could never find their way out.

"Shall I go investigate?" George's eyes glinted with the promise of adventure.

I nearly stopped him, but I was too curious, and he too quick.

He was only gone a matter of twenty seconds before slipping through the door, his breath coming quickly and his eyes still bright as they always were when he engaged in mischief.

"The windows are all closed."

"Then, what in the world—"

I clamped my mouth shut at the sound of footsteps in the corridor. "...Can at least make yourself useful."

George and I looked at one another, our brows knitting as the footsteps drew even with the room we were in, then passed.

"George!" I hissed as he pulled the door open.

But my curiosity drew me toward it, and I came up behind him to peer through the space.

I covered my mouth with a hand to prevent the laugh. In his hands, Mr. Donovan held a cat, his arms extended as far in front of him as they would reach. The cat's body stretched toward the floor, legs dangling strangely.

"Capital," George whispered with a growing grin.

When Mr. Donovan reached his door, he paused, for his hands were both occupied holding the cat, but the door was closed.

"You will run away the moment I let you down," Mr. Donovan said, fixing a censuring gaze on the cat. "But you must believe me when I tell you that would be a mistake."

I watched with unveiled curiosity. He meant to employ the cat in the task of fly-catching.

George rushed into the corridor. "I shall open the door for you!"

Mr. Donovan's gaze moved to George, and I hurried to step back, concealing myself from view.

"Thank you, my lord," Mr. Donovan said, as though he found George's presence and offer of help no surprise. "It is very kind of you."

Was he unaware George had caused his troubles? Or did he simply not care? For two reasons, I hoped it was the former, for that would mean he was far stupider than I had thought. No person of sound mind would truly believe the sudden presence of ten flies in his bedchamber was a matter of chance. The latter would mean he was a more formidable foe than I had anticipated, and spending half an hour amidst the compost had already stretched the limits of what I would do to aid George in his pranks.

The two of them disappeared into the bedchamber, leaving me to wonder what might next transpire. I cocked an ear but was met with only silence.

A few moments later, George's laughter sailed through the corridor.

Traitor.

This was followed by a string of strange noises: surprise, censure, more laughter.

I hesitated for a moment, then opened the door and made my way toward Mr. Donovan's room. I had promised myself to oversee George's tutelage; it would be remiss of me not to see precisely what was happening to elicit such passionate reactions from him.

I walked toward the door to Mr. Donovan's bedchamber, just far enough that I could see inside. Books were stacked neatly in one corner of the room, distracting me for a moment with a desire to explore the pile, to know which works Mr. Donovan had thought worthy of bringing.

I pulled my eyes away from the books. Mr. Donovan and George were on the other side of the room by the windows, facing away from me. In the space between them, I could see the swishing tail of the cat. It was standing on the floor, looking up at the nearby curtain.

The tail stilled, and the cat lowered its head, utter silence permeating the air except for the subtle but constant buzz in the room. A glance toward the ceiling told me the flies George had released were still at large.

The cat pounced at a curtain, falling to the floor with its front paws pressed together. George and Mr. Donovan cheered, looking at each other with smiles stretched across their faces. My own mouth drew up at one edge. It had become rarer to see George's genuine smile recently. As for Mr. Donovan, he was wearing glasses again, and the studious air they gave him, combined with the first unrestrained smile I had encountered from him was… well, if I had my notebook just now, I would certainly add two entries: *no spectacles. A toothless smile.*

A rational woman didn't need such distractions.

The cat's paws danced a bit as he played with his prey. Then, after a moment of stillness, he lowered his head to his paws and began nibbling.

George made a sound of disgust, while Mr. Donovan folded his arms and tipped his head to the side, as though he was observing a curiosity.

I narrowed my eyes at the way his shirt stretched over his shoulders and hugged his arms. It was decidedly *not* the frame of a tutor, which should be slight, lean—emaciated, even, from long hours spent poring over books, with no thought of physical food or drink to disturb the nourishment the mind was receiving. Phineas Donovan had no business calling himself a tutor with such a shape to his body.

He glanced over at George, an eyebrow cocked. "What did you imagine he would do once he caught it?"

George's nose wrinkled. "Not *that*."

"He does what he has learned will lead to his survival. Catching insects keeps his mind and body sharp."

"Yes, but he needn't *eat* it."

Mr. Donovan smiled slightly, reaffirming my desire for a husband who found no joy at all in life. Hearts shouldn't skitter at the sight of a smile, but if mine insisted on doing so, I would do what I could to prevent the stimulus from occurring at all. Avoiding marriage altogether would be the preferred way of accomplishing such a thing.

"Perhaps if Chester watched you eating *your* dinner, he would be every bit as disgusted by your choice of food as you are by his."

George gave a hmph. "Perhaps I shall eat *him* for dinner."

"You could, but I wouldn't recommend it. The meat of a cat is not only sparing, but sour."

George looked up at him with patent interest. "You have eaten cat?"

"Once. We had an old cat on board the *Dominance,* and when it died, some of the other midshipmen insisted on cooking it." He chuckled softly while I tried to imagine him aboard a ship. Perhaps that explained the muscular form. I had assumed he had been educated at Eton or Harrow. What *was* his education, then? It was certainly a point that should be addressed.

"You were in the Navy?" The reverence in George's voice had me abandoning my position and stepping into the room. The last thing I needed was for him to regard Mr. Donovan as an idol.

Mr. Donovan looked over at my entrance, his smile disappearing in an instant. He brought a fist to his mouth and cleared his throat. "We should leave Chester to his business and see to today's lessons."

George followed his gaze to me, then waved a dismissive hand. "Sarah doesn't mind if we watch the flies getting caught. She's the reason they're here in the first place."

"George!" I said, my cheeks a bonfire of betraying heat. I should have known he would throw me to the wolves the moment it served him.

Mr. Donovan observed me, his brow knit. It gave me the sensation of being scrutinized like one of his books, and from our conversation about *Ajax*, I had an idea how closely he studied those.

No scrutinizing. I would add that to the other requirements later. Perhaps there was a phrase I could find that would cover all the things that made my heart unstable.

"Can I help you, Lady Sarah?" Mr. Donovan asked, his voice ever-serene.

"I merely heard the commotion and came to see what it was about. I cannot think George's education requires such tumult." I sounded like a shrew, and it made me want to shift under Mr. Donovan's gaze. But if a shrew would rid us of him sooner, so be it.

"Of course," he said. "Shall we go to the library, my lord? Chester seems to have things well in hand—or paw. I imagine the room shall be rid of most of these flies by the time we are done."

George sent me a look full of complaint—or vengeance, perhaps. I would have to be careful not to antagonize him further, or he would not submit to *my* efforts to tutor him, either.

Mr. Donovan set to opening the windows, the movements providing another demonstration of the entirely gratuitous amount of muscle he possessed. I debated for a moment between observing just how extensive it was—a way to estimate just how much time he had neglected books in favor of less cultured pursuits—and sparing myself such a display. It took time, of course, to weigh the merits of each option, and by the time I had decided to pull my gaze away from the bunching and stretching of such muscles, Mr. Donovan had finished his work and turned toward me.

I lifted my chin, spun on my heel, and left, making my way to my bedchamber, wondering if Mr. Donovan had spent any of his time studying at all. The physical evidence suggested otherwise.

I picked up the notebook sitting on the writing desk, pulling the pencil marking my place from within its pages and scribbling my earlier thoughts below those I had already added.

No spectacles

A toothless smile

Does not scrutinize me

A cultivated mind rather than a cultivated body

I stared at the growing list, aware that it was becoming quite specific. Well, so much the better. Mother and Father would find it all the more difficult to select someone who conformed to my requirements.

In the meantime, I was doing my best to distract myself from the thought of my letter arriving at Cousin Arthur's home in London. He was a rising star in the House of Commons; some had even mentioned him as a future prospect for prime minister. Father's comments on the subject had given me to believe he was a confirmed bachelor, which was precisely the situation that served my interests—and his, as I had attempted to persuade him in my letter.

He could retain his status as a bachelor while taking me in to act as a sort of hostess, just as Lady Hester had done for her uncle, William Pitt. Perhaps I could even advise him on matters coming before Parliament.

It would be the perfect situation, the ideal entrance into the wider world, placing me in situations that would display everything I had to offer and giving me the means whereby I could pursue my interests, preferably in Athens or Rome.

M r. Donovan continued to be absent from dinners, an encouraging fact all on its own. It also provided the opportunity to acquaint Father with the less desirable aspects of the tutor's approach to education. When I ventured to mention the incident with the cat and flies at one point during the meal, Father's brow furrowed pensively.

Mercifully, George was quiet. I had spoken with him before the meal, reminding him Mr. Donovan's departure was a goal we shared. However interesting it might have been to see a cat catch flies, my tutelage would be far preferable for George, and he knew that. But that could not happen without proving to Father that Mr. Donovan was unable to provide the sort of education necessary for a Danneville of Bettencourt Court.

"I am surprised by what you say, Sarah," Father said. "Mr. Donovan does not seem the sort of man to seek such childish diversions."

"A childish diversion or a resourceful solution to an annoyance?" Mother cut her potatoes with her usual grace, her gaze on her plate.

I pinched my lips together as Father considered this.

"Was it successful?" he asked.

"Yes!" George said, breaking the silence we had agreed he should observe. "When we returned after my lessons, there was but one fly left of the ten. Mr. Donovan killed that one himself, for he told me that one fly may lay thousands of eggs in just a month!" He looked around to see the effect such information exercised upon us. His smile fell as his gaze met mine, and he resumed his precarious silence, pushing the food around on his plate.

"Well, then," Father said, setting his napkin on his plate. "No harm done. One might even go so far as to call it a resourceful solution. A testament to his quick-thinking."

I glanced at Mother, who gave no indication she noticed the way Father had repeated her words as if they had been a novel idea, all his own. I had pointed out such an occurrence before, but Father would never accept that any good idea had not originated with his own mind.

"By the by, Sarah," Father said. "Mrs. Bamford was absent from church on Sunday. I wish you will make her a visit this week. Her health is declining."

"Her health or her memory?" I said with a smile. Mrs. Bamford had lived in the parish for scores of years, and her advancing age had only somewhat dimmed her tendency to say precisely the sort of things others kept to themselves. I quite liked her for it.

Father squared me with an unamused look, clearly confirming it was the latter. "Sarah," Father chastised, "it is our duty to—"

"Be at ease, Father," I said. "I *shall* visit her and take her a basket, though she will be quite disappointed our strawberry crop has been such a failure this year." She had a particular liking for strawberry jam.

Mother rose, signaling it was time for George to retire and

for she and I to make our way to the withdrawing room, leaving Father to his port.

As she closed the door behind us, Mother wrapped her arm around mine. "Have you had any time to consider our discussion, my dear?"

"A bit," I replied noncommittally.

She sent me a sidelong glance. "With the time you have been spending in the library observing Mr. Donovan, *a bit* is less than I had expected. Perhaps I should arrange a dinner party to give you an opportunity for interaction with more gentlemen."

"I have interacted with plenty of gentlemen, Mother," I said, ignoring her pointed reference to my time overseeing George's education. Between the seasons we had spent in London and the parties we had hosted and attended, I had met more eligible gentlemen than I could count.

"Yes," she said, "but not since attuning your mind more fully to the matter of marriage. Or perhaps you are too distracted by George's schooling to set your mind to it."

"A woman may hold more than one thing in her mind at once."

Mother knew it well. She was an intelligent woman. Her father had been a member of the Royal Society, and she herself had been one of the Bluestockings, only to fade away from such a life after marriage. It drove me mad she let her intellectual abilities lay dormant and, even worse, that she let Father take her ideas as his own.

If I ever did marry, I would not sit idly by, my intellect consumed and subsumed into a man's, indistinguishable from his own. Better to marry a fool than accept such a fate.

PHINEAS

There were no flies left in my bedchamber. Chester had taken care of all but the last one, which had stayed in its place on the ceiling for an admirable amount of time in an attempt to evade the same fate as its fellows.

Chester had lost interest, which meant I had been obliged to finish his work for him, during which time he disappeared— back to the vicarage, I could only assume.

The result of his fly-catching efforts, though, was an eruption of cat hair all over my bedchamber. I was still trying to garner the courage to ask one of the servants to clean it up. I had sensed the way many of them looked at me askance for the superior position I held, and I was reluctant to do anything to antagonize them unnecessarily. In the end, I would likely clean the hair myself.

In any case, the explosion of feline hair was the reason I was in the library so early this morning. Having been obliged to change my clothing once already due to the amount of hair that had found its way to my small escritoire, I had surrendered and left my bedchamber.

It was still early—a few minutes after seven o'clock. Lord

Danneville wouldn't come down for our lessons to begin until eight, giving me plenty of time to prepare for the day.

A half-dozen books were stacked to my right, while *The Odyssey* lay open before me on the table. After the interest Lord Danneville expressed in the Navy, I thought perhaps he would enjoy the adventure in Homer. I would have preferred to study *The Iliad* first, but perhaps the viscount's interest in *The Odyssey* would lead to interest in its precursor. And if Lady Sarah happened to be present while Lord Danneville and I discussed the adventures of Odysseus, well, she could decide whether to provide her input.

I was not generally one who enjoyed exhibits of passion, and I certainly didn't seek conflict. But something about the zeal with which she had argued with me the other day... it had been both impressive and intriguing. I wanted to know more of her mind, to challenge and be challenged by her. And yes, perhaps a part of me wished to see the fire lit in those blue eyes of hers.

But that was beside the point. I found her mere presence during lessons distracting, and if she was going to distract, she might as well play a more active role in the lessons. She could demonstrate to her brother the passion the *intolerably insipid works*, as he described them, could inspire in people. It would be a valuable lesson.

At the moment, though, I was finding *The Odyssey* to be less engaging than usual. Through the corner of my eye, I glanced at the stack of books beside me, my gaze fixing on the book third from the top. It stood out, for all the other books were organized by size, creating a sort of pyramid. That one, though, was the smallest of them all, and it belonged at the top. I had put it lower in the stack to conceal it, but rather than being inconspicuous as I had hoped, it taunted me with its disregard for order.

Unable to abide it any longer, I took the top two books in hand and moved them beneath the third one. Sighing with satisfaction at restored balance, I returned my gaze to the text before me.

But it was drawn again and again to the small book. Pulling my spectacles from my face, I reached for the cloth in my pocket and wiped them. I returned them to their perch on my nose, hoping the act would refocus me, but it was no use. Staring at the title, I tapped my thumb on the desk.

I should never have brought it down. It certainly didn't belong amongst the classics. I should return it to its place in my bedchamber to remove the disturbance.

I stood, straightening my shoulders. I was much too rational to pay heed to a frivolous romance novel's clarion call to open its pages—and in preference to Homer, no less. Homer!

I shot out a hand to it, and it slipped from its place atop the stack and onto the floor, landing with its pages open.

"Oh"—I glanced around in the unlikely event anyone had managed to enter the library without my awareness—"how terribly clumsy of me." Satisfied I was indeed alone, I stooped to pick it up.

My eyes explored the page, landing squarely on a bit of dialogue.

> "All this she must possess," added Darcy, "and to all this she must yet add something more substantial, in the improvement of her mind by extensive reading."

My brows went up. This Darcy figure at least knew a thing or two. But what did he mean when he said *to all this*? What could possibly be considered as important as extensive reading? It was a mystery which needed to be solved.

And solve it I did by starting at the beginning of the page, but no sooner was *that* mystery solved—I was rather inclined to agree with Miss Elizabeth Bennet that such a list of accomplishments as Mr. Darcy and Miss Bingley provided was excessive—then a whole host of new mysteries demanded my attention.

There was nothing for it but to start at the beginning. A half an hour's reading couldn't hurt, for I knew *The Odyssey* well already. I rose slowly, my eyes on the text.

"Mr. Donovan?"

I shot up and whirled around, concealing the book behind my back as Lady Sarah stood in the doorway.

"Lady Sarah," I said, my voice emerging high and strange. I cleared my throat. "Good day to you."

She looked around the room as though in search of her brother. "It is early for lessons, is it not?"

"Yes. I was merely preparing."

Her gaze moved to the arms I still held behind my back, and I gripped the book more tightly. The last thing I needed was for her to think I was reading romance novels. "I thought I would explore your father's collection to see if there was anything that might add to today's topic of study." I turned toward the nearest bookcase, transferring the book I held to my right side, where it remained out of her sight.

"And were you successful?" She walked over to join me.

My muscles tightened instinctively as she came up on my right, placing the book between us. "Yes," I hurried to say, passing the book behind me and into my other hand.

Her face turned toward me, and I met it, breathless, certain she had noticed my efforts to conceal the novel from her. But her brows were merely raised questioningly. "And which book was it?"

I watched for any sign she could hear my heart thumping against my chest. Her blue eyes met mine squarely. Gone was the bright energy that had been there when we had disputed *Ajax* two days ago, but I found myself unable to look away, all the same.

One of her brows inched up even higher.

Tearing my gaze away from her to the bookshelf before us, I reached out to the shelf at eye level. "This one."

She stepped toward the bookcase. "*Miscellanies?* By Armstrong?"

I cleared my throat, cursing my luck. "Yes. I thought it would be useful for..." I pulled my spectacles from my face to clean them only to realize that, given the novel I still held, I hadn't two free hands for the task. I had no choice but to return them to their place. "As I was saying, I thought it would be useful for Lord Danneville to compare the poetic styles of Homer and Armstrong."

By the way Lady Sarah's lips pinched together, I could see she did not think highly of my reasoning. Little wonder. I was like a bumbling schoolboy. If I intended to be taken seriously by her—and, as a result, by Lord Bettencourt—this was assuredly not the way, but I found it difficult to maintain my composure when she looked at me so frankly with those blue eyes, or when my heart beat so erratically. If I let myself be dazzled by her beauty, though, I was no better than Ajax, bamboozled by Athena.

"And here I thought you had *already* found something you liked." She leaned back, peering around me in an effort to see what I held in my left hand. "You were reading a book when I arrived—quite intently. I had assumed *that* was the one you had taken an interest in."

I hesitated for a moment. I could pretend I had found the novel amongst all the books in this extensive library, but something told me Lady Sarah would know if I was lying, that she was acutely aware of all the books her father possessed and would know immediately that *Pride and Prejudice* was not one of them.

Even if that were not the case, I had been using Rebecca's note to me as a bookmark of sorts, which meant that, within those pages was irrefutable evidence the book belonged to me.

No, I would have to take a different approach. And if I had learned anything from Valentine over the years, it was what could be accomplished with a bit—or a great deal—of confidence.

"Ah, this one, you mean?" I raised the book from my left side, determined not to betray how nervous I was. "Yes, it was after a quick perusal of *Miscellanies* that I decided this one would better serve my purposes, after all." The cogs in my brain whirled round and round, searching for a way to connect Mr. Darcy to *The Odyssey*.

Lady Sarah tipped her head to the side to read the title, her delicate brows furrowing. *"Pride and Prejudice?"*

This was it—the moment that would decide everything.

"Yes. Have you not heard of it?" It was amazing how my voice could sound so clear when my mind was abuzz with doubt and with visions of being pushed over the threshold of Bettencourt Court, my trunks thrown unceremoniously after me. That was the most chilling part of all. If my trunks were being thrown, that meant they were empty of books.

"I have not heard of it," she said. "May I?"

Only with the greatest effort did I manage to cede the book to her. She let it fall open in her hands, and I watched on tenterhooks as her eyes skimmed over the pages, well aware that my continued presence at Bettencourt Court required me to defend my choice in book.

She frowned and, after a pause, turned the pages until she found the one she was looking for: the title page, which said, *Pride and Prejudice: A Novel*.

Chapter Nine

SARAH

I read the two words again to be sure I was not imagining things, but there they were, clear as the glass on Mr. Donovan's spectacles: *A Novel*.

My gaze flicked up to him. He was watching me with an impassive expression, for all things as though I hadn't just found him guilty of the pastime of silly schoolgirls and fainting misses. It had been strange enough to discover the man crouched with a book in hand—*I* had never seen anyone read a book in such a position—but to discover it was a *novel*?

The man tutoring George Danneville, the next Earl of Bettencourt, the man whose tutelage was preferred over my own, was a reader of romance novels?

Most shocking of all, perhaps, was that he had been doing so in the morning, in plain view. When he had hidden the book upon seeing me, I had been determined to discover what it was, for his demeanor had been undeniably guilty. But he had shown it to me without hesitation when I had asked.

It was... peculiar.

It was also precisely what I needed to convince Father Mr. Donovan was entirely unsuitable. Father abhorred novels.

"Mr. Donovan," I said, unable to mask the satisfaction in my tone, "you are a reader of novels?"

"Naturally," he said. "You are not?"

My lips parted at the unexpected response. *Naturally?* There was nothing natural about a learned man reading such stuff. And yet, I couldn't help but feel a sliver of doubt at the way he said it, as though he suddenly doubted *my* intelligence. Neither could I stop feeling a hint of intrigue to know why on earth he valued such drivel. "Of course not." I handed the book back to him.

"Hm."

I narrowed my eyes. That little *hm* seemed to hold a great deal within it. "What?"

He lifted a shoulder, rubbing a thumb along the spine of the book in his hand. "I admit I do not see why it would be a matter of course not to read novels."

I stared at him. Had Father known what sort of man he was employing when he had agreed for Mr. Donovan to come to Bettencourt Court? Impossible.

"Forgive me, Mr. Donovan, but I must ask... *why* have you come here?"

There was a pause.

"I have come to tutor your brother, Lady Sarah."

"Yet you appear wholly unfit for the job."

His brows drew together. "Because I read novels?"

"That is part of it, certainly."

"And the rest?"

"Without wishing to give offense," I said, my gaze dropping to his well-shaped jaw and then to his broad shoulders, "you have the appearance of a sporting gentleman, not a tutor."

"A... sporting gentleman?" His mouth stretched into a wide smile before being masked by a hand, which insufficiently muffled the subsequent chuckle.

I watched as he attempted to gain control of himself, part of me wishing he would drop the hand covering his mouth to reveal that warm and handsome smile of his.

Mr. Crooke had been George's first tutor. He was a short, stout man of no less than four-and-fifty, with a face that had turned impressively vibrant shades of red whenever George had crossed him or made the man a victim of his antics. Mr. Swain, on the other hand, had been nine-and-thirty, but his cold, calculating manner had meant that George's boisterous laughter after he had slipped one of Gillray's more vulgar caricatures into the man's copy of *Othello* had been unbearable enough to send Swain complaining straight to Father, and then home.

Mr. Donovan removed his glasses, wiping at his eyes. "Forgive me, my lady. I am not laughing at *you*. It is just that I have never in my life been accused of being a *sporting gentleman*, as you put it. I assure you, my family would be equally amused if they heard such a description."

"Forgive me if I lack the knowledge to properly describe you," I said with a touch of impatience. "A Corinthian, then."

He seemed to bite his lip to prevent another onset of laughter, but behind his spectacles, his eyes twinkled merrily. It was endearing—and annoying. "You must acquit me."

"How, then, do you explain *that*?" I nodded at his form.

He glanced at his side, trying to follow my gaze, the smile fading from his mouth. "What?"

"Your... your *muscular* physique."

Mr. Donovan's gaze flicked to mine, something in his eyes I couldn't identify. "From anyone else, I would imagine that to be a compliment, but you say it with a hint of disdain, I think."

Well, he wasn't entirely beef-witted, at least. "I have little admiration for men whose pursuits lie in that vein—hunting and boxing and riding to hounds."

"My lady, I have never hunted. I have never boxed. And I have never ridden to hounds."

A likely story. "Then how do you explain your"—my gaze went again to those well-formed arms—"self?"

He looked as though he might laugh again. But he did not. He glanced at his arms as though he had never considered them before, as though they had come formed in such a way. Unfortunately, the gesture gave *me* ample opportunity to take note of their shape and size, too.

"I spent most of my life as a sailor, my lady." His mouth quirked up at one side. "And I make a practice of regularly carrying substantial books."

I cocked a brow and directed my gaze at the one he held. "I would not call novels *substantial*, sir."

"Oh?" He looked genuinely curious. "Which ones have you read to lead you to such a conclusion?"

I stumbled over my words. "I… that is… I have not read any, of course."

His curiosity morphed into a frown. "Hm."

There was that *hm* again. An aggravating syllable if I had ever heard one. I wished I could simply ignore it, but I was too curious. "What?"

He shook his head, the sides of his mouth turned down in a pensive expression. "I simply do not see how one can hold an informed opinion on any subject without personally acquainting oneself with it."

Far from holding a challenge, his gaze met mine calmly and frankly. But the implication that I held a position of ignorance was not one I appreciated. "Perhaps some subjects are not worth acquainting oneself with."

He inclined his head, granting my point. "Perhaps. But you will never know for certain unless you take that chance yourself, will you? Until then, you are simply relying on the opinions of others—or perhaps avoiding the subject out of fear."

I smiled at the subtle insult. "Fear?"

He shrugged but did not retract his statement.

"I am not afraid of novels, Mr. Donovan."

"That is well, for one should never be afraid of words on a page."

"Yes, but surely some words on a page are more worthy of our time than others."

"Oh, inarguably."

Now we were making progress. "And yet you choose to spend your time in novels."

"Some of it, yes. I try to adopt an expansive approach to learning."

I cocked a brow, still smiling. Yet another subtle insult. "As do I."

"Undoubtedly." The polite smile which accompanied the response told me clearly he *did* doubt that fact.

"Very well." I extended a hand.

He raised a brow, not understanding me.

"I shall read it." I gestured with a nod at the book.

"Oh, but *I* am reading this one, my lady."

I stared at him for a sign that he was teasing. But there was no glint in his eye this time, no trace of amusement in the way he regarded me.

"I will gladly lend you one of the others in my collection," he offered.

"Collection?" He had—and was admitting to possessing—a *collection* of novels?

He nodded. Unapologetic, unembarrassed as ever. "Which one would you like?"

"I could hardly say. I am unfamiliar with the titles. I cannot think it matters much." I had every intention of reading a few pages of the novel and tearing it—and him—to shreds afterward. Metaphorically. Violence should always be carried out metaphorically.

"I shall bring one down later today, if it suits you."

"It suits me perfectly," I said, just as George appeared in the doorway.

With a polite smile, Mr. Donovan turned away and addressed himself to my brother.

And I... I stared at his broad back, vaguely wondering how many books one would need to carry to acquire such dimensions. But more importantly, I stared at Mr. Donovan with a creeping feeling of failure.

I had begun the conversation with every intention of seeing him dismissed for his unsophisticated habit. Somehow, though, I had ended it with a promise to read one of the ridiculous novels myself.

W hile Mr. Donovan's figure might give some to believe he had neglected his mind in favor of his body, another morning spent listening to him teach George put any such thoughts to rest.

His mind was every bit as sound as his body appeared, which was a compliment indeed.

George, while more agreeable and somewhat more pliable than he had been for the past two tutors, was still disinclined to take Mr. Donovan seriously. As they sat discussing Heroditus— "discussing" in this context meaning Mr. Donovan asked questions and prodded George through the answers in a way I found simultaneously humorous and painful—George's focus was squarely upon the paper before him, which he was folding and refolding. From my place near the window, I could not decipher what precisely his goal was except perhaps to irritate his tutor.

But Mr. Donovan was not irritated. He supported a large, open book with both hands, training his gaze on it and adjusting his spectacles as he read sentences aloud. It was a sight I tried not to pay heed to, for it couldn't but affect an intelligent woman to see a man reading so studiously. I was only human, after all.

He glanced up at George after each sentence, his eyes going to the folds George was making.

"My lord?" Mr. Donovan finally said.

George gave no indication he had heard himself addressed.

Mr. Donovan glanced at me, and I raised my brows slightly. It was clear he viewed my presence in the library as an added pressure. Part of me wanted to reassure him he was doing far better than the other tutors had, but that was counterproductive. The more a person focused on whether their efforts were being met with approval rather than focusing on the activity itself, the worse their performance became.

And *that* was precisely what I was hoping would happen with Mr. Donovan.

In fact, this seemed a very good opportunity to introduce an added element of stress to his teaching.

I marked my place with a frayed ribbon and set my book down, rising and making my way out of the library. Before closing the door, I glanced at Mr. Donovan, whose shoulders seemed to relax at my departure.

I smiled and shut the door. He would do well to revel in my absence, temporary though it would be.

PHINEAS

Lady Sarah's departure freed me to do something I would not have felt capable of doing in her presence.

Setting down the book on the edge of the table, I walked over to Lord Danneville, who had not responded to me in the last five minutes, so enthralled was he with his folding. The fact that he did not react at all to the cessation of my speaking was all I needed in order to know I was wasting my breath trying to teach or discuss Heroditus with him.

He made a noise of frustration and undid the most recent fold.

"Is that a dart?"

He startled, as though he had not even realized I was in the library with him.

What a testament to my success.

"That was what I was *attempting,* yes." He tried to recreate a new crease near the last one. "But it is getting too small and unmanageable." He struck a hand on the paper in frustration as it unfolded of its own accord.

"It is difficult to make a new crease when one has already been made nearby." I took up a piece of paper of my own and carefully began folding it down the center, noting from the corner of my eye how Lord Danneville watched with begrudging interest. "Like water in a riverbed, it will follow the path of least resistance. The trick is to ensure that your folds are both precise and firm. Feel this." I ran my finger along the fold I had made, and he followed suit.

Then I took the magnifying glass on the desk and used the edge to press the length of the fold. "*Now* feel it."

The viscount ran his finger along it.

"Much sharper, isn't it?"

He nodded quickly, curiosity lighting his eyes. It was the second time I had managed to garner such a reaction from him, and I would not let it go to waste.

"You try now." I gave him the magnifying glass. "I would suggest unfolding it entirely and starting with your first fold."

By the time he had done four folds, his mouth was turned in a smile. "It is working!"

"Is it?" I said, feeling satisfied for him to exhibit such energy, even if it was not regarding the subject I had intended to discuss. For now, it was more important to gain the viscount's good favor and trust. If I was able to do that, he would be more likely to listen and engage on other topics. I hoped.

He shot me a strange look, and I smiled. "How shall you know for certain unless you try throwing it?"

His eyes widened, and I was left to infer he had never been given license to throw a paper dart—or anything, perhaps—by one of his tutors. Whether that should fill me with pride or concern was yet to be determined.

He stood and, bringing his arm back, cast the paper dart forward. It sailed a few feet, then dove onto the floor.

"Bravo," I said. "Only imagine how it will be when you use a fresh paper with no old folds to mar it."

Lord Danneville took that as an invitation, opening the drawer nearest him and removing a sheet.

"Perhaps you could try a different method of folding this time."

He set the sheet on the desk and sat down. "But I do not know a different method."

"I know one or two, but I imagine there are others we could discover together." I retrieved one of the chairs that sat along the wall and brought it next to the viscount. I took the paper I had folded and created a new fold along the bottom. "Have you heard of Sir Isaac Newton, my lord?"

He shook his head, watching my hands as I used the magnifying glass for its new purpose.

"He would be a helpful person to have here with us, for he discovered the physical laws which determine how far and how long these darts sail through the air. They are the laws of motion."

We worked alongside one another, folding and pressing, as I described the laws, trying not to overwhelm him, and asked him how each might relate to a paper dart.

Lord Danneville stood with his prepared dart, and I finished the last precise fold on mine just as the door opened. I swung my head around, my eyes widening as my gaze fell upon Lady Sarah, Lord Bettencourt, and Lady Bettencourt entering.

Their eyes took in the scene—the viscount preparing to throw his dart, me with my own in hand, one lying a dozen feet from us on the floor—and a flash of victory passed over Lady Sarah's face, only to be quickly veiled. Lord Bettencourt's brows pulled together in a deep frown, while Lady Bettencourt's impassive gaze surveyed the room.

I awaited my inevitable dismissal. The Earl of Bettencourt was not employing me to make paper darts with his son, and as my predecessors had already cast grave doubts upon the value of the tutoring profession, I recognized my time had come.

"Oh, jolly good!" Lord Danneville said, smiling at them as though we had been awaiting their appearance. "Now you can all see whether this one fares better than the last." He threw the dart, which flew forward, briefly tipped upward, then dove down to the floor, three feet past its precursor.

He turned toward me, and I could not have kept myself from congratulating him on his victory for all the tutoring positions in the world, so pleased did he look.

"Very well done," I said, fully embracing the coming ignominy.

"I shall call that one Newton," he said, grinning widely, "in honor of good Sir Isaac." His eyes went to my own dart. "Go on, then, sir. Your turn. You mustn't let the first law of motion keep the dart inert."

Pride and victory filled my chest. He had listened. And learned.

Refusing to let myself look at our audience, I nodded and let my first, last, and only dart take flight. It took a steep route upward, then, after a moment suspended, dove to the rug while I winced.

It was a metaphor for my time as a tutor. An abrupt, hopeful climb, only to end in disaster.

Lord Danneville looked at me thoughtfully. "What went wrong? You folded it so carefully."

I chuckled softly. "I believe the fault was in the person exerting the force, my lord, rather than in the object itself."

The viscount smiled slyly. "You can teach the principles, but you need me to show you how to execute them."

"Perhaps so." I had always been better at the logical than the practical, but I was coming to suspect that my charge was my opposite in that way.

"What is the meaning of this, Mr. Donovan?" Lord Bettencourt asked.

I took in a breath and turned to face him, with his deeply furrowed brow.

"I think it is quite obvious," Lady Bettencourt said, her face still impassive. "It is a practical exploration of Newton's laws of motion."

Lady Sarah's gaze flitted to her mother, her lips pinching slightly. There was no doubt in my mind she had orchestrated this little gathering. I only wished I understood why she so persistently desired my failure.

"Father, perhaps you can do better than Mr. Donovan." Lord Danneville picked up my failed dart from the floor and straightened out the dented front. "You need to hold your arm like th—"

"I know how to throw a paper dart, my boy," the earl said testily, striding over and taking it from his son.

"We'll see about that," the viscount said softly, shooting me a skeptical look.

The short but private exchange made my heart twinge. It was evidence of how things might have changed between us, of the possibilities before us, if only I were allowed to continue with him. I understood it now: Lord Danneville required everything I had never required or wanted as a young boy—practical experience of principles.

Perhaps my departure was for the best, then. But I couldn't help regretting it.

Lord Bettencourt's attempt fell short of the dart his son had dubbed "Newton." Far from taking this in stride, he insisted on making his own dart. To his credit, it was more successful, landing nearly even with Newton.

He brushed his hands together, apparently satisfied with the result. "A very interesting exploration of Newtonian's physical laws, one might say."

I glanced at Lady Bettencourt, who had said just such a thing not five minutes ago. She reacted not at all to this redundant comment, stated as it was like a revelation. Lady Sarah, however, looked less pleased than ever.

"Come, my dear," Lady Bettencourt said to her daughter.

"We should be going. The journey will take at least an hour, and I have no desire to be late. We hope to return in time for dinner," she said to her husband.

"Very good. Perhaps you would care to join us tonight, Mr. Donovan?"

I blinked. Somehow, I had gone from standing at the precipice of dismissal to being invited to dine with the family. It was an indubitable honor, and I formed a halting acceptance.

"Six o'clock, then," Lord Bettencourt said.

I met eyes with Lady Sarah, who held my gaze calmly and impassively. It was a short moment that seemed to stretch on for half a minute, though that was laughable. Time did not stretch.

I watched as Lady Sarah followed her mother and father through the door. It was a strange thing to feel drawn to someone who so obviously held me in disdain.

"Mr. Donovan?"

I turned to Lord Danneville, who was looking at me as though perhaps that was not the first time he had attempted to garner my attention.

"Can we make more?" he asked.

I cleared my throat. "Perhaps we should study a bit more first. Daniel Bernoulli discussed a few things that just might help us in our quest for a steady, far-flying vessel."

Lord Danneville's mouth turned into a frown, and I sensed myself losing him.

"But," I hurried to say, "I propose that tomorrow, we hold a competition."

"A competition?"

"Today we shall do all we can to understand and study Newton and Bernoulli so that tomorrow, we may make twenty variations of dart and see which one works best. What do you say?"

"Capital!"

SARAH

After leaving the library, the carriage was brought around, and I went to fetch my bonnet in my bedchamber. I was in no humor for social engagements, but that made little difference. I had been trained to engage in polite discourse no matter my mood, and I had promised Mother that my overseeing of George's tutoring would not interfere with my social obligations.

Perhaps a respite from the library would be good for me. I was particularly out of humor with Mr. Donovan at the moment, and, for whatever reason, I was struggling to maintain my composure in his company.

When I had returned to the library with Mother and Father in my wake, I had been delighted to discover that, not only was George paying no attention at all to Mr. Donovan's lessons, they had abandoned them altogether, replacing them with child's play. Father had been suitably annoyed at the sight—and Mr. Donovan deliciously embarrassed—until Mother had stepped in and ruined things.

As was so often the case, Father unwittingly took Mother's lead, going so far as to create his own paper dart and engage in the silliness of tossing them about a room meant for somber study and reflection. It was akin to sacrilege.

And, as though that had not been enough, he had invited Mr. Donovan to dine with us this evening! It was the perfect opportunity for him to demonstrate his intellect, further solidifying his place at Bettencourt Court.

Eyeing my notebook on the escritoire against the wall, I walked over and opened it, quickly scribbling my next requirement: *an average mind.* I did not wish for a husband whose intellect eclipsed my own. I would be forever overshadowed.

After a moment of thought, I added *an average frame.* Not too muscular. I still very much doubted Mr. Donovan's assertion that he was not a sporting gentleman. He claimed he had never hunted, boxed, or ridden to hounds. Perhaps he was telling the truth. But what of fencing? Shooting? Driving to an inch? Granted, given the depth of understanding he displayed of classical texts and other topics of interest to me, I could only infer that, if he *had* made a practice of something like fencing, it must have been with a rapier in one hand and a book in the other.

The image danced about in my head for a moment, intriguing me against my will.

It was nonsensical, and I pushed it aside, pressing the notebook closed and going to join Mother in the carriage, wondering if Mr. Donovan and George were still engaging in dart throwing. The way Mr. Donovan had looked at me just before I left the library had been—

"You look flushed, my dear," Mother said as I took my seat across from her.

"This heat is unbearable," I said, well aware that it was not nearly as hot here as it had been in London. I was wearing my coolest dress, in fact, and I was not particularly hot. If I appeared flushed, it must be a result of the hurry I had been in to descend from my bedchamber.

"Hopefully, the company at the picnic will make up for that," Mother said, smiling a bit too pointedly for my taste.

I stared at her, waiting for her to expound.

"Lady Violet is always careful to ensure there are plenty of young people to enliven things. It will be a splendid opportunity for you to converse with eligible gentlemen, and I hope you will take advantage of the opportunity to make the very astute observations you are so capable of. It is much easier to do so in an environment like this one than when you are cooped up at home with no male company to speak of."

I nearly mentioned Mr. Donovan, but thought better of it. Mother was referring to *eligible* male company, and he certainly did not fall into that category. One need look no farther than the number of observations he had motivated to see that. Each and every entry I had made was a requirement for a husband quite opposite of him. And then, of course, there was the fact that he was but a tutor.

Mother seemed to hope I would be inspired by today's young people, but *young* was not one of the desirable attributes I wished for in a hypothetical husband. I was more likely to find someone who appealed to me by frequenting the nearest spa town or putting an advertisement for wealthy gentlemen expected to die in the next few months in the *Daily Advertiser*.

That wasn't a terrible idea, in fact. Perhaps I could advertise as a solicitor looking to help gentlemen arrange their final affairs, then manage an introduction to the most promising candidates. Promising meaning least likely to survive through Christmas.

That made me sound terribly heartless, didn't it? But I would be perfectly honest with the man. He would be under no impression it was a match motivated by anything other than mutual benefit—my future in exchange for an heir.

Of course, this was only supposing my preferred plan was rendered unachievable, and I trusted that would not happen.

L ady Violet's picnic, held at her estate in Milldale, was a wilderness, full of young and spry men and women and their middle-aged parents but severely lacking in the old and decrepit.

Her arm threaded through mine, Mother pulled me nearer as we approached Lady Violet and Sir Thomas. "I charge you to find the least objectionable young man here, my dear."

"Is that what Father was for you?"

Mother was prevented from responding, as we came before our hosts just then.

Once that was accomplished, she took it upon herself to foster conversation between every bachelor in attendance and myself. Though part of me wished to disappoint her by making no observations at all, my mind was a force to be reckoned with, and it insisted upon making them without any prodding—or even permission.

The truth was, I found all of them highly objectionable. There was no choosing between them. Vapid, grinning dandies, the lot of them.

Well, not the lot of them. Mr. Clements was dour and somberly dressed. He was also a foot shorter than I, and his breath reeked of anise. But he was on the shady side of thirty, which was more than I could say for the other men in attendance, all of whom seemed to be mere babes of five-and-twenty or thereabouts.

Sufferable. That was the word I had first inscribed in my notebook, and as our anise-filled conversation progressed, I tried to determine whether Mr. Clements met such a requirement. I could not decide such a thing for certain, so I moved on to another of my requirements.

His body had certainly not been cultivated, unless perhaps a steady diet of mutton, port, and anise were considered cultivation. As for his mind... a bit of prodding would be necessary to discover that.

"Mr. Clements," I said, as he wiped the sweat from his brow with a handkerchief. "Who do you consider the hero of Sophocles' *Ajax*?"

I might as well cross two items off my list. Efficiency was the mark of a strong mind.

Mr. Clements's brow knit for a moment at my strange and abrupt question, and I envisioned his name, written in my notebook, my pencil poised next to it, prepared to strike it through or circle it.

"Ajax," he said, as though it was the most obvious thing in the world.

And it was. It was the correct answer. And yet, I found it supremely dissatisfying. It was so terribly obvious and boring.

Excusing myself a moment later, I made my way to the drink table. My progress was impeded, though, when a young brunette woman stepped in front of me.

I blinked, surprised at the almost aggressive behavior, but the genuine smile she wore as she stared at me laid some of my qualms to rest.

"Forgive me," she said in a voice full of energy, "but are you Lady Sarah Danneville?"

"Yes," I said with a hint of wariness and a dash of curiosity.

She placed a hand on the front of her dress, which protruded slightly, betraying she was with child. "How delightful! It is quite wrong of me to introduce myself to you like this, of course"—she looked around as though someone might detain her for her impertinence—"but I could not resist."

I smiled a bit. I couldn't help but like her artless manner, unusual though it was. "But *you* have not introduced yourself to me yet."

She laughed. "I suppose I haven't. I am Rebecca Donovan." She gave a curtsy.

My brows went up as I returned it with my own casual one. "Donovan..."

She nodded quickly. "Yes, my brother-in-law is tutoring your brother."

My gaze intensified, for I found her more interesting than ever. This spritely young woman who approached strangers was the sister-in-law of the staid tutor?

She glanced behind her and smiled guiltily at the man approaching. "And here is my husband to chastise me for my forwardness."

He was a handsome man, dark in coloring and expression, providing a striking contrast to his exuberant wife... and to his brother, the tutor, for that matter.

"Isn't that right?" she said, taking him by the arm.

"Probably not," he said, "but it is difficult to say without being told what I am agreeing to."

"I was just telling Lady Sarah that you had come to censure me for introducing myself."

"Have I ever censured you for anything, my love?"

It was strange to hear the endearment from a man with such an aloof expression. Was this a love match or one of convenience? The way he tenderly—and quite needlessly—brushed at one of the hairs in her coiffure told me it was the former.

Mrs. Donovan smiled up at him, a warm and loving light in her eyes. "No. I suppose not. You are far too indulgent."

I observed the brief holding of gazes between them as I always observed such displays of romance: with a mixture of curiosity and distaste. Nothing could induce me to look at a man in such a sickly and adoring way.

"Now that I have transgressed custom," Mrs. Donovan said, "I may as well introduce you, as well, do you not agree? Lady Sarah, this is my husband, Mr. Valentine Donovan."

He bowed.

"Very pleased to meet you, Mr. Donovan," I said.

"And now that that is taken care of," Mrs. Donovan said, "you must tell us how Phineas is faring, my lady. I had hoped he would write us immediately upon his arrival to Bettencourt Court, but alas, we have not heard a peep from him."

I hesitated, unsure how to communicate that, though I had spent an appreciable amount of time in the same room as him, I not only was unaware how he was truly faring, but had been doing my utmost to see that he would fare *ill.* "I believe," I said, "that he is doing well."

"I doubt she has conversed much with him, my love. It has only been three days, after all." Mr. Donovan's gaze moved to me, regarding me as though he was taking my measure. Had the hedging in my tone betrayed that I was being intentionally vague? His gaze seemed inordinately piercing, but I met it the only way I knew how: unflinchingly.

Now that I came to think of it, I had heard of Valentine Donovan. But I could have sworn his rakish reputation had been what set him apart. Here he was, though, married to the most spritely of women, and apparently in love with her.

There was something disappointing in that. Bluestockings and rakes were opposites in most ways, the former dedicating themselves to the pursuit of knowledge and the practice of logic, while the latter let themselves be consumed by their carnal appetites, but at least in one thing they often agreed: love was to be avoided. But Mr. Donovan here was unfortunate evidence that even rakes fell prey to their emotions sometimes.

"A great deal can happen in three days," his wife responded. "The third day after meeting you, I was already halfway in love."

He smiled slightly, glancing at her in affectionate amusement. "Yes, but Phineas is not nearly as intelligent as you."

My ears perked up. *Not nearly as intelligent as you.* That was certainly interesting. Without wishing to offend Mrs. Donovan, I did not take her for a bluestocking by any stretch of the imagination. And if her brother-in-law was not even as intelligent as *her*...

My good fortune suddenly occurred to me. This was my opportunity to learn things about Mr. Donovan I didn't dare ask him myself and to verify the truth of what he had told me.

Mrs. Donovan turned to me. "You mustn't listen to my husband, Lady Sarah. He is forever teasing Phineas. Brothers are wont to do such things, I believe. Phineas is terribly bright."

Terribly bright. The question remained what qualified as "bright" to Mrs. Donovan.

But rather than refine upon that, I seized my opportunity. "I admit, when I first saw him, I took him for more of a sporting gentleman."

Mr. Donovan stared at me blankly. His wife's eyes widened. Then, the two of them erupted into laughter, Mr. Donovan covering his mouth and his wife hanging on his arm as they exhausted their amusement.

I managed a smile, remembering how Mr. Donovan—*my* Mr. Donovan—no, not *my* Mr. Donovan, but Mr. Phineas Donovan—had predicted just such a reaction to my comment.

"That is quite enough," Mrs. Donovan said, though the chastisement in her voice was weakened significantly by the way it trembled with the remnants of her laughter. "Forgive us, Lady Sarah. It is only that Phineas is... well, he is—"

"He hasn't a sporting bone in his body," her husband stated baldly. "What in the world would have made you think such a thing?"

Heat trickled into my cheeks. How precisely was I to say I found his brother's body an ideal specimen of the male form? At least, as far as one could tell when a body was encased in pantaloons and a coat rather than fully displayed like the entirely unclad statues in a museu—

Oh, dear. If this was how I was phrasing things in my head,

it would be better not to venture into the topic at all. Thankfully, Mrs. Donovan saved me the trouble of responding.

"Nonsense! Phineas may care for books more than anything else in this world, and I would never call him a *sporting gentleman*, but you must admit he has a fine set of shoulders despite that. Perhaps we know less about him than we think. Everyone has their secrets, you know. It is possible he is a better shot than even you, dear."

"Yes. About as possible as *you* being a better shot than me." He looked at me. "Content yourself, my lady, that *my* brother is perfectly suited to be tutoring *your* brother. If you want someone to ride to hounds with you or to take your place as a second in a duel, leave Phineas to his books for the safety of everyone involved. But if you wish to discuss or be taught anything of an intellectual nature—from poetry to politics to arithmetic—you could not find a better candidate."

I manufactured a smile, though I was secretly annoyed. "While I appreciate your fraternal praises, surely you cannot truly mean to say that, in the whole of England, there is no one who might be better suited to a tutoring position."

Mr. Donovan's lips curled up at one edge, a sardonic half-smile. "If you knew me better, my lady, you would not accuse me of *fraternal praise*. Or of hyperbole, for that matter. I meant what I said." He held my gaze for another moment. "If you will excuse me, now, my lady. It was a pleasure to meet you."

Mrs. Donovan squeezed his hand and smiled, but did not follow him. Once he had moved a dozen feet away, she looked up at me with a sheepish smile. "My husband cannot abide being accused of sentimentality, you know, though he cares for his brother deeply. But despite that private brotherly affection, he is quite right about Phineas."

I wanted to prod her to expound, but I had no desire to seem overly inquisitive. Happily for me, Mrs. Donovan was inclined to satisfy my curiosity.

"Of course, I was not there for any of this, but I have pieced together a great deal despite that. Phineas's mother always indulged his bookishness while she was alive. He suffered greatly at the hands of the other ship's boys, though, for he was always sneaking away to read. His father, too—the admiral—could never abide his preference for reading over sailing, and when Phineas begged to attend the Naval Academy rather than continue sailing, the admiral flatly refused. Phineas resigned the moment he reached his twenty-first birthday, studying on his own and working to gain a scholarship to Cambridge, as his father refused to pay the fees." She let out a large breath. "All of this to say, Phineas has fought harder and endured more bullying and abuse than anyone I know in his quest for learning. Your brother is in the best—and kindest—of hands."

Well.

That was not at all what I had been hoping to hear. Neither did I particularly care for the way Mrs. Donovan's words moved me to compassion for the man. But how could one not be inspired to hear of those who suffered in the cause and pursuit of knowledge?

Guilt for my treatment of him, for the way I had encouraged George in his pranks niggled at me.

It was possible Mr. and Mrs. Donovan were merely saying what they believed would assure their brother's place at Bettencourt Court, but it did not seem that way. He already *had* the position, after all, and they had been eager enough to point out where he was lacking.

Which led me to an uncomfortable question: *was* it in George's best interest to be taught by Mr. Donovan rather than by me? This was the first time I had considered such an idea, and it sat ill with me, bitter on my tongue.

He did seem to have more patience for George than I had expected. Cruelty seemed antithetical to his nature, and that was an even greater fear for me than the possibility that my brother's education would be lacking. And according to Mr. Donovan's family, he was well-qualified.

Besides, if I was to follow Lady Harriet Stanhope's path, I would not be able to tutor George for long, and then what would become of him? I would not even be present to advocate for him, to see that any lacking tutors were dismissed, to ensure he was not sent to Harrow out of Father's frustration.

Perhaps it was time to consider stepping back from my plan to oust Mr. Donovan.

Chapter Twelve

SARAH

I watched Mr. Donovan carefully at dinner. That he was uncomfortable was obvious to anyone with eyes. He was not adept in the art of polite conversation, and that endeared him to me against my will—an occurrence which was becoming altogether too regular.

He cleaned his glasses using his napkin no less than four times, despite their looking quite immaculate to me—two perfectly clear conduits to his blue eyes. But even when his spectacles rested on his nose, he often readjusted them. These were nervous habits, I could only assume.

I could see no resemblance at all between him and his brother, Valentine. They were both handsome, of course—at least I imagined those who took notice of such things would have said as much—but in entirely different ways.

I tried to picture Mr. Donovan as a young ship's boy, reading books through crooked spectacles while the others taunted him. Was his suggestion of melted tallow to obscure his lenses a suggestion from his own personal experience? The image my mind created tugged at my heartstrings a bit, making me wish his brother and sister-in-law had resisted telling me any of his history. It was far easier to dislike a person when one was not aware of their hardships.

More regret for having encouraged George in his pranks niggled me. Of course, Mr. Donovan had not seemed terribly troubled by them; he had responded with an aggravating amount of patience and equanimity. But perhaps he was adept at hiding his feelings. That was certainly something I could appreciate.

He seemed most at ease when addressed by George, with whom he seemed to have reached some sort of understanding, such that George was in very good humor, constantly speaking of the plans they had to test Newtonian laws and Bernoulli's theories in a dart throwing competition tomorrow.

Mother, too, seemed intent on putting him at his ease, and when she asked him about his time at Cambridge, he was able to speak easily on a number of topics. I envied him his time at Cambridge, with such a grand library at his disposal and such an abundance of strong minds to interact with.

Over the course of the meal, I chimed in several times with my opinions. When I did so, Mr. Donovan's gaze would settle on me, his hands stationary as he listened. I had to resist the urge to squirm under his eye, for not only was I unused to being regarded in such an intent way when offering my thoughts, his expression was impossible to decipher.

I was almost regretful by the time Mother, George, and I withdrew, for Mr. Donovan and Father continued their conversation about the unrest fomenting in the north, a topic I had been following for some months.

I was mending a pair of stockings later when the doors to the drawing room opened and Father entered. He shut the door behind himself, and I frowned. Perhaps Mr. Donovan had tired of polite conversation. Or, just as likely, he wished to spend his evening reading those frivolous novels of his.

Apparently, he had forgotten his offer to lend me one. I

stamped out the regret and the spark of curiosity such a thought produced. I had far better things to occupy my time and mind than reminding him of his offer.

I paused on the next stitch.

Mr. Donovan did not strike me as the forgetful type, though. Perhaps he knew I would find the novels ridiculous and beneath me, and he hoped I would simply forget our interaction this morning.

I smiled. If he thought *I* was the sort to forget, he was very wrong indeed. I would not encourage George in pranking Mr. Donovan anymore, but it was my responsibility to ensure the man tutoring my brother—the future Earl of Bettencourt—was not filling his own mind and, consequently, my brother's, with utter nonsense.

While I would have liked to march straight to his bedchamber and confront him about the unfulfilled promise, I would have to wait until the library tomorrow morning.

I finished a few more stitches in the stocking, then set it aside, feeling restless. Mother was sorting the tangle of threads in the sewing box, while Father had opened a copy of *The Globe* in his favorite chair by the fire.

"Father," I said. "Have we any novels?"

He looked up, brow knit. "Novels?" I might as well have asked him whether he intended to sleep in the stables. "Of course not. Why in heaven's name should we—"

"We do, my dear," Mother said placidly.

"We do not," Father insisted.

Mother smiled serenely. "Not in the library, no. But I have one or two in my sitting room." She turned her attention to me. "Why do you ask?" Was I mistaken, or was there a hopeful light in her eyes as she waited for me to answer?

"Surely you have not taken to reading novels, Sarah." Father looked at me over the top of his reading glasses, visibly concerned. That certainly did not bode well for Mr. Donovan.

"Why shouldn't she?" Mother asked.

"Novels," he replied firmly, "are for silly girls."

"And you fear Sarah is likely to become a silly girl if she reads one?" Based on the way her eyes smiled, Mother found this an amusing idea.

"She reads far too much as is, but at least there is substance to such books rather than vulgar novels written by vulgar persons."

"Content yourselves," I intervened. "My question was a mere matter of curiosity." And my curiosity had only grown, but I did not care to encourage either Father or Mother in whatever they had inferred from my question. I rose. "If you will excuse me, I shall turn in early tonight, I think."

Mother generally stayed in the drawing room until ten o'clock, which meant I had enough time to pay a quick visit to her sitting room to see precisely which novels she kept there.

I closed the drawing room door behind me and made my way down the corridor, looking back just as I turned the corner to ensure Mother had not taken it in her head to follow my example and retire early.

I collided with something solid, stumbling a bit. Mr. Donovan did the same, though he stabilized me with a hand on my arm.

"Forgive me, my lady," he said, blinking in surprise.

I pulled my arm gently but firmly from his, annoyed at the unnecessary reminder of his solid frame and firm grip.

"Mr. Donovan," I said, taking a further step back. "I thought you had retired for the evening." I glanced at his hand, which held a book. My lip pulled up at the corner. He *was* spending his evening reading a novel.

"I merely went to fetch this from my bedchamber for you." He held the book toward me.

My smile disintegrated, and I read the spine. *Sense and Sensibility*.

He had not forgotten. In fact, it looked as though he had intended to bring it to the drawing room, where he would have given it to me in full view of Father. If only I had waited instead of giving in to my restlessness, it was entirely possible Father would have dismissed him then and there.

Strangely, I felt a shred of relief such a thing had not transpired. I needed to understand why someone like Mr. Donovan felt devoting time to novel reading a worthy pursuit.

"This is only the first of three volumes, of course," he said, still holding it out awkwardly.

I raised my brows and took it from him. "Should I not be judging the work in its entirety?"

He held my gaze, and the corridor suddenly felt narrower. I scoffed inwardly at my own thought. Corridors did not simply become narrower. That sort of observation was precisely what I expected to find in a romance novel.

"Of course," he said. "That is, I thought we might discuss this volume before you continue to the next one. If you choose to continue, that is."

It took me a moment to respond. I had not at all been expecting such a response. "Is there so much to discuss after one volume?"

"I rather think so." The hint of a smile pulled at one corner of his mouth. "But something tells me that you and I could discuss one simple *line* for hours."

I swallowed with difficulty. *You and I.* He said it as though it was the most natural thing in the world to speak of us in such a way—together. I should give him a set down for his presumption.

But it did not feel like presumption. Instead, it made me feel breathless. "Discuss it? Or quarrel over it?"

He held my gaze in his particular way, as though those perfectly clear spectacles allowed him to see more of me than he otherwise could have. "Discuss it," he said.

"And when do you propose we carry out such *discussions?*"

He inclined his head. "At your convenience, my lady. If you continue to spend time in the library, I imagine we will find plenty of opportunity while Lord Danneville applies himself to some of the exercises I have in mind."

Well. That was quite optimistic of him. George was not at all the type to sit quietly and do arithmetic. He was more likely to write an impish message for his tutor to read. But Mr. Donovan would discover that soon enough.

"Certainly," I said, looking at the book.

"I hope you enjoy reading *Sense and Sensibility*, my lady," he said. "I look forward to hearing your honest opinions, whatever they may be."

Oh, I would be quite honest with him. And I doubted he would enjoy it.

Chapter Thirteen

PHINEAS

The sun had reached its apex an hour ago and was beginning its slow descent toward the horizon, passing behind swathes of clouds and casting shadows over the lawns behind Bettencourt Court.

Lord Danneville skipped ahead of me, holding one of the two baskets of darts we had spent the last hour folding in the library. Lady Sarah had not made an appearance this morning, and I tried not to wonder if I had overstepped in mentioning the possibility of discussing the novel together. I hoped not, for I was looking forward to it as I had not looked forward to anything for quite some time.

Handing her *Sense and Sensibility* was one of the more terrifying things I had done in my life, though. I had personally given her the means to have me dismissed. Suggesting we discuss it together was the only way I knew to prevent that. I needed her to see the value in the books, which meant I myself was obliged to acknowledge their value. I was finding the task much easier than I had thought, catching glimpses of the truths Rebecca had mentioned, even. These were not equations or laws of physics; they were truths about humanity.

"Just there, I think," I called to the viscount as we came to a small rise in the lawn.

"A fine place for the competition," he said as he set down the basket.

He had complained at first when I had insisted he apply himself to some Latin and arithmetic this morning, but with the promise of a dart-flying competition urging him along, he had capitulated. Enough, in fact, that I had been able to peruse the book of sermons Mr. Vickers had recommended on my visit to the vicarage.

I came abreast of Lord Danneville and set my own basket next to his. In my other hand, I held a brief-bag, containing the pencil and papers we would use to note which darts performed best. It would not be the most scientific of exercises, but it was my goal to help engender Lord Danneville with a greater curiosity to learn, and this, I hoped, would accomplish that, allowing him to see the value in Newtonian laws and the like, while satisfying his desire for fresh air and entertainment.

Each day, I learned more about my charge. He was impatient with learning and quick to become angry when he did not find immediate success at something. He had no patience for arithmetic, for instance, when his answers were incorrect. In fact, he had made intentional errors when I had tried to explain how to correct the previous faults.

He took very well to the competition, however, noting the distances—marked by buttons and measured by string—between the various darts with high precision and willingly doing the arithmetic to determine the differences between them.

In fact, it was he who suggested we throw each dart three separate times, then take the mean distance to determine its overall score. Was it possible the suggestion was grounded in a desire to prolong the competition and avoid less desirable learning endeavors? I had no doubt at all of it. But I would not discourage him in anything that would lead to a greater understanding of physics and arithmetic.

There *was* something invigorating about seeing Bernoulli's principle and Newton's laws at work—and to see the satisfaction they produced in Lord Danneville.

We were nearly through the second round of throwing when Lady Sarah emerged on horseback from the trees that lined the lawn on all but one side. A groom followed her a short distance behind.

I suppressed a sigh. Naturally, she would find us when we were engaged in the least studious of our endeavors today.

But her eyes were trained on the path before her, giving me hope she would not see us at all. It also gave me the opportunity to admire her for a moment. The deep blue skirts of her riding habit spilled over the hindquarters of her bay mount, perfectly matching the hat set at a jaunty angle atop her glinting hair. Her cheeks were becomingly flushed, and though I could only see her profile, I could imagine her blue eyes would be bright.

"Mr. Donovan!"

I blinked and turned to the viscount, who was frowning at me, annoyed by my lack of attention—or that it had been trained on his sister.

I cleared my throat, hoping my cravat adequately concealed the heat creeping into my neck.

"Euclid went a far greater distance this time," he said, pointing to where it lay past the other four. I had convinced him to name the darts based on significant figures in the history of physics and arithmetic. "An interesting development, don't you think?"

"Yes, yes," I concurred, forcing myself not to look in Lady Sarah's direction.

"It is your turn now."

"So it is." I picked up Galileo the Dart, focusing my mind on my throwing technique. A dart was only as good as the force that launched it into the air, after all.

I was not a good force, as it turned out. The dart dove for the ground, landing far short of its fellows.

"Apparently, the force applied was not sufficient."

My head whirled around.

Lady Sarah pulled on the reins, bringing her horse to a stop a dozen feet away. She wore a smile that tripped my heart, a strangely physical reaction. Her groom descended from his mount, but she slipped down from hers without his assistance, handing him the reins and striding toward us.

Her brother shot her a glance but otherwise ignored her, picking up his next dart.

"Archimedes," he called out just as he launched it into the air. It sailed well past mine, gliding elegantly and evenly toward the ground, where it landed just behind his last attempt.

"What interesting educational practices you espouse, Mr. Donovan," Lady Sarah said, coming up beside me as George picked up the brief-bag and string and ran toward the darts scattered across the lawn. "George will never want to open a book again."

I looked over at her and found her eyes on me. Behind her, the groom made his way toward the stables with both horses. "That is quite the opposite of what I hope for, my lady. Do you not find it valuable to put knowledge into practice?"

"Certainly I find it valuable," she replied, "but not at the expense of spending time with the texts themselves, which is something George could use more of."

I watched as he carefully measured the distance between buttons, then wrote on the paper. "Yes, I think you are right. But, in my experience, not all students respond equally well to the same teaching methods. Some students of learning must be shown its value through the application of principles."

"Yourself, for instance?"

I chuckled and clasped my hands behind my back. "No, I have always fallen quite firmly in the other camp. I had little interest in hoisting the sails of a ship, but if you gave me a book about navigation or maps—something most of my fellow sailors would have gladly thrown overboard or used as kindling—I would happily read it from cover to cover in a matter of hours."

"You did not enjoy your time in the Navy, then?"

My mouth turned down at the edges in contemplation. No one had ever asked me such a question. "I found it... difficult."

"Is that not merely another way of saying you did not enjoy it?"

She had taken off her hat, leaving her hair in a state of subtle unruliness I found my gaze drawn to. She looked at me frankly, and I found it simultaneously unnerving and flattering. Most women's gazes paused on me for only the briefest of moments, if at all. Lady Sarah looked at me as though she was trying to divine my thoughts.

"In a sense, perhaps," I said. "At least at the time. I am better able to appreciate it in retrospect. That is how it is with challenges, I suppose. I did things in the Navy I would never otherwise have known myself capable of—things I would only have known in theory."

"But you *prefer* theory."

"Infinitely."

"That was apparent from the dart you threw," she said with dry humor.

I chuckled softly. "I shan't pretend to be adept at throwing darts, my lady, but surely, by looking at the others, you can see that dart was an exception."

She kept her lips pressed together, making no response, though there was a slight twinkle in her eye that told me she was merely trying to goad me.

I was not one to be goaded. But there were exceptions to every rule, and for whatever reason, I felt inclined to play this game with Lady Sarah. "Lord Danneville," I said as he made his way toward us, "your sister has just informed me that we have been using the incorrect form while throwing these darts. She has graciously offered to instruct us in the proper method."

The viscount scoffed. "She will ruin our mean distances, more likely!"

"Come, now," I said, watching as Lady Sarah shot her brother a look. "Surely, she deserves an opportunity to prove her claims."

Lord Danneville seemed unconvinced, but he set down the brief-bag and string in exchange for the basket. Taking it with him, he went to collect the darts.

"If you recall," Lady Sarah said slowly, her gaze fixed on me, "I made no claim at all. I merely remarked that your preference for theory over practice was evident in the way you threw the last dart."

"Implying you are familiar enough with the proper method to execute it with greater success."

"Tell me, Mr. Donovan," she said in a tone of false fascination, "do you always make such unsupported leaps of logic from simple observations?"

"When there is a hypothesis to test *and* entertainment to be had?" I unsuccessfully suppressed a smile. "Without exception. Though, I take issue with your characterization of it as a *leap of logic*. It seems quite a reasonable one to me."

Lady Sarah smiled amusedly but said nothing, staring forward as her brother collected dart after dart.

Normally, I would assist him, but at the moment, I found it suited me that he carry out the task himself. It was important for him to learn to see through even the dullest bits of an experiment. This had nothing to do with wanting to remain in his sister's presence. Or at least not much.

"Your smile tells me you disagree with me yet again," I

commented. "I wish you will tell me the reason for it. I assure you I am well able to withstand any criticism you might have."

She looked at me for a moment. "Very well. It was only a thought I had that what is reasonable to a man whose study material includes romance novels might not be considered reasonable to others."

"Others such as yourself?"

She gave an acknowledging nod. It was a subtle, graceful gesture, and it struck me.

I looked at the grass at my feet, which trembled slightly in the breeze. The fact that Lady Sarah spent a great deal of her time between the pages of the same books I valued had made me feel a level of kinship with her. Granted, she had shown a strong inclination to disagree with me on every topic we had discussed, but that did not bother me. Indeed, I found it enlivening. In many ways, I had more in common with someone who vehemently disagreed with me on a host of topics than with someone who regarded all such topics with ignorance or apathy. It was that feeling of kinship which had encouraged me to suggest discussing the novels together.

But I had been deluded.

Lady Sarah Danneville was just that: *Lady* Sarah Danneville. She was the daughter of an earl, gently bred, raised with an innate sense of her superiority and duty.

I, on the other hand, was a tutor, the third son of an admiral, however respected he might be. To her, I was more servant than friend. And that was the proper way of things. I should be more concerned with educating Lord Danneville than with convincing his sister not to regard my novel-reading with contempt.

"Lady Sarah," I said, "there is no obligation whatsoever for you to read the volume I gave you. And there is certainly none to discuss it with me." She looked at me strangely.

"You wish for me to return it to you?" Was there a touch of annoyance in her question?

"I wish," I said slowly, "for you to do what pleases you, my lady"—I smiled wryly—"and neither of us can pretend you believe reading *Sense and Sensibility* will accomplish such a thing."

She was silent for a moment, and the hairs which her removed bonnet had disturbed fluttered with the breeze, quivering threads of spun gold, highlighted by the sun.

I looked away, for it was too easy to admire Lady Sarah if I allowed myself the opportunity.

"So," she said on a sigh, "I read an entire volume for naught."

I whipped my head around.

She smiled, as though she could see the thoughts I was having. "I am a fast reader, Mr. Donovan. Yet, now you mean to deprive me of your opinion of the Dashwoods and the Ferrars. I feel as though I have been tricked."

"My lady," I said, "I assure you I am more than happy to discuss anything you wish—"

"Very good. Tomorrow morning, then, in the library, while George throws darts or"—she waved a hand in the air—"whatever unconventional activities you prescribe."

I couldn't help laughing, feeling a lightness in my chest. "Tomorrow is Sunday, my lady."

"So it is. All the better, for George shan't disturb us."

I grimaced. "I *did* tell him we would go for a walk after church, assuming the weather agrees."

"Then I shall join you."

Somewhat breathless, Lord Danneville trudged to us with his basket full of darts. "You may throw, Sarah," he said resignedly, "but I shall fetch the dart after and throw it myself to preserve the integrity of our experiment."

Proud to hear such a loyalty to accuracy on Lord Danneville's lips, I gave an approving nod and caught Lady Sarah's eye, which held as much reluctant amusement as I felt.

"And what if I manage to throw the dart farther than *all* of yours?" she said as her brother handed her the first one from the basket.

Lord Danneville only snorted in response, and I watched determination ignite in her eyes as Lady Sarah took the dart. I put out a hand, offering to take her bonnet, and she thanked me with a small smile that, scientifically speaking, shouldn't have affected the rate at which my heart beat.

"You must stand just behind there." The viscount stood a few feet in front of her and pointed to a place where a string had been stretched across the grass.

Lady Sarah complied, standing just behind the mark and rolling her shoulders as she looked at the lawn before her.

"Go on, then," her brother said impatiently.

Her gaze flicked to me, and I tried to control my desire to smile. Lady Sarah might be the daughter of an earl, but her younger brother was the *future* earl, and he had no compunction speaking to her in such a way, despite the fact that he was more than a decade her junior.

Lady Sarah reached her arm back, then thrust it forward, releasing the dart into the air.

Chapter Fourteen

SARAH

T he dart flew forward, carrying the weight of my hopes on its frail wings.

The weight was too great. And unbalanced, apparently, for it veered to the right and straight into George's face.

He cried out, grasping at his eye and stumbling backward as the dart plummeted to the grass.

"George!" I rushed over and fell to my knees, and Mr. Donovan followed suit, joining me at his side.

"My eye," George said, pain making his voice tight and breathy.

"My dear George," I said, putting a hand to his and imagining the worst behind them. "I am so very sorry! How very stupid of me! Will you let me see?"

After a moment, he removed his hands from his face. His left eye was pinched shut, but there was no blood—thank heaven. It was entirely possible I had blinded him, though.

"Can you see, my lord?" Mr. Donovan's hand on George's shoulder, and his even voice settled my nerves, if only slightly.

George's lids blinked in quick succession as he attempted to open his injured eye. The short glimpses I had of it were enough to tell me it was terribly bloodshot.

"It does not want to open," George said in frustration. "And it hurts to try."

Swallowing, I glanced at Mr. Donovan, who set a reassuring hand on my arm. "Let us give it a moment's rest rather than trying to force it open."

I nodded, my conscience writhing. I worried for George as it was, for he had such difficulty learning. The last thing he needed was another difficulty, another reason for people to tease him.

George rubbed at his eye, but Mr. Donovan gently pulled his hand away. "It will only agitate it more. Try to let it be."

"It hurts!" George yelled in frustration, batting the tutor's hand away.

Mr. Donovan was unperturbed by the aggressiveness of the gesture and merely retreated. "I am certain it does."

"Well," George said, his tone still savage, "I think we can safely say you have no knowledge at all of how to throw a dart, Sarah."

"None at all," I agreed, sitting beside him and putting my arm around his shoulders. I glanced at Mr. Donovan, and our gazes met, his warm and appreciative.

I felt a wretch. I had let my competitiveness be drawn out by Mr. Donovan, and George had been the casualty. I rested my head against his, and though he pulled his head away a bit at first, he allowed it.

"I accept my punishment," I said.

"Punishment?" George asked testily, though there was a sliver of interest in his voice.

"It is only just."

"What sort of punishment?" His expression softened, and Mr. Donovan smiled at me.

"I shall... I shall stand before you and... allow you to throw the other darts at me."

George removed his head from under mine, his left eye still shut. "In the eye?"

"Good heavens, George," I said.

"Mosaic Law reigns supreme," Mr. Donovan said softly. The glass of his spectacles seemed to amplify the twinkling of his eyes. "Perhaps you should invest in a pair of spectacles, my lady."

I stared at him. Had he read my mind?

His smile fell slightly. "To act as a shield against the darts."

"Ah," I said, laughing. "Yes, indeed. But, George, you don't truly mean to throw a dart at my eye, do you?"

His brow furrowed as he thought for far longer about the matter than should have been necessary. "I suppose not," he said reluctantly. "I shall have my revenge when you least expect it." He blinked a few times, finally opening the injured lid.

"There!" I said, putting out my hands. "It is perfectly fine now! No harm done." A threat of revenge from George was enough to make one's blood curdle. "Come now," I said, making to rise from the ground and hoping to change the subject so that George would forget his oath of vengeance. "You still have an experiment to finish, do you not?"

My skirts stuck under my foot, and Mr. Donovan rushed from the ground, offering me his hand.

I accepted his offer, and he pulled me up with ease.

I hadn't meant to tell him I had read the entire volume of *Sense and Sensibility* over the course of last night and this morning, but the prospect of shocking him had been too enticing. And I hadn't wanted to give up the discussions he had promised. I was very interested indeed in what he had to say about the story.

It had been quite different from what I had expected. There was nothing gothic in the story, nothing overly sentimental, and, if I was being truthful, I had been pleasantly surprised by the author's wit.

But I did not intend to let Mr. Donovan know such a thing. He would still have to fight to persuade me that such books were more worthy of my time than Dante or Plutarch.

I stayed to observe while he and George finished their experiment. George managed to throw a dart at me in one of my less attentive moments, though it only hit me in the back of the head. He assured me it did not count as his revenge, successfully ridding me of the hope he would forget his sworn oath.

As for Mr. Donovan... I sighed as I watched him clap while George threw the tenth and final dart. I was finding it harder and harder to dislike him. And, even if that had not been true, George seemed to have taken to him quite well, which made the likelihood of getting rid of him far smaller.

"A fine experiment, my lord," said Mr. Donovan once George had written all the entries on the paper they had brought.

I took the paper from George to take a look at it myself. It was quite impressive, actually—all the more so because it was George who had carried it out. He was not one for completing tasks.

"Perhaps we should do a fourth round," George said. "Surely that would make the results even more reliable."

I glanced at Mr. Donovan, curious to see if he would give in to George's obvious desire to prolong the activity. In my experience, people reacted in one of two ways to him: either they gave in to his whims, letting him rule the roost, or they lost all patience with him and became autocratic. Which route would Mr. Donovan choose? Or would he find a different way entirely?

"It would indeed make the results more reliable," Mr. Donovan acknowledged.

I felt a strange disappointment at the realization that he was going to let George overrule him.

"But why stop at four rounds?" Mr. Donovan continued. "Why not ten?"

George's eyes lit up with the promise of dart flying.

"Why not a hundred?" Mr. Donovan continued. "A thousand, even?"

I quite saw Mr. Donovan's point; I could even agree with it—at some point, observation had to cease so that the findings could be studied for insight—but the method of conveying it was wasted on George. It was worse than wasted, in fact.

George's hope gave way to annoyance, making his brow dark and pouty. "I don't *want* to go back to books."

"You have collected a great deal of information, my lord, and now we must try to decipher its meaning."

"I don't want to," George said, staring at Mr. Donovan with the mulish set to his jaw that foretold trouble.

Mr. Donovan was quiet, watching his charge as though trying to decide how to approach this sudden stubbornness. "This was the agreement we had, my lord."

I couldn't help admiring his calm but forthright words. He struck a fine balance between overindulgence and harshness. But George did not take the same view, his expression growing more foreboding and ominous.

All this time, I had been hoping to create just such a situation between him and Mr. Donovan, but now that it was before me, I found it less satisfying than anticipated. In fact, I was inclined to run to Mr. Donovan's rescue.

Well… rescue was perhaps too strong a word. I wouldn't mind causing a bit of mischief amidst the assistance I meant to give. And why not? His calmness under pressure couldn't but make me wish to test and try him a bit.

"George," I said, "if you are not careful, you will change Mr. Donovan's mind about the other enjoyable activities he has in store for you."

Mr. Donovan's head turned toward me, his brow furrowing slightly.

"Activities?" George said in a question, his face transforming with a swiftness only a child could manage.

"Yes," I said, my brain working quickly to decide how to save and challenge Mr. Donovan in one stroke. "He mentioned to me earlier that he intended to teach you a bit of... fencing, was it?" I looked to the tutor, who, to his credit, gave no outward indication that my fabrication was unwelcome.

"Fencing!" George exclaimed. "That is capital, Mr. Donovan!"

His eyes didn't stray from mine. It was quite impressive, in fact, the way he kept his equilibrium. I couldn't imagine him showing *any* strong emotion.

"It is, isn't it?" I said, continuing my mischief with zeal. "Mr. Donovan is a great proponent of putting knowledge into practice. I believe he mentioned something, too, about making a study of Greek tragedy through performance. Apparently, he is quite a skilled performer."

George's eyes widened further. "A play?" There was no mistaking the excitement in his voice.

Mr. Donovan held my gaze for a moment, a mixture of appreciation and amusement there—and perhaps a bit of promised vengeance—before he turned to his student. "I thought we could combine fencing and performance by making a study of *Ajax*. The reason I thought to mention it to your sister is that we can hardly perform Sophocles's *Ajax* with only the two of us." He turned his eyes on me again. "She kindly offered to join us, playing the role of Athena."

My eyes narrowed. There was no doubt in my mind that the role was chosen with significance. Athena played the part of deceiver in *Ajax*. "The goddess of wisdom," I said, smiling. "Of course, I did point out to Mr. Donovan there *is* no swordfighting in the story of *Ajax*, only the slaying of cattle—"

"To which I offered the reminder that Ajax *believes* himself to be fighting and slaying Agamemnon and Menelaus—a perfect opportunity for fencing. And as there are only three of us and far more roles than that, your sister offered to play Agamemnon and Menelaus, as well as Athena—"

"Though after further reflection," I said firmly, "I realized how *nonsensical* it would be to play the parts of two people who share the stage at one ti—"

"I want to be Ajax!" George cried out. "You can be Agamemnon, Mr. Donovan, and Sarah will be Menelaus, for then I shall be able to fight *both* of you." He suddenly stilled, looking back and forth between us as though he had realized something.

He stood straighter, his chin lifted, his eyes looking ahead at some point in the distance. "I shall use Father's sword," he said with reverence.

Mr. Donovan and I shared a look of horror, both of us no doubt imagining the damage a ten-year-old like George could do with the hefty sword Father displayed in his study.

"*Fencing*, George," I hurried to say. "One does not fence with a sword."

George was crestfallen, his newly envisioned dreams shattered to bits.

"No," Mr. Donovan said, "and as I imagine any épées your father possesses are meant for someone a great deal older than you, my lord, I thought we might search for the perfect sticks on our walk tomorrow after church."

"Sticks?" George spat out the word with contempt.

Oh, dear. There we were again, on the brink of one of George's outbursts. There was nothing a child disliked more than being made to *feel* like a child.

Mr. Donovan raised his brows. "You think yourself incapable of defeating me with a stick-sword?"

George scoffed.

"I assure you, my lord, that before Ajax became the warrior he is now known as, he practiced with sticks."

George seemed to consider this for a moment. "Very well. Let us find our sticks, then. I know just the place."

"Tomorrow," Mr. Donovan said. "And before we can do any practicing of the play, you must become acquainted with the text, of course." He looked at me. "Thankfully, your sister has read it four—*was* it four?—times, so she will be able to help us select the parts most worthy of performance."

And just like that, he placed my time at his disposal. I couldn't manage to be angry, though; I looked forward to seeing Mr. Donovan wield a stick and perform the part of Agamemnon.

As I watched him help George gather up their things, the words Dares the Phrygian used to describe Agamemnon came to mind: "…blond, large, and powerful. He was eloquent, wise, and noble, a man richly endowed."

Devil take Dares the Phrygian.

SARAH

Mr. Donovan was at dinner again that evening, and I resigned myself to the fact that he would be a fixture there going forward. Mother and Father both seemed to enjoy conversing with him, and now that the initial social niceties had given way to a more natural relationship, Mr. Donovan appeared more at ease.

Unexpectedly, I found his presence at dinner a relief in many ways, for it ensured a more interesting discussion while also acting as a safeguard against topics which would be deemed too personal to hold with a tutor in our midst.

When George retired to bed and Mother and I to the drawing room, however, the spell was broken, and Mother insisted on speaking on the topic I least wished to discuss: marriage.

"I am doing what I can to hold your father at bay, Sarah, but he is losing patience."

"Did he have any to begin with?" I said under my breath, pulling my needlework from the basket next to the sofa.

"He wants what is best for you, my dear."

"Which I very much appreciate." I took my seat. "But I am content as I am, Mother, and I am also quite capable of deciding the future for myself. He has enough to occupy him without needlessly saddling himself with that burden."

"It is not a burden. That is, not unless you make it one."

I cocked a brow. "Meaning?"

She met my gaze for a moment. "He worries you shall do something... unwise to ostracize yourself from polite society, making it more difficult to make a smart match."

"He shouldn't put ideas into my head," I said, trying not to imagine what Father would think if he knew I meant to follow in the footsteps of Lady Hester. It was inevitable, perhaps, but I hoped to delay that moment until everything was well in order. That way, he wouldn't be able to thwart me. He certainly had enough influence to do so if he had a mind to.

"Did you find anyone to your liking at the picnic yesterday?" Mother asked. "I saw you speaking with Mr. Clements for longer than most."

I repressed a shudder, almost able to smell the anise at the mere mention of him. "The people in attendance offered me plenty of things to contemplate."

I was being aggravatingly opaque, but I wished to delay any real conversation on this topic, for I had hopes this would be the week I heard from Cousin Arthur.

"Sarah," Mother said in a voice that told me she recognized what I was doing. "I know at this stage of your life and, given your interests, you feel that marriage is the last thing you wish for. I cannot blame you, but as your mother, I would be remiss if I did not warn you."

She took the seat beside me, facing her knees toward me as I worked to thread a new needle.

She waited until I looked up at her to continue. "Independence is a wonderful thing, but, as with anything, it does not come without sacrifice. I fear you may at some point realize the path you have chosen is a lonely one—and perhaps not as satisfying as it first seemed."

"And agreeing to chain myself to a man, to make myself and all I have his, *would* be satisfying? *That* would not be a sacrifice?"

Mother sighed.

"I merely want you to consider whether the goals you have for yourself, the things you wish to accomplish, are in fact achievable—perhaps even *more* achievable—within the safety of marriage. That is all."

She returned to her sewing and I to mine, though my mind lingered on her words.

Mr. Donovan did not come to the drawing room with Father, and I found myself fighting off annoyance. After finishing my sewing and spending half an hour at the piano, I retired for the evening.

Two books awaited me in front of the door to my bedchamber. Inside the cover of the top one was a note.

Lady Sarah,

I look forward to discussing Volume I with you tomorrow—and finding proper stick-swords—if you are still willing.

Your servant,

Phineas Donovan

I closed the cover and smiled.

There was little semblance of reverence in the church when I arrived with my brother and parents ten minutes before the beginning of the service. Soft chatter echoed amongst the tall stone walls of the nave. A certain amount of socializing was normal, but this was out of the ordinary.

It took only a moment for me to recognize the cause of the unusual volume of conversation, for heads turned again and again toward the chancel, where Mr. Vickers and Mr. Donovan stood talking. *Ah, yes.* Mr. Donovan. He was a new face amongst people who had spent the better part of the summer deprived of such a thing.

No sooner had I made the connection than the Misses Linton scurried over to me, their slippers shuffling over the stone floors.

"Lady Sarah," they whispered in near unison, executing quick curtsies. The Lintons were the only other landowning family in the parish. They lived at Henby Hall with Mr. Linton's unmarried sister. The younger brother, Frederick, had begun at Harrow a year ago, and his visits home were highly unwelcome, for when he returned to school, George was always itching to join him. In any case, Harriet and Maria supplied the parish with enough girlish silliness that I felt at peace with my utter lack of such traits.

"Is it true he is living at Bettencourt Court?" Harriet asked.

"Who?" I asked in blinking confusion, pretending ignorance merely to be difficult.

"Mr. Donovan," Harriet said, looking in his direction.

"Only the most handsome man in the room," Maria added.

I took my time allowing my gaze to trail over to him. He wore a crisp black coat and matching breeches, and next to the aging Mr. Vickers, he did indeed look "blond, large, and power-ful." He *was* the most handsome man in the room, but I would not acknowledge such a thing to these girls.

"Yes," I said, pulling my gaze away. "He is acting as tutor for my brother."

I was not even certain they heard me, for their eyes fixed on Mr. Donovan, who nodded at something the vicar said. His gaze flicked in our direction, finding the Linton twins first, then shifting to me, where it settled for a moment, lighting his eyes with recognition.

I gave a discreet nod, and he returned it with a small smile, then turned to the vicar.

I could almost hear the twins sigh, overcome with admiration for him.

"Is it true his father is a rear admiral?" Maria asked.

I opened my mouth to respond.

"And his brother, the infamous Valentine Donovan?"

Again, I moved to speak.

"And his sister none other than Diana Russell?" Harriet said.

I waited a moment before attempting to speak again. It was well, for they had apparently not exhausted their description of his family tree.

"Yes, and Father said his oldest brother is Captain Theo Donovan—one of the more promising young gentlemen the Navy had seen until he resigned and bought his own ship."

"You are very well-acquainted with Mr. Donovan's situation, then," I said.

"But not with Mr. Donovan *himself*."

"Will you introduce us, my lady? It is so rare that there are gentlemen of eligible situation in the district."

I bit my tongue to stop my excuses. It was so tempting to refuse their request. A hint of possessiveness rose in me.

Mr. Donovan was eligible indeed for the Lintons, but certainly not for me. If I married—which I sincerely hoped would not be the case—it would be a man of title or wealth. Or both, based on the few suggestions Father had presented over the past few years.

There was no need for me to guard Mr. Donovan from the Linton twins. I remembered our first encounter in the library and smiled. I suspected he had little experience with young women. It could be quite amusing to see how he handled their advances.

He would *have* to do so if he meant to take Mr. Vickers's place in the parish, so, really, I was assisting him.

I returned my focus to the Lintons. "Of course. I imagine he is every bit as anxious for the introduction. After the services?"

They nodded quickly, their eyes sparkling with anticipation. Neither of them seemed worried over the fact that, even if Mr. Donovan welcomed their interest in him, he would have to choose between them at some point. Could their sisterly bond withstand such a thing?

A s promised, I left my family's box pew after the service to make the introduction. The task was more difficult than anticipated, though. Everyone seemed to be intent on an introduction to Mr. Donovan.

I watched with mixed sympathy and amusement as he handled the polite conversation required of one introduction after another, and the delicacy needed to end one exchange in favor of another—a necessary skill when there was a line of people awaiting his attention.

The Lintons waited patiently behind me—if one could call such incessant fiddling with their gloves and bonnets *patient*—until finally, Mrs. Reeves ended her conversation with Mr. Donovan. He was looking harried and flushed, beads of sweat beginning to form at his forehead.

He bade farewell to Mrs. Reeves, then turned his resigned gaze toward us. When his eyes met mine, the relief in his expression was palpable, as though there was no face he would rather see in that moment. A strange wave of pleasure rolled over me, making me reluctant to perform the task I had come to carry out. It would put a quick end to his relief.

But that was preferable to this strange sensation, this thread of connection I was feeling.

I stepped aside to reveal the Linton twins.

Phineas Donovan was not a man who wore his emotions on his face, but I knew him well enough now to see his chagrin.

I performed the introduction, trying not to take pleasure in the way Mr. Donovan's gaze shifted to me frequently as he tried to navigate the twins' enthusiastic and overlapping dialogue. I merely smiled serenely at him, ignoring how my mind insisted on pointing out how much more at ease he was with me than with the Lintons, or how I could stand back from the conversation at hand with the assurance that I would be spending time with Mr. Donovan later today.

Evidently, I was beginning to consider him as a friend.

That was certainly unexpected.

Chapter Sixteen

PHINEAS

I f Lady Sarah's habit of holding my gaze directly came as a surprise, it was nothing compared with the way the Linton girls engaged with me. Their substantial amount of energy drew entirely from my small reserves—the more docile my response, the more lively theirs.

Lady Sarah stood nearby, but her involvement in the conversation was confined to short responses and the same faint smiles I had known her to give from the first day of meeting her. They seemed to mock me until we met eyes, and I thought she might be laughing *with* me.

In any event, I had little doubt she was enjoying my discomfiture. Perhaps I deserved it after forcing her into the performance of *Ajax*, but both of us had landed a blow or two during that exchange. It was unlike me to engage in such a way, but Lady Sarah brought it out of me. She seemed to enjoy causing me mischief. But as long as she did so with an amused glint in her eye, I felt no real need to fear.

In the end, she *did* put a stop to the conversation with the Linton twins. She managed it so deftly, so gently, that I felt a stab of envy. How could she be skilled at so many things at once? It seemed unfair that one woman could possess a sharp mind, a pleasing appearance, *and* such easy manners.

I anticipated our discussions about the first volume of *Sense and Sensibility* would be quite lively later on, and I looked forward to the prospect more than I had looked forward to anything in weeks.

———

"You two are so slow," Lord Danneville complained. The path we were taking led through the kitchen gardens and away from the imposing exterior of Bettencourt Court. The viscount insisted he knew the best place on the estate to find sticks for swords, and since I hadn't explored the expansive grounds yet, I had agreed for him to lead the way.

Lord Danneville didn't bother trying to match the pace Lady Sarah and I had adopted, instead staying in front of us and picking up whatever small twigs had been blown down recently.

"You have made quite an impression on the parish, Mr. Donovan," Lady Sarah said, as her brother picked up a stray cabbage leaf, threw it in the air, and whacked it with the twig he held. "I understand you are to take charge of next week's services. I would not be surprised if attendance was double what it normally is."

"Heaven forbid," I blurted. The thought of standing before such a large crowd of people made my stomach churn.

Lady Sarah raised her brows. "I rather think heaven would approve. Is it not a vicar's goal to encourage his parishioners in their worship?"

"Provided their motivations are proper, certainly."

"*Or,*" she said, "perhaps what begins as an intent to ogle you may shift to a more sincere and pure-hearted worship."

The amount of heat in my neck and cheeks was fast

becoming unbearable. Had Lady Sarah ever… *ogled* me, as she put it?

"Take care, my lord," I said as the viscount reached over into the bed of spices to retrieve a stick. There was no real fear of him falling, but I needed something to save me the task of responding to Lady Sarah's comments.

"A timely intervention, even if somewhat unnecessary," she said. "If you wish to change the subject, you need only say so."

I laughed shakily, pulling the spectacles from my face and cleaning them with my cloth. "You seem to delight in discomfiting me, my lady."

"Perhaps you should not make it so easy." She smiled as we stepped under the canopy of trees that marked the edge of Bettencourt Wood. "But let us rather turn to our promised discussion."

"Happily," I said, trying to pay no heed to the anxiousness I felt to hear her thoughts on the subject. What if she despised it? Despised *me*? "What are your opinions, my lady?"

"Well," she said in a voice that made it clear she had no shortage of such things, "where to begin?"

I had a fair idea what would have elicited her strongest opinions. "Perhaps we could start with Miss Marianne."

"Marianne," Lady Sarah said with a hint of contempt. "*Marianne!*"

I turned my head away to hide a smile.

"A sillier, more frustrating young woman, you would be hard-pressed to find. And yet, the sad truth is she accurately represents so many of my sex—willing to make fools of themselves in the name of a bit of romance."

We slowed as we waited for Lord Danneville, who had left the path and was searching amongst the bracken nearby.

"Perhaps you will feel differently about her as you continue your reading," I said.

"Unless there is a fourth volume, I should think that quite

impossible. She is certainly improved by the end of the story—or at least expresses the intention to act in a more sensible manner—but convincing evidence of that is yet to be seen."

I looked at her in surprise. Had she truly finished the other two volumes since my leaving them at her door after dinner yesterday?

"Nothing useful here," Lord Danneville said, traipsing toward us and onto the path again. "We shall have to continue on, just as I expected."

"Lead the way, good Ajax," Lady Sarah said, putting out a hand to invite him to precede us. "We must find Achilles' sword."

The viscount scoffed. "In the play, Ajax never *has* Achilles' sword, Sarah. It is given to Odysseus. That is the entire premise of the story." He stepped in front of us and went on his way, giving his sister no chance to defend herself against his castigation of her ignorance.

We both stared after him for a moment, and then the humor of the situation pressed itself upon me, and I covered a laugh with a hand.

"Well," Lady Sarah said, blinking. "I have certainly been put in my place. I take it you did, in fact, convince him to read through the play yesterday?"

"Yes, but I did not think he had truly paid it any attention."

"Well done, then, Mr. Donovan."

Her praise, unexpected as it was, struck me silent, filling me with a curious warmth. I cleared my throat, forcing my focus to our discussion—and wondering if I had wrongly inferred she had finished all three volumes of *Sense and Sensibility*. "You do not find Miss Marianne's change convincing, then?"

"What? Because of her marriage to Colonel Brandon?"

Well, that answered my question sufficiently; she *had* finished the entire book. "Surely, that is evidence she has learned to control her tendency toward romanticism and sensibility."

"Is it?" she asked, tilting her head to the side in consideration. The cover of trees we passed under allowed bits of sunlight to filter through, illuminating her and our path with dappled light. "I find Colonel Brandon to be quite like Marianne."

I frowned. "In what way?"

"He is not so open with his sensibility, perhaps, but it drives everything he does—from his initial infatuation with Eliza, to his caring for her illegitimate daughter, to his becoming enamored with someone as silly as Marianne."

A recently fallen tree intersected our path, and Lord Danneville hopped over it deftly. When Lady Sarah and I reached it, I offered her my hand, which she took as she held up her skirts to keep them from tangling in the protruding branches.

"I had not considered it in that light," I said as she stepped over with one foot, then the other, "but I cannot disagree with your analysis."

"And *I* cannot fail to acknowledge the sense in your conclusion." Her hand still in mine, she smiled teasingly.

My heart stuttered, and I let my eyes explore her face, trying to understand the physical response I was having to her. Her gaze locked more intently on mine, and the stutter of my heart was followed by uncomfortable rapid beating.

"Over here!" Lord Danneville called to us.

She dropped my hand, and I cleared my throat.

"And what of Elinor?" I said.

Lady Sarah sighed. "Ah, Elinor. She is portrayed as her sister's opposite in many ways—the *sense* part of *Sense and Sensibility*, we are made to believe—but particularly in the end with Mr. Ferrars' visit, we see she is hardly without that strength of sentiment which characterizes her sister. She merely conceals it more effectively."

I did not respond immediately, taking time to consider her opinion. We passed a small mound amongst the trees that marked the estate's ice house. It was covered in dirt and plants, its short door opening into darkness.

"But that is the lesson of the story, is it not?" I said. "That sense and sensibility must be balanced?"

"It is not the lesson *I* took," Lady Sarah replied. "The abundance of sentiment in the story was also the source of all conflict and pain, even for Elinor. If reason had prevailed, imagine how different things would have been."

"Now, there I cannot agree with you."

"A dangerous proclamation, Mr. Donovan, which you must now expound on."

I smiled, clasping my hands behind my back as we continued at our sedate pace with Lord Danneville scouring the surroundings. "In a way, you are correct; the characters face adversity because of their sensibilities, and yes, in some cases, an excess of it. But when all is said and done, it is those who act *without* regard to sentiment who are most unhappy."

"Namely…?"

"Willoughby, for one. He disregards his feelings for Marianne in favor of the more sensible path granting him Miss Grey's fortune. But does that serve him well in the end? The answer is certainly *no*."

For a moment, silence succeeded my words, the only sound our footsteps on the dirt.

"And yet," Lady Sarah said after some thought, "we are ignorant of the future of these characters. Who is to say Willoughby did not come to be glad for his decision to marry Miss Grey? If he had chosen sensibility and married Marianne, they would have been poor and perhaps come to resent one another."

I smiled slightly at her practical assessment. "You haven't a romantic bone in your body, have you, my lady?"

"Not that I am aware of. I find such sentiments difficult to understand."

"As do I."

"Here it is!" Lord Danneville said, turning toward us. "Only look—an entire *pile* of proper stick-swords. We must all find three, I think, in case any are broken in our skirmishes." He set to the task immediately, leaving Lady Sarah and I to smile.

Once again, our gazes held for a moment, as though both of us were trying to understand the shift occurring between us— from subtle foes to... friends? I didn't know if she would deign to consider me thus, but I found myself greatly wishing for just that.

She pulled her gaze away from me, and we proceeded toward the pile. It was nearly as tall as I. The viscount was on the opposite side, picking out sticks one by one, inspecting them, then executing a few thrusts with them to test their desirability.

"You surprise me, Mr. Donovan." Lady Sarah picked up a stick. "You seem to be a great proponent of sensibility and romance."

"Do I?" I followed suit, pulling a long, knobbly one from beneath a few others. "Appearances can be deceiving. I share your reservations on this topic, my lady, and the difficulty in understanding those who rely upon sentiment so willingly. It is difficult for those of us who place such value on the workings of the mind to submit to the workings of the heart. I have merely been advocating for the other side of the argument, which I find a necessary part of understanding my own position and its possible weaknesses." My eyes settled on an uneven line running diagonally across the stick I had chosen. With one hand on either end, I pried at the stick, and it snapped along the line.

"And what *is* your position?" She watched as I tossed the broken stick into the pile.

I brushed my hands off and faced her. "I suppose it has been that the mind is a more reliable vessel for truth than the heart."

"*Has been*? Does that mean you have undergone a change of opinion?" There was no accusation in her tone, merely curiosity.

A rush of nerves coursed through me at the thought of conveying my recent ruminations to her. "Not a change of opinion. I have been playing host to a suspicion, rather." I paused, still unsure whether it was wise of me to make this admission to her, of all people. But part of me wanted—needed, even—to know whether she, who was like me in many ways, had felt something similar.

And though I would not have felt comfortable having such a conversation with her even yesterday, today felt different, as though both of us had agreed to put down our weapons—even as we searched for stick-swords.

"Suspicion?" Her curiosity shone through her eyes.

I nodded.

"Are you searching or not?" Lord Danneville said, outraged at our inactivity.

"Of course, my lord." I crouched before the pile and rifled through sticks. "We were merely making a visual surveyal of the options."

He gave a *hmph* and stayed where he was to supervise our efforts. Amidst our rifling, Lady Sarah and I shared a quick, amused glance, like schoolchildren being watched by a demanding master.

Finally satisfied we could be left to our own devices, the viscount returned to his place, though not without shooting us a chastising glance first.

"What suspicion?" Lady Sarah asked in a low voice, her eyes flitting to our taskmaster, then back to me.

I pulled a stick from the pile and took a moment before responding, choosing my words carefully. "Have you ever wondered if you are missing something?"

She searched my eyes, her brows delicately furrowed. "Missing what?"

I lifted a shoulder. "Missing whatever it is that those of more sensibility enjoy, I suppose."

Chapter Seventeen

SARAH

Mr. Donovan's gaze was a mixture of wary and hopeful. "Have you ever felt such an inclination?"

I swallowed.

I could laugh at him for his comment and assert myself as the more reasonable of the two of us; it would be easy and effective.

But it would be a lie. I *had* felt what Mr. Donovan spoke of—I felt it now. A strange and increasingly familiar pull toward him. I was drawn to his calm demeanor, challenged by his bright mind, enticed by his genuine smile.

That was why my notebook was full of requirements so opposite of everything he encompassed.

But I did not wish to put myself at the mercy of such sentiments. Of course, his status as a tutor with no future beyond a vicaracy protected me from any real danger—a connection between us was unthinkable—but if I could feel such stirrings for *him*, it was conceivable that I might feel them for someone else. Someone more suitable.

I needed to find someone as unlike Mr. Donovan as I could manage.

Someone whose clear blue eyes didn't look at me so piercingly, whose smile didn't elicit one of my own, whose mind didn't make me feel a kinship I hadn't known until now.

"What are you two talking about?"

I startled.

George had returned and was watching us, his arms folded across his chest, two sticks in one hand.

Mr. Donovan opened his mouth, but I hurried to speak before him. "Stick-swords, of course. What else? I think this one is quite good." I pulled a stick from the pile at random. It was much longer than I had anticipated, and removing it disturbed the rest of those around it, sending other sticks and twigs tumbling down the stack. Ignoring the inauspicious choice and the clumsiness of its removal, I stood, well aware that the way I was acting would make most people more, not less, suspicious.

George stepped toward me, looking at my stick with skepticism. "It is crooked. And too long."

So it was. A large knot intersected it, acting like a crossroads which sent a longer branch in one direction and a stub in the other.

I couldn't stop a glance at Mr. Donovan, who was watching me with an impassive expression. He cleared his throat.

"A wise selection, my lady. It is difficult indeed for a foe to defend against such an unexpected weapon."

I masked a smile and looked at the unwieldy branch, for it really was more of a branch than a stick. I resisted the urge to glance at Mr. Donovan. When had we become allies?

I let out a shriek and dropped the branch as a spider crawled along it and toward my hand.

Mr. Donovan scrambled to his feet. "What is it?"

Heart thrumming inside me, I forced myself to take a calming breath. "A spider. It was just a spider."

"Where?" George asked, showing aggravating enthusiasm as he bent to examine the branch.

"On your sister's skirts," Mr. Donovan said, looking at them.

I jumped back, as though that would do anything at all to put distance between me and the creature.

"You needn't fear," he said, coming for a closer look. "It is only *Trochosa ruricola*. Harmless to humans."

"Oh!" I said with feigned nonchalance. "How reassuring. Shall I let it crawl on me indefinitely, then?" It scaled higher, reaching my waist, and I barely suppressed another shriek. "Get it off, George!"

He shrank back. "I hate spiders."

"You were just trying to find it!"

"To see it! Not to touch it."

It continued its climb, making its way up the bodice of my dress, and I tried to garner the courage to push it away.

Mr. Donovan reached over and brushed it from my midsection, sending a trill of bumps across my skin and the breath out of my lungs. And just like that, all of my fear was forgotten.

"There." Spider on his hand, Mr. Donovan crouched for it to crawl onto the dirt. It stayed in place for a moment, and Mr. Donovan sucked in a breath, his forehead pinching.

He flung the spider from his hand, and it went sailing into the air, landing on the ground and immediately blending in so that I lost track of it.

"It bit me." Mr. Donovan said it as though it was the most surprising turn of events imaginable.

"You needn't fear," I said. "It is only *Trochosa ruricola*. Harmless to humans."

His eyes twinkled as he chuckled, shaking out his hand, then bringing it up for inspection.

The spider incident turned into a discussion of the different types of spiders, which morphed into a discussion of taxonomy. Mr. Donovan was adept at that, I found—making experiences educational for George without George realizing it. He played to my brother's interests, leaving George curious for more. It was quite impressive.

But George could only be distracted for so long by discussion of genus and species. He had come for swords, and he refused to let us leave until we had each found three. And once that was accomplished, he insisted on practicing the swordfight scene—a fiction of Mr. Donovan's imagination.

"George," I said as we stood on the lawn in front of the house, each holding our spoils, which I had insisted Mr. Donovan inspect for spiders. "I doubt whether a sword fight is the proper activity for a curate to engage in on the Sabbath."

George looked at Mr. Donovan, as though seeing him for the first time. "Do you mean to become vicar, then?"

Mr. Donovan nodded. "I hope to, yes."

"Does that mean you shall become as stuffy and strange as Mr. Vickers?"

"George," I said censuringly.

"What?" George said in a complaining voice that made it clear he saw nothing wrong with his comment. "You must admit Mr. Vickers is both things. He chastised me for picking a flower outside of the church today, warning me against becoming like Eve. And he smells like cats. Every time I see him, he is either holding one or trying to lure it with a bit of food. It is no wonder he is a lonely old man!"

"George, *hold your tongue.*"

His brows drew together. "I am only trying to help Mr. Donovan. If he thinks a harmless stick-sword fight is inappropriate on Sunday, though, perhaps he is too far down the road to Mr. Vickers already."

Exasperated beyond anything, I looked at Mr. Donovan to apologize.

But Mr. Donovan dropped two of the sticks in his hand and yelled, "En guarde, Ajax!"

M r. Donovan brushed at his forehead with the sleeve of his shirt, then picked up the coat he had shed some time ago—and risked nearly being gored by George in doing so.

All of us were breathing quickly, for George had insisted on fighting both of us at the same time, and though he lacked skill, his determination nearly made up for it. In his zeal for victory, he had broken one of his sticks.

At one point when George was retrieving a new sword, I had turned to Mr. Donovan, engaging him in battle. It had been a thrilling bout. We had both begun it smiling, but as we continued, the skirmish took on a more intense tenor, as though our earlier clashes of the mind were now being played out in this physical arena.

There had been no victor, though, for George had interrupted, reminding us that Agamemnon and Menelaus do not fight each other in *Ajax*. I bit my tongue rather than remind him that neither did Ajax fight them in the play.

"I think you have successfully persuaded George you shan't be strange and stuffy," I said as a welcome breeze licked at my hair and brow. There had been nothing at all stuffy about Mr. Donovan as he had sparred and laughed and tossed his head to keep his hair from falling into his face and over his spectacles.

It was an image I would not soon forget, though I wished I could. I liked every bit of Mr. Donovan I had seen—the studious man, the bumbling converser, the kind and deliberate tutor, the competitive stick-swordsman.

"Stuffy, perhaps." Mr. Donovan glanced at George, who was searching the grass for his other stick. Mr. Donovan leaned toward me, his breathing still a bit labored. "I suspect you were right to say it was not an appropriate activity for the Sabbath, though. I doubt Mr. Vickers would approve." Behind his spectacles, his eyes were bright and his cheeks slightly pink. I suspected he had enjoyed himself nearly as much as George had.

I had to admit that I, too, had found a great deal of pleasure in it. And in the discussion preceding it.

George traipsed over to us with his two sticks. "I think I will be very good at fencing. Frederick Linton says they have a prime fencing instructor at Harrow."

I stiffened.

"Do you intend to go to Harrow?" Mr. Donovan asked with interest.

"I do," George said firmly. He looked at me, his face set in defiant lines. I merely held his gaze.

Mr. Donovan seemed to note the silent exchange, and he looked at me, a question in his eyes.

"Sarah doesn't wish for me to go to Harrow," George explained. "She wishes for me to stay here and be miserable."

"You were hardly miserable while attempting to slay Agamemnon and Menelaus," I said as I picked up my other sticks.

"But I should be far happier at Harrow. And if Mr. Donovan means to become a vicar, he shan't be my tutor for long. Yet another reason for me to go!" He looked to Mr. Donovan. "*You* haven't anything against Harrow, have you, sir?"

Mr. Donovan glanced at me, and I sent him a warning look. The last thing I needed was someone else to encourage George in something that could mean his ruin. George didn't understand that my dislike of Harrow had more to do with his own personality than with Harrow itself.

"I do not," Mr. Donovan said.

"Ha!" George said victoriously. "You shan't try to keep me from going to Harrow, shall you, Mr. Donovan?"

"No. I shan't."

And just like that, my charity for Mr. Donovan vanished.

Chapter Eighteen

SARAH

I hardly saw Mr. Donovan that evening, for we dined with the Lintons at Henby Hall. I was glad for it, for my sentiments toward the tutor were becoming thoroughly confusing and convoluted. He was both friend and foe, particularly when it came to George. I wished to assert myself as the more intelligent and reasonable, but I also wanted to question him, to acquaint myself with his mind and understand his innermost thoughts.

As the twins were eager to make Mr. Donovan the subject of discussion at the dinner table, I was given the doubtful pleasure of hearing every person's opinion of him. Father was pleased with his tutelage, for George hadn't carried out any great mischief since his arrival. Mother was very complimentary indeed, stating him to be a kind, well-informed gentleman with whom she felt very comfortable entrusting her son's care. Both of them found his dinner conversation enlivening.

Mr. and Mrs. Linton had very high opinions indeed for people who had never spoken to Mr. Donovan directly. Those opinions seemed to originate with the respected position of his father, Admiral Donovan. The view their daughters took of him, of course, was in no doubt at all, and they begged their parents to invite him for dinner as soon as could be arranged.

I smiled at the thought, well aware that such an invitation would not be welcomed by Mr. Donovan.

On the carriage ride home, I contemplated what I would read during the time before I retired to bed. I almost regretted that I had read *Sense and Sensibility* so quickly.

Despite what I had expressed to Mr. Donovan, I had very much enjoyed the book. The author had a wittiness to her writing I found singularly engaging and quite unlike anything I had ever before read. And after the discussion Mr. Donovan and I had engaged in, I found it even more interesting.

My heart skittered as my mind offered the image of Mr. Donovan, the question he had asked hanging in the air and reflecting in his eyes, as if to say, *Do you feel what I am feeling right now?*

I disposed hurriedly of such thoughts. Evidently, Mother's amusement at the implication that reading novels would turn me into a silly girl had been misplaced. I was becoming precisely that, not least of all because I wished to read more of the silly romances. I had none, of course, and I toyed with the prospect of seeing whether the nearest lending library carried the author's other works.

That was unthinkable. I could not have it be bandied about that I was visiting the library for romances. And even if that was not the case, it did not help me tonight. But nothing else appealed to me at the moment. Perhaps I could sneak into Mother's parlor and see what selection she possessed there.

Good heavens. What was I becoming? Mr. Donovan might be exercising a beneficial effect upon George, but his effect upon me left much to be desired. And increasingly, it was *him* I found myself desiring.

When we arrived home and I reached my bedchamber, I

found another stack of books in front of my bedroom and my maid bending to pick them up.

"I can take those, Sutton," I hurried to say.

She paused, looking at me questioningly.

I owed her no explanation, that was certain. "They are just a few… military histories," I said as I picked them up ungracefully, for it was a tall stack.

She moved out of the way. "Of course, my lady."

The top few books teetered dangerously, and I shifted my position to keep them from falling.

Sutton put her hands out to help.

"I have it under control," I said with unnecessary force, barely maintaining my hold on the stack. I didn't wish to risk having gossip spread amongst the servants that I was reading romances. I took in a breath and smiled. "Thank you."

She nodded and stepped aside, waiting for me to pass into the room, then closed the door behind us.

I set the books in the darkest corner of the room where there was no fear of Sutton seeing them, then allowed her to help me prepare for sleep. Once my hair was brushed and tied in cloth and my clothes put away in favor of my shift and dressing gown, I bid Sutton goodnight and waited for the click of the door.

I hurried to the corner and picked up the top book, looking at the spine. *Pride and Prejudice*, it read.

I opened the cover and tried not to feel pleased at the note there—or that it was far longer than the last one.

My lady,

I hope you will forgive the liberty I have taken in bringing these to you. After our discussion today, I am not even certain whether you wish to read more of the author's works, but, as I have finished all of them, I thought I would leave that choice to you.

I imagine you will enjoy Miss Elizabeth Bennet far better

than you enjoyed Marianne, though I fear Misses Kitty and Lydia are likely to inspire you with intense dislike.

As always, I look forward to hearing your opinion on the stories if you choose to read them.

Your servant,

Phineas Donovan

My candle guttered just after I finished the first volume of *Pride and Prejudice*.

———

"While I was at Cambridge, there was no shortage of newspapers to read," Mr. Donovan said, cutting his meat in a slow, precise motion. "But I am afraid my knowledge of the issue at hand is outdated now."

"You are welcome to my copy of *The Chronicle* if you care for it," Father said.

I frowned, for I had asked to take it from him in the past, and he had refused.

"I wouldn't wish to trouble you, my lord," Mr. Donovan said.

"It is no trouble. I am generally through with it by ten, you know. I shall just have Collins bring it to you in the library."

"A kind offer, my lord. I would very much appreciate it. I thought perhaps Lord Danneville and I might take some time each day to discuss parliamentary matters."

Father looked very pleased with this idea indeed. "A very good notion." His brow furrowed as he sliced through the pota-toes on his plate. "Though I can promise you there is nothing in today's installment to make you feel anything but thoroughly frustrated. Things in the north will be coming to a head soon, I'm afraid. And as for the rest of it? Well, I would not be at all surprised if we were drawn into some conflict or another in Sidon. Lady Hester is causing trouble there."

My hands stilled, and I looked up from my plate. "Lady Hester Stanhope?" I had never heard her mentioned in my home —did not even know Father was aware of her existence.

"Yes," he said darkly. "Apparently, she has gathered a great deal of influence there."

"Which you dislike?" I tried to keep my tone disinterested, but it was annoyingly predictable that people would resent a woman garnering power and prestige in her own right.

"She is capricious and of unstable character! That apparent the moment she left her brother's care and continued traveling—unchaperoned and in the presence of unmarried men." He turned his attention to Mr. Donovan. "Are you aware she had a priceless statue smashed to bits?"

"Ah, yes. I heard about that incident. A monumental discovery she destroyed, wasn't it? Isn't it thought to have been one of Alexander the Great's successors? Nothing like it has been uncovered in that region before."

Father nodded darkly. "All for naught."

"A show of loyalty to the sultan, I take it."

"And a slap in the face of England—the country that gave her everything she has, she would do well to remember."

I stared between them, shocked. I knew of Lady Hester's archeological excavation, of course, for it was one of the reasons I so admired her. She was all the things I hoped to be: intelligent, dedicated to natural philosophy, independent. But to have a statue beyond price destroyed?

The revelation made me sick to my stomach.

"Perhaps it is for the best the Earl of Stanhope is not alive to witness it," Mr. Donovan said.

Father gave a scoffing laugh. "Stanhope was a loose screw himself. A supporter of the French Revolution, you know. It is little wonder his daughter would have strange ideas, but her conduct has been beyond the pale."

"She does seem to be becoming more and more erratic," Mr. Donovan conceded.

I bit my tongue. I had long since learned that arguing with Father was an exercise in futility. And when there were other men present to bolster his opinions, I would sooner find success flying to the moon than making any headway with him.

I was accustomed to being at odds with others in my opinions, but I found myself more than usually frustrated by the knowledge that Mr. Donovan agreed with Father. It felt like a betrayal, and since I was already bothered by his offer to help George to Harrow...

There had been no time for our discussions earlier. The only time I had been able to spend with him over the course of the day had been occupied with helping George and him decide which parts of *Ajax* most merited being included in our brief performance. Mother had pulled me away from that for an unexpected caller—the very worst type of caller.

"My lord," Mr. Donovan said, "I meant to speak to you on the matter of Lord Danneville's instruction this week. Mr. Vickers is traveling to his other parish—he left today, I understand—so I shall be responsible for overseeing any matters that might present themselves during his absence."

Father nodded curtly. "That is quite all right. If you are needed, Sarah may stay with George until you are able to return."

My jaw slipped open. So, I was not permitted to instruct George as a tutor would, but I could play nursemaid to him while Mr. Donovan was called away on other business?

Mr. Donovan's eyes searched my face. "I wouldn't wish to inconvenience Lady Sarah. I hope that the work required of me will be minimal, but the vicar did specifically request I pay a visit to Mrs. Bamford tomorrow. Is she in the village?"

"Yes," Mother said. "In fact, Sarah has been meaning to pay her a visit. Perhaps she can accompany you."

I stared at her. It was like Father to dispose of my time as he pleased, but Mother was usually more considerate. "Of course," I said with false cheeriness, "but how am I to do so when I am playing nursemaid to George?"

"He might go along with you," Mother said. "A healthy dose of fresh air and a bit of social interaction would do him good, I imagine."

"You might take George with you," Father said, as though it was the most obvious thing in the world. "It would be good for him to have some insight into the workings of the parish and to socialize. I fear having him here for his education has deprived him too much of such a thing. He must learn how to go on in polite society somehow."

"I *do* know how!" George protested. Seeming to realize he was arguing against a respite from his studies, though, he hurried to add, "but I could always use more practice."

I met Mr. Donovan's gaze and found that, to his credit, he was looking at me apologetically, as though the conversation had got away from him, but he didn't feel at liberty to counter Father's wishes.

"How is my son faring in his studies, Mr. Donovan?"

The conversation turned to different channels, and it wasn't long before the covers were removed, and Mother and I left for the drawing room.

After spending what I felt an acceptable amount of time with Mother there, I made my way toward my bedroom, trying to decide whether I should heed my desire to continue reading *Pride and Prejudice,* or if I should instead decline to read any more of it in protest.

Such a battle was raging in my mind when I passed the door to the library just as it opened.

"Lady Sarah," Mr. Donovan said, and from the way he looked

at me, I suspected he had perhaps been waiting for my passing. "Forgive me for alarming you. I merely wished to apologize for what had occurred at dinner. It was not my intention to inconvenience you, and I assure you that, if you will tell me where Mrs. Bamford lives, I may save you the trouble of accompanying me. I will convey your regards, and of course, take Lord Danneville with me."

I hesitated before responding. Drat him for being considerate when I wished to be annoyed with him. And drat him for making me wonder if he was trying to be considerate or whether he didn't wish for me to join him on the visit.

The reasonable thing would be for me to accept his apology and tell him the direction of Mrs. Bamford.

But I was not feeling particularly reasonable. "You do not wish for my company?"

He blinked. "No, no. That is not what I meant. Far from it! Believe me, I would like nothing more than—" He shut his mouth.

I wished he hadn't, for I was quite curious what would have followed.

He proceeded more slowly. "That is to say, I would be glad for your company, my lady. I merely didn't wish to presume upon your time or to assume you would share my... what I mean to say is that I—"

"I am happy to accompany you into the village, Mr. Donovan," I said. His scrambling speech was strangely charming. It meant I was not the only one to blunder about when we were in company.

He took in a deep breath, as though I had relieved a burden from his shoulders. "Perhaps tomorrow you can inform me when would be most convenient for you."

"I shall do so."

"Then I shall bid you goodnight." He bowed, and I could have sworn he was trying to dampen a smile.

I turned away and began walking, only to stop. "Oh, Mr. Donovan?"

He stopped in the act of closing the library door, eyes wide and questioning as he met my gaze.

"I *do* like Miss Elizabeth."

The smile that met my spontaneous comment made me look forward to our walk to Mrs. Bamford's and whatever other time we would spend together.

Chapter Nineteen

PHINEAS

I pulled the spectacles from my face and rubbed the lenses with the cloth in my pocket as we approached the door of Mrs. Bamford's home. As always, Lord Danneville led the way.

We came to a stop in front of the door just as I finished the cleaning.

Lady Sarah glanced at me as I set the cloth back in my pocket and put the spectacles in place. "You are nervous." Over her arm, she held a basket of bread and preserves.

I gave an anxious smile. "Shocking as it may be, my lady, I am not known for my social graces."

The smile she returned was warm, a glint of amusement in her eyes. "You have come to the right place, then. You may rest assured that, if you do commit some error, Mrs. Bamford shan't remember it. I have no doubt that is why Mother and Father agreed for George to come along. Of all the people in the parish, Mrs. Bamford is the safest audience, for her memory is very poor indeed."

Lord Danneville shot her a look of resentment and rapped on the door with far more force than I thought necessary.

"A bit firmer, George. Mrs. Bamford is hard of hearing," Lady Sarah explained to me.

The door opened before Lord Danneville could set his fist to it again, though, revealing a middle-aged woman wearing a cap and apron. She looked far from pleased.

"Mrs. Bamford," I said when no one else stepped into the silence. Remembering that Lady Sarah had said the woman was hard of hearing, I raised my voice. "Good day to you."

Lady Sarah grabbed my arm while Lord Danneville sniggered. "Mr. Donovan, this is Jane Hicks. She lives just a few doors away with her family. Perhaps you noticed her on Sunday."

I nearly stole the basket from her arm, discarded the contents, and turned it upside down over my head. Not only had I assumed she was the wrong person and nearly yelled at her, I had failed to recognize her from church. What a vicar I would make!

"Are you helping Mrs. Bamford now, Jane?" Lady Sarah asked.

The woman nodded. "Aye, m'lady. Mrs. Bamford's memory is worse than ever, so she be forgettin' to eat and put out candles and the like."

"That is very kind of you. Is she feeling well enough for a visit? We shan't stay long."

Jane nodded and moved to let us into the house. She led us into a very small sitting area, dim except for the light one small window provided. Near the fire, seated on a worn chaise-lounge of nondescript color, was a petite, elderly woman, wrapped in a blanket.

"Would you like some tea?" Jane asked, looking between Lady Sarah, Lord Danneville, and me.

"That would be very nice, thank you," Lady Sarah said as she took a seat.

Lord Danneville was walking around the room, but he stopped to scratch at something on the wall.

"George," Lady Sarah hissed.

Sulking, he came and took a seat on the opposite end from her of the small sofa. The only place left for me was the place in between them, and Lady Sarah motioned for me to take it.

No matter how I shifted, I could not prevent being pressed up against her. The sofa was made for two, and though Lord Danneville was smaller than I, he was accustomed to taking up as much space as he needed. "I am mortified," I whispered to Lady Sarah.

She laughed softly. "You needn't be. It was quite amusing."

All of us looked to Mrs. Bamford, who was staring at the empty fireplace, yet to acknowledge our presence.

"I think she is sleeping," Lord Danneville whispered.

"She is not," Lady Sarah said. "Her eyes are open." She cleared her throat. "How are you faring, Mrs. Bamford?" The volume of her voice made me blink.

Mrs. Bamford snorted, her head turning this way and that until her gaze landed upon me. Apparently, the viscount had been correct, and Mrs. Bamford possessed the skill of sleeping with her eyes partially open.

It took a moment before she said anything, but once her gaze found Lady Sarah, her mouth pulled into a smile, displaying the spots where two teeth were missing. "My lady. How happy I am to see you." She looked at George, then to me, her eyes widening as comprehension dawned. "And you have brought your family! Look how tall your son has grown—and how handsome your husband is. Forgive me, sir, but I have forgotten your name." She leaned forward and put a hand beside her mouth as though to tell me a secret. "Between the two of us, I sometimes suspect my memory is beginning to fail me."

Not comprehension, then.

"Oh," I said, glancing at Lady Sarah as an amount of heat I

would have previously thought physiologically impossible flooded my face. "I am not—"

Lady Sarah grabbed my arm. "He is not one to gab, so you needn't worry he shall tell anyone about your memory." She rose and held out the basket on her arm. "We brought you some bread and preserves."

"You did?" Mrs. Bamford took the basket and pulled it onto her lap, smiling. "How thoughtful of you." She took the two jars of preserves in hand, holding them so that the light from the window illuminated the labels. "No strawberry?" The disappointment in her expression was comical.

"I am afraid not," Lady Sarah said, her voice still raised to an unnatural level. "They did not take well this year. But I assure you these are every bit as delicious, for I had some this morning with my breakfast."

Mrs. Bamford looked doubtful, but she set the jars in the basket and thanked Lady Sarah again. As Jane came in at that moment with the tea tray, conversation was restricted to the subject of tea for a few minutes.

Once we all had a teacup in hand, Jane took the basket of bread and preserves and left us to ourselves.

"Now," Mrs. Bamford said, motioning to me with a hand, "come over here so I may look at you properly."

Hesitating slightly but unable to think of a way of refusing, I set down my teacup on the table and went over to her.

"Now, what did you do to deserve our ladyship here?"

I looked at Lady Sarah on the sofa, who was removing her bonnet. Even in the dusty dimness of the room, her eyes sparkled with amusement. It was an enchanting picture, as she unveiled her golden hair and smoothed the ribbons of the bonnet.

Mrs. Bamford's question, ridiculous as it was, hovered in my mind. We had spent the majority of the walk here discussing *Pride and Prejudice*, debating the characters and their actions, both agreeing and disagreeing, being interrupted from time to time by Lord Danneville, but always returning to our conversation afterward with ease.

It occurred to me that I would never, *could* never deserve Lady Sarah Danneville. I was not part of her world. I might be able to persuade myself otherwise for a time as we interacted as mistress and a servant of sorts, but that was the extent of our relationship.

Regret and a pang of anguish filled me.

Under my sustained gaze, her amusement took on a more questioning and intent look, as though she could divine the direction of my thoughts.

I faced Mrs. Bamford. "Nothing at all," I said softly, calmly.

She took my hand in her weak, wrinkled one and pulled downward so that I was obliged to kneel on the thin rug. "I have forgotten your name, and I am terrible with names, so you may save yourself the trouble of telling me again." She leaned farther toward me. "Between the two of us, I suspect my memory is beginning to fail me."

I couldn't help a smile.

"I like your eyes," she said, letting hers run over my face. "That must be how you captured her heart."

I had a fair idea I had done nothing at all to Lady Sarah's heart, but my own beat erratically. "Is there anything we can do for you, Mrs. Bamford? I am here on behalf of the parish and Mr. Vickers."

She patted my hand, and I tried not to betray how it hurt for her to press the place where the spider had bitten me. "Very kind of you, but I am quite self-sufficient, I assure you. And what of you, my boy?" She turned her eyes to Lord Danneville.

He looked at his sister, who shot him a glance both pleading and warning, no doubt fearing he would burst this fragile bubble by telling her he was not our son but my student—and a viscount.

But he only smiled. "I am ten years old, ma'am. And soon to go to Harrow."

"Harrow, is it?" She kept her hold on my hand, which meant I could do nothing but remain by her side, kneeling on knees that ached.

"Yes, Harrow." He looked at his sister, as though willing her to challenge him.

What reason Lady Sarah had for disliking his wish to attend Harrow, I didn't know. Until a day or two ago, I would have thought her glad for a reason to be rid of me, and the viscount attending Harrow would certainly accomplish that.

"We shouldn't take any more of your time," Lady Sarah said, rising. "We merely wished to give you our best—including our best bread and preserves."

Chapter Twenty

PHINEAS

Lord Danneville was snickering before Jane even shut the door. "Married, are you? Shall I tell Papa?"

"Not unless you wish me to tell him you lied to poor Mrs. Bamford."

"*You* lied first!"

"I did no such thing. I merely refrained from correcting her. It is quite different."

"Well, I *am* going to Harrow, so it is *not* a lie. Mr. Donovan has promised to help me persuade Father, and Father likes him very much. You *shall* help me, shan't you, Mr. Donovan?"

I opened my mouth, but I hadn't any idea what to say to the viscount's request for confirmation or the accusatory expression on Lady Sarah's face. It was obvious Lord Danneville was quite set on Harrow, and after all the progress I had made with him this week, the last thing I wanted was to set him against me. Besides, I knew firsthand what it was like to be refused the one thing I wished for at an age where it seemed the world would end if I did not have it.

Lord Danneville had a personality closer to Valentine's, though, which meant that setting up his back could mean putting him on the road to a place I was certain Lady Sarah would not wish for him to go.

"I certainly shan't stand in your way, my lord," I said, hoping Lady Sarah would see the balance I was attempting to strike.

Her lips pinched together, and her stride became quicker, forcing both her brother and me to exert ourselves to keep up. The viscount decided he might as well run.

No sooner had he gone twenty yards ahead of us than he slipped and fell on the road. Lady Sarah and I rushed toward him just as he was pushing himself to his feet, his pantaloons and coat covered in mud.

"Are you hurt?" I asked at the same time as Lady Sarah.

Both of us took one of his arms to assist him while keeping our feet well out of the mud.

"It is only a bit of dirt," the viscount said, pulling his arms away in annoyance.

I glanced at Lady Sarah, waiting for her rejoinder, for it was *not* just a bit of dirt, and his ungratefulness was likely to elicit chastisement. But there *was* no rejoinder.

She merely watched him in silence as he walked ahead of us again. Was she hurt by his dismissiveness?

"He is merely embarrassed," I said as we started walking.

She continued to look ahead. "He is getting too old to accept help. Soon he shan't need me… or anyone."

Lord Danneville passed through the gates that led onto the tree-lined drive of Bettencourt Court.

"Is that why you do not wish for him to go to Harrow?"

She hesitated for a moment before answering. "No." She turned her focus to her brother, who kicked at some of the grass growing up near one of the tall beech trees on the side of the drive.

I didn't know that I believed her. Was she afraid of admitting she loved her brother enough to wish for him to stay near her?

"At least, it is not the primary reason," she added, as though she sensed my skepticism.

"And what *is* the primary reason, if I may ask?"

"The primary reason, Mr. Donovan, is that Harrow might well spell George's ruin." She stopped, her frank gaze meeting mine. "So, when you encourage him in his desire to go there, when you tell him you will assist him in convincing my father to allow it, you may feel you are acting in his best interests, but I assure you, you are not."

I held her gaze, frowning, but she turned away and continued to walk toward the house. I skipped up beside her, but as we reached the gravel courtyard at the front of the house, and the viscount was waiting for us there, I was prevented from pursuing the subject.

Lord Danneville's face, which had recently been set in stubborn lines, was more uncertain now. He looked at his sister, as though waiting for I knew not what.

"I *should* force you to go through the front door where Father shall see you and chastise you for becoming so dirty. And I *should* tell him you lied to Mrs. Bamford."

"But I did not—" He stopped himself, pressing his lips together. He let out a frustrated sigh.

Lady Sarah stepped toward him and put out a hand, extending her pinky.

The viscount looked at it for a moment, then smiled slightly, the drying mud on his cheek cracking with the expression. He wrapped his own pinky with hers.

"Go through the servant entrance, and I shall send Sutton to help you clean up. She shan't tell Father."

Still smiling conspiratorially, Lord Danneville ran off in the direction of the servant door.

Lady Sarah observed him go, a small smile on her face.

And I watched *her*, transfixed by the glimpse of the warmth and affection I was being offered.

She glanced over at me and found my gaze on her.

Embarrassed to be discovered, I hurried to speak. "You said Harrow might be his lordship's ruin, my lady. What makes you think such a thing?"

She evaluated me, as though deciding whether she wished to answer my question. "It cannot have escaped your notice that my brother struggles with learning."

I *had* noticed it. Not only did his attention wander frequently, he struggled to remember things he had learned only minutes ago. "I have. But he does much better with a more practical approach."

"He does indeed. But do you think he will be given such an opportunity at a place like Harrow?"

I didn't answer because I didn't need to; he would not.

"George knows he is deficient in that way, and he cannot bear it. That is why he misbehaves—to take the attention away from his failings."

I made a mental review of my time at Bettencourt Court. "I have not seen him do anything outside the range of normal activities for a child his age."

"That is because he hasn't *done* such things during your presence here. Believe me, Mr. Donovan, you have been fortunate to escape the worst of George's antics. You have connected with him in a way that no one else has. But Harrow will not be so kind to him."

"Perhaps Harrow will teach him other valuable lessons."

"But at what cost?"

"I believe Harrow's fees are somewhere in the range of fifty pounds per year."

My attempt at a joke elicited the smile I had been hoping for. I hated to see her preoccupied.

She sighed. "Would that fifty pounds was the only cost. George has been raised to think highly of himself, to expect others to do so as well, and he cannot bear to be thought badly of. Harrow would give him the opportunity and means of making the sort of mistakes and allying himself with the sort of young men who would bring out the very worst in him. Absent someone like you to help him learn in the way that most benefits him, he would fall far behind his peers. To make up for and distract from such a lack in the classroom, he would fraternize with the worst of the students, asserting his place by whatever means necessary, inevitably leading to severe discipline. And you may be unfamiliar with the medieval methods used at Harrow, Mr. Donovan, but *I* am not."

Her reasoning was sound, and I couldn't help but agree with it. "I quite see what you mean, my lady."

"But…?"

I met her gaze.

"I can see you have reservations," she said.

"It is hardly my affair."

"Perhaps not, but I should like to hear what you have to say all the same, for I know you have his best interests at heart."

"I do." She had complimented me twice in the last two minutes, and I feared the effect such words were having on my heart, giving it hope it did not have any right to.

"Shall we walk?" she asked.

I nodded, wishing I could offer her my arm, but I kept my hands clasped behind my back instead. We began our stroll on the path that led toward the side of the house, the gravel crunching under our feet.

"I was raised in a naval family, my lady, and it was assumed I would make a career for myself there. My true interests, however, were far less practical. I preferred books and found no joy in the hardships of life at sea. I begged my father to let me attend the Naval Academy, where my involvement in his preferred profession would better intersect with my interests. But he was staunchly against it. I hated him for it, but I did so in secret, finding ways to rebel."

155

She put a hand on my arm to stop me, then apparently thinking better of it, removed it. "Mr. Donovan, rebelling? I must hear more of this."

I laughed, trying to brush away the disappointment I felt at her reaction. "I shirked my duties in favor of reading in a rarely frequented corner of the ship, stole candles to allow me to read after the other midshipmen were asleep, and begged my mother to sneak books onto the ship whenever we were ashore."

"A veritable criminal, in fact," she said with her wide, engaging smile. "I am astounded Father agreed for you to tutor George with such a history."

"I imagine my brother-in-law conveniently failed to mention such things when he recommended me for the position. In any case, my father hoped I would come around to the life of a sailor, make him proud as I rose through the ranks, but I resigned my position the moment I turned twenty-one, still a lowly midshipman—the only one of my brothers not to achieve at least lieutenant."

We turned the corner of Bettencourt Court, bringing into view the lake, shimmering deep blue in the afternoon light. Beyond it lay the woods where we had found our stick-swords.

"My father's stubbornness on the subject only drove me to want the Academy more. I resented him terribly. In truth, I doubt I would have enjoyed the Academy, but his absolute refusal to consider it kept me from seeing that."

"And you think my being so against Harrow only drives George to want it more?"

I sent her a sympathetic grimace. "Human nature is not exempt from Newton's laws, my lady. You are providing a force, and your brother is returning with an equal amount of force."

She was silent for a moment. "But surely it is cruel to let him think he shall be able to attend Harrow when I have no intention of allowing such a thing happen?"

"It *would* be cruel."

"You mean I must truly allow him to attend?"

"I am not certain what you should do, my lady. That is not for me to decide. I merely wished for you to understand why I have not joined your efforts to stop the viscount—and to warn you, perhaps."

"I see."

I smiled ruefully. "I have not managed to convince you, have I?"

"You offer your own experience as evidence of what not to do, Mr. Donovan, but I find you far from a convincing example. Only look at you now." And she did. She stopped walking, turning toward me and studying my face with a keen eye. "You are intelligent, caring, and reliable, even if you *do* read romance novels in your spare time. I would be quite content if George grew to be like you." She smiled and turned to the path, leaving me speechless and breathless.

I liked Lady Sarah Danneville. I liked her much too well for my own good. And in my affinity for her, I was too quick to see in her increasing kindness to me something that was not—and could not be.

Chapter Twenty-One

SARAH

I tapped the end of my quill distractedly on the half-sheet of paper to my side while I stared at the blank page of my notebook. It was just after the one where I had written the things I wished for in my hypothetical husband. The problem was that all I could see when I looked at it now was Mr. Donovan. He was the one who had inspired every entry, and I could not base my list off of my brother's tutor.

I needed to see things afresh, but I was struggling to do so. I hardly knew what I wished for. Perhaps that was because I primarily wished for a response from Cousin Arthur. I had yet to hear from him, and I was beginning to wonder if he had not received my letter. The thought that Father might have intercepted it was dismissed quickly. He would not have remained silent if that had happened.

I would wait two more days, and if I had no response by then, I would write Cousin Arthur again.

I glanced at the unsightly bubble of ink at the tip of the quill. I was making no progress—none at all. I let out a sigh of frustration, replaced the quill in the stand, and put the cap on the ink before rising and leaving my bedchamber.

I had seen precious little of Mr. Donovan since our walk around the house three days ago. A number of issues had arisen in the parish which required his attention. Each time, he and George had come in search of me, the former's eyes full of apology. He would tell me what they had been studying or discussing before the interruption, and I would take charge.

While I inevitably sighed as though I was very put-upon, I took secret pleasure in taking over—and in the complete trust Mr. Donovan had expressed in my abilities to continue his efforts.

When I reached the bottom of the staircase, Hughes was walking across the entry hall.

"Any post today?" I asked.

"Yes, my lady," he replied. "Though nothing for your ladyship."

"Thank you, Hughes." I suppressed a sigh as he bowed and continued on his way.

Behind me, Mr. Donovan emerged from the library. He had a paper in hand, but he stilled as his gaze found me. "Good day, my lady."

He was looking very handsome—more so than usual, even, with a lock of hair dropping onto his forehead. What was it about the veriest hint of disarray in a man so contained that I found so alluring?

A thought occurred to me. "Have you been practicing *Ajax* without me?" The play had been delayed with the busyness of Mr. Donovan's schedule this week.

He smiled and brushed the hair from his face. "No. Though it is not for lack of Lord Danneville requesting to do so."

"*That* I have no difficulty believing." I glanced at the paper in his hand. "Are you needed again? I never knew a parish to have so many urgent matters in a week. I suspect it is due to the fact that they know *you* will be the one to carry out such visits. Mr.

Vickers will be astounded by the increase in his obligations when he returns."

Mr. Donovan laughed genially. He did so much more often than when he had first arrived at Bettencourt Court. He was becoming less awkward by the day, and that fact was hardly conducive to helping me turn my thoughts from him.

"I hope I shall not be obliged to bother you today, my lady, though I must say the viscount's grasp on Latin numerals is far better after your time with him."

I tried not to let him see how well this pleased me.

"I was just going to seek your father," he said. "I received a letter from my sister. She seems to be under the impression that she and my brother-in-law have an invitation to pay a visit on—"

"Sarah." Father's voice interrupted Mr. Donovan unceremoniously, his tone dark and foreboding. And yet, his brow was even more so as he stood a dozen feet away, his eyes squarely upon me. Was he upset to find me talking to Mr. Donovan?

"Come to the study," he said in a peremptory voice.

It was not an infrequent occurrence that Father became annoyed with me, but it had been some time since he had spoken to me so forcefully.

I glanced at Mr. Donovan, whose alert expression made it clear he realized something was amiss.

"Of course," I said calmly, giving the tutor a little nod, then following Father toward the study. The silence between us continued once the door was shut. I had never seen Father look so grim, and I combatted a surge of nerves.

He went to his desk, setting the tips of his fingers on an open letter. They pressed upon it, turning white as his jaw flexed and hardened. "What the *devil* is the matter with you?" The words were an explosion of anger, a rush of water breaking through a dam.

I looked at Father and then the letter, my mind working quickly as it tried to discern to what he was referring. Was this a letter from Mr. Donovan's sister? I scoured my mind for what I might have done to anger him and remembered my parting words to Mrs. Donovan at the picnic, inviting her to visit her brother at Bettencourt Court.

"I did not do it with an intent to anger you, Father," I said slowly.

"With an int—" He clamped his mouth shut, his face turning the color of a beet. "What the devil *was* your intent?"

I lifted my shoulders, scrambling for words. "I considered it a harmless kindness."

"Harmless? Have you so little regard for your family? You should be thanking the heavens Fox is discreet! If word of this got out…" He scrubbed a hand over his jaw and swore.

My stomach tightened, roiling with a torrent of nausea, and I looked at the letter again. "Arthur Fox?" I swallowed. "Cousin Arthur?"

"What might have happened if he were a loose screw and had agreed to your… *scheme?*" He picked up the letter, his face screwing up. "It is the behavior of a harlot, Sarah, not the decorum I expect of my daughter—the daughter of the Earl of Bettencourt." He slammed the paper down. "How dared you?"

Words failed me. Cousin Arthur *had* received my letter. But rather than responding to it, he had borne the tale to Father.

"Even if he had agreed to your proposition, did you truly think I would have allowed it?"

I brought my gaze from the letter to Father, my jaw hardening. "You could not have stopped me."

"You may be of age, Sarah, but do not think for a second I cannot make the future miserable for you. I have borne with your stubbornness to this point, but by Jove, if you insist on humiliating this family in this manner"—he crumpled up the letter—"I shall have no choice but to protect the Danneville name by employing methods that, believe you me, you shall not like."

We stared at one another in silence, both of us trembling at an impasse of wills.

Chapter Twenty-Two

PHINEAS

I glanced at the door of the library, listening in vain for any sign of Lady Sarah's footsteps. I had felt unsettled since the earl had interrupted our conversation in the entry hall. Did I bear some responsibility in her father's anger? Perhaps he had noticed the time we had been spending together. Perhaps he suspected how I was beginning to feel for her.

Surely he would address such concerns with *me*, though.

Lord Danneville was hunched over at the desk in the library, practicing his Latin. There had been a distinct improvement in him this week. Whether that was because I had assured him I would not stand in the way of him going to Harrow or because he responded particularly well to his sister's teaching methods, I didn't know.

Lady Sarah was certainly a skilled teacher. Each time I had left her brother in her care, informing her what we had been studying, I had returned to find progress made. Of course, we still spent an appreciable amount of the day doing things most tutors would consider well outside the normal methods of instruction.

This was a challenge for me as well. It was not in my nature to think in terms of practical applications as a method of learning, but I found my own understanding of each topic solidified by the activities.

"Very good," I said, looking over the viscount's work. He still had more than half of the exercise remaining, and I was feeling impatient. It had been long enough that Lord Bettencourt would likely be at liberty to discuss my sister's letter with me. "Continue as you are, my lord, and I shall return shortly."

Lord Danneville nodded distractedly, and taking Diana's letter in hand again, I strode to the door. I slipped out of the library just as Lady Sarah emerged into the entry hall from the corridor behind the stairs. Walking toward the front door, she dashed at her eye with a finger, pulled the front door open, and disappeared outside in a hurry, without a bonnet or a shawl or gloves.

My heart constricted, the sight of her pink cheeks and pained expression swimming in front of me.

Standing in the doorway, I addressed the viscount. "If I have not returned by the time you finish, my lord, you may take a half-hour respite." Without waiting for a response, I opened the door and hurried into the entry hall, then through the front door.

My eyes scoured the scene for Lady Sarah and caught sight of her rounding the corner of the house, where she disappeared.

I hesitated for the briefest of moments, but after what I had seen of her face, I couldn't stop myself from following her. Folding my sister's letter, I hurried after her. She had a significant advantage over me, though, and it was not until I was warm and breathless and just twenty yards shy of the lake that I was able to gain enough ground to say her name without yelling.

"Lady Sarah," I said, raising my voice just enough to be heard.

She was nearing the edge of the lake, but she turned. A glistening on her red cheeks made me glad I had heeded the impulse to follow her, but I struggled with what to say next, how to explain my presence.

"I… I saw you leave and"—I tried to catch my breath, using it as an excuse to choose my words with care as I drew nearer— "I wanted to ascertain whether you were well." The words came out lame. Ridiculous, even. It was obvious, despite her efforts to brush away evidence of tears, that she was not well. But what did I intend to do now that such a thing was clear?

"You needn't trouble yourself on my account, Mr. Donovan." Her voice trembled slightly, and she turned toward the lake. It glimmered a slate gray in the cloudy afternoon light, its surface rippling gently with the breeze.

She walked to one of the stone benches that punctuated the banks of the lake every hundred feet and took a seat.

I stopped where I was, trying to decide what I should do. Did she wish for me to leave? I couldn't leave her in such distress. "It is no trouble, my lady." I hesitated. "Forgive me, but… do I bear some responsibility in this grief?"

Her head whipped toward me, her brow pursed. "What? No, of course not. Why would you think such a thing?"

"I…" How was I to tell her I had been worried her father's anger had been caused by her interactions with me? It would be presumptuous at best.

"Rest easy, Mr. Donovan," she said. "My father is angry with no one but me, and my current state has nothing to do with you."

The words were simultaneously reassuring and painful, though I couldn't say precisely why. It was not as though I wanted to be the source of distress in her life. Far from it. But she said it almost as though it had been ridiculous for me to even consider having the power to affect her.

"I *cannot* rest easy, my lady," I said. "Not when I see you so distressed."

"My father's anger is not what distresses me." Her jaw tightened as she said the words.

I took a step closer. "Then what is it?"

She studied my face for a moment before returning her gaze to the lake. "If I tell you the whole of it, you shall never think of me the same way."

Part of me hoped that was true, for the way I thought of her now—the way my eyes insisted on studying every detail of her face, the way my thoughts strayed to her when I was teaching the viscount or visiting one of the parishioners—*needed* to change.

"Are you an avid reader of gothic romance novels?"

She glanced at me, the hint of a smile on her lips. "No. That is not what I mean, Mr. Donovan."

I took another step toward her, and her eyes watched my progress, but she gave no indication that it was unwelcome. "Then we have already exhausted the list of possible things you could tell me that would change the way I think of you."

"I disagree."

I held her gaze for a moment. "May I sit?" It was bold. And I was not a bold man—not by any stretch of the imagination. But if Lady Sarah needed someone to be bold, to sit with her when she doubted anyone would want to sit with her, I could be bold enough for that.

Her eyes met mine for a moment, and I thought she would surely refuse. But she nodded and moved aside, making room for me.

I took the place, remarking how unhealthy boldness seemed to be for my heart. It was whacking about in a way that couldn't possibly be good for it. How strong *was* the human heart? Perhaps I would find out today.

Lady Sarah sniffed subtly beside me. She wiped a tear from her eye, and a few of her lashes stuck together. The muted daylight fell upon her face, casting gentle shadows on her features, and I realized then that I had never seen her from so near. Had there always been such a sadness in her eyes?

"What has distressed you, my lady?"

Her chin trembled for the briefest moment as she smoothed a wrinkle in her skirts. "Naught but the end of a dream."

"What dream is that?"

A group of ducks quacked in the sky above us, descending toward the lake until they landed one by one, grazing with grace across the surface and leaving the water disrupted in their wake.

"Freedom." Lady Sarah watched them glide along the lake. "Like Lady Hester's."

I studied her face, trying to understand.

"The first time I heard of her, she had just left England. There was much talk of her accomplishments, of how she had excelled at hosting for Pitt, making a place for herself where no other woman had. Of course, there was talk, too, of the scandal she had created in doing so, but I paid that no heed. All I knew was she was everything I wished to be: intelligent, refined, unmarried, ambitious. And just like me, she was the daughter of an earl. And then I heard of her bravery during her travels—the shipwreck at Rhodes, continuing on without her brother, her archeological excavation at Ashkelon. Everything I heard gave me hope that the constraints around me could be overcome, that I could leave a mark on the world."

I kept my silence, remembering the dinner conversation the earl and I had a few evenings ago. I had agreed with Lord Bettencourt's opinion of Lady Hester—and I had done so genuinely, for Lady Hester had been much discussed during my time in the Navy and at Cambridge. She was ambitious, certainly, and intelligent, too. But I couldn't think highly of her despite that. Her failings seemed to me too great.

But Lady Sarah saw her as an example, a beacon of possibility.

"I thought if I could only follow in her footsteps, I could have everything she had."

Silence followed her words, punctuated by the ducks dipping their heads into the water, searching for food and bathing their brown feathers.

"I wrote to a relative of Father's, an unmarried man of great influence in the world of politics, much like Lady Hester's uncle. To him, I proposed a similar situation: I could act as his hostess. My hope was that, through the connections I would make in such a role, I would be able to organize an expedition to Athens —perhaps even live there."

I had been listening in silence, but my curiosity was piqued. "You wish to live in Athens?" I would not have guessed such a thing.

"Perhaps. But it matters little now. Father received a letter today from his cousin Arthur, informing him of what I had done. Father…" She swallowed and shook her head. "Well, he made it clear he would allow no such thing. And he has the power to ensure it."

I didn't doubt it. I knew what could be done—or prevented— with the proper influence.

"I am sorry, Lady Sarah."

She smiled wryly. "You needn't pretend. I know your opinion of Lady Hester."

"I shan't pretend I hold her in the same esteem you do, but I can understand why you would admire her."

"Can you?" The glistening of coming tears filled her eyes to the brim. Her words, though, were full of energy. "Can you understand what it is to be a woman, Mr. Donovan? To be allowed no real aspirations of your own? To be shut out from learning by both culture and institution? To have nothing to offer the world but a set of pretty accomplishments? With no prospects or expectations except to be swallowed up into the life of a man? To become entirely his, to be at his every whim?"

I met the intensity of her eyes, transfixed by her sudden passion, convicted by her questions. When *had* I truly considered the plight of women?

"I..." I struggled to find the words to respond, to convey how I felt. "No, I cannot understand it as you can. But I am sorry for it, my lady. Truly sorry."

The energy in her eyes dissipated, and she took in a large breath that shook slightly, turning her gaze to the lake. "You are fortunate. You may be a third son, but the only true limits to your intellectual aspirations are the ones you set on yourself. I might read all the books in Father's library, but there are doors which, no matter how deserving I am, will remain closed to me."

She was right. I couldn't blame her for doing what lay in her power to break free of the bonds constraining her. I wished it was in my power to open every door to her, to give her the opportunity to prove what she was capable of.

We sat in thoughtful silence, and I took the handkerchief from my pocket, offering it to her.

She smiled weakly at the gesture and accepted it. "Do you know the most aggravating part of all?" She played with the folds of the handkerchief, and I refrained from filling the silence, worried I might say or do something to break the spell allowing her to treat me as a confidant.

"The worst part," she finally continued, "is the relief I feel."

"Relief?"

She nodded. "To know I shan't have to be brave the way following after Lady Hester would have required me to be. To know I will not be gossiped about or thought badly of. It is almost as though I was privately hoping Father would stop me all along."

She dropped a hand to her side, and it brushed my leg. I had the impulse to touch it, to hold it in my own. "There is no shame in that, my lady."

"Is there not? I have always prided myself on being superior to most of my sex—more intelligent, more daring and determined. But I am no different. I am worse, for I am a hypocrite. It is the disappointment I feel in myself that I can barely stand."

I shifted my legs more fully toward her, nervous energy demanding I move, but reason insisting that taking her hand would be a mistake. "You needn't be, my lady. What if the relief you feel is your intuition telling you this is for the best?"

Her eyes searched me. "You believe in such things? In intuition?"

I tried to breathe steadily, but I found her more captivating than ever in such proximity. I might have expected as much; the nearer I studied anything, the more I came to appreciate it. Why should it not be so with her?

But the strength of the pull I felt toward her now was *not* reasonable. I doubted it was something I could understand with my mind, and that was both exhilarating and terrifying. "I hardly know what to believe anymore."

Her eyelids fluttered ever so slightly, her body completely still.

Something dropped onto the ground nearby, and we broke eye contact to see what it was. My handkerchief lay on the ground, and I stooped to pick it up.

So did she.

A pang shot through my skull as our heads collided with a sickening thud.

I touched a hand to her head and one to my spectacles, wincing.

"This is becoming a habit," she said in a pained voice, though the glimmer of a smile told me she was not angry.

"I am truly sorry," I said, looking at the pink spot on her forehead. My hand lingered just beside it, the tips of my fingers touching her hair. The time had come to pull my hand away, but it remained there, defying me. "Does it hurt terribly?"

"Only as much as yours, I imagine." She smiled, but in her eyes, I saw the awareness of my hand. It cradled her head as her hair beckoned me to slide my hand across it, to feel its softness. She hadn't yet moved away, and though I didn't know what that meant, I couldn't bring myself to be the one to initiate a distance I didn't wish for.

I glanced at the ground, where the handkerchief still lay.

"Do you dare?" Her eyes held mine, a playful glint in them, until her gaze dropped to my lips, and her smile wavered.

SARAH

I had only meant to tease him, to see whether he dared to reach for the handkerchief, but as I looked at him, the words took on a new meaning, as though I was daring him to kiss me.

I had never been touched as he touched me now, with such care and concern. I had never been regarded as he regarded me now, with something I could only describe as desire.

Its effect was to ignite something in me, too. Something new, something full of curiosity and want that made my body tremble.

An obnoxious quacking sounded nearby, and we broke gazes to see a duck toddling swiftly toward us, a purposefulness to its waddle. It was somewhat threatening, in fact—enough to pull us from whatever had been happening.

"She is intent upon your handkerchief, I think," I said, my pounding heart at odds with my calm voice.

"It appears so. Please, for both of our sakes, my lady, remain precisely where you are."

I nodded, smiling.

Dropping his hand from my hair, he reached for the handkerchief just as the duck neared, still quacking animatedly. He grasped the square first, but the duck spread its wings and flapped them swiftly, producing a flurry of air and the release of a few small feathers.

I retreated from the angry chaos, leaning into Mr. Donovan for refuge.

He raised the handkerchief as though he might throw it toward the creature as a peace offering, but it settled its wings and turned, waddling toward the lake and complaining noisily.

"Good heavens," I said, watching the duck as though it might change its mind and return to finish its business. "I am tempted to have Father's hunting rifle fetched. Perhaps that can be your next practical lesson with George."

He laughed and gave me the handkerchief. "I am no hunter."

"Yes, I know." My breath caught at the sight of him so close again. It frightened me how much I wanted to close the last bit of distance between us, and I shifted away, taking a more normal seat—one that didn't rely on Mr. Donovan to keep me upright.

"*You* would do a much better job of teaching him to hunt," he said, adjusting his own position as well.

"I would do a better job of teaching him *everything*." I sent him a playful glance.

He laughed ruefully. "I think I might agree with you. He has made a great deal of progress this week."

"I was only teasing, Mr. Donovan. George was making progress *before* I began helping, though it pains me to admit such a thing." I glanced over at him, remembering our first encounter. "I was quite determined to get rid of you when you first arrived, you know."

"Yes, I am well aware. What I do not understand is why."

I gave a soft laugh. "I had been asking Father to allow me to tutor George for months, and I thought he had finally agreed to it, only for you to appear in the library that day. I thought you would be just like the other tutors."

"Which is to say…?"

"Unable to manage George, impatient with his slowness to learn."

"I am not impatient with him, but I do not know I can say I have learned to manage him." His brows drew together. "I am sorry to be the source of your disappointment, my lady. I hadn't any notion."

I shook my head. I did not think of Mr. Donovan as a disappointment anymore. I wished I *could,* though. It would be far simpler than what I did feel for him, whatever that was. "You have done things with him I would never have thought to do. He needs you."

"Perhaps he needs us both. I would share the burden of teaching him with you if you wished to do so."

The thought was appealing. Perhaps not for the right reasons.

"I shall think on it." I held out the handkerchief to him. "I do not think I stand in need of it any longer." It was true. I no longer felt the need to cry. "Thank you, Mr. Donovan. For sitting with me."

He nodded as he took the handkerchief, and our fingers brushed in the process, sending an increasingly familiar pulse through me.

I stood, but his hand grasped mine. "Lady Sarah?"

I turned toward him, my gloveless fingers surrounded by his warm ones.

He stood. "You *will* make your mark on the world. But you will make it in your own way, without following in the footsteps of any other man or woman. I have no doubt of that at all. You are too remarkable not to."

I couldn't breathe. His words washed over me, slipping into cracks in my heart I hadn't realized were there.

A rustling sounded, and we both whipped toward it, our hands dropping.

"George," I said in surprise.

He stood a dozen feet away, looking at us with round, curious eyes.

Mr. Donovan cleared his throat and walked toward him. "You finished your exercises?"

George's eyes remained on me. "I did. *And* I took the respite, but you did not return, so I came to find you."

Mr. Donovan's color was heightened, and his hand moved to his pocket, as though his impulse was driving him to clean his spectacles. But he refrained. "Yes, I apologize for that. But we may resume now if you are ready."

"I would rather stay outside. We haven't even practiced *Ajax* since deciding on the script."

Mr. Donovan looked to me as though asking whether I cared to participate in such a practice at the moment.

But I couldn't. My mind was abuzz, my heart confused.

What had I been doing, permitting myself such proximity to Mr. Donovan? George's expression—*shocked* was putting it lightly—acted like smelling salts, reviving me from whatever had come over me.

"I have some things I must attend to," I said, my voice tighter than usual.

Mr. Donovan's eyes lingered on me for a moment, as though he could sense a shift in me. Those spectacles made him far too perceptive for his own good. Certainly too perceptive for *mine.*

"Of course," he said.

George complained, and though I felt guilty Mr. Donovan had the unenviable task of tending to him, I hoped George's frustration would cause him to forget what he had seen. Not that there had been anything to see; I had merely been shaking hands—briefly—with Mr. Donovan, which was a perfectly acceptable thing to do with the tutor of one's brother. And if he thought he saw me looking at Mr. Donovan's lips or my body leaning ever so slightly in his direction, well, perhaps he needed spectacles as much as Mr. Donovan did.

I hurried toward the house, my fingers trembling. How different things were from this morning. Then, I still had hope of arranging my own future. Then, I hadn't fully realized the attraction Mr. Donovan held for me.

Or perhaps I was being too rash. What if it was not attraction but merely a moment of weakness? I had allowed my emotions to overcome me, leading me to make unwise decisions.

Well, no more. I might not be able to sail to Athens and study ancient texts, but some things still remained in my control, and I would do anything but fall prey to my emotions. My mind *would* reign supreme.

I would marry, just as my parents and society expected of me, but I would do it on my terms.

———

"I am ready, Mama."

Mother was in the sitting room connected to her bedchamber, sipping from a cup of tea with a magazine before her, but she looked up at my sudden appearance and declaration.

"Ready?" She set down the teacup.

Clenching my jaw determinedly, I stepped into the room, a small piece of paper in hand. It was the result of a great deal of work. My fire grate was full of a half-dozen others just like it.

"Ready to marry."

Her brows shot up, and there was silence for a few moments as she surveyed my face as though looking for evidence I was not in earnest. "Is there someone in particular you *wish* to marry?"

"No." *Why* did my mind immediately turn to Mr. Donovan? "I suppose what I should have said is I am ready to be serious about marrying. I have made a list, as promised, of the qualities I value in a potential husband." I extended the paper to her, and she took it from me, her eyes fixed on my face before they turned to the list.

"A marriage of convenience," she read.

I gave a firm nod. "I have no desire to be… *accosted* by a man who fancies himself in love with me."

She regarded me a moment longer, then returned her gaze to the paper. "Over the age of fifty. Is this out of a hope he will die soon?"

"It should come as no surprise, for we discussed it before."

"Yes, but I did not think you were serious."

"I was."

She looked as though she might say more, but she pinched her lips together and returned to the list. "Untitled. Wealth acquired from trade." Her brows pulled together.

"Someone who has not been raised by peers will be less likely to take issue with my ambitions," I explained.

She sighed, no doubt contemplating how she would convey my requirements to Father. "A widower with an heir." She cleared her throat. "I rather think I understand *that* one without needing to ask any questions."

"Very good, for I do not particularly wish to discuss it."

"And finally"—she took a sip of her tea, then frowned—"no spectacles?" Her gaze flitted up to mine, complete and utter bafflement in her eyes.

I lifted my chin, keenly aware the final requirement was strangely specific and not entirely reasonable. "You will see it is my only requirement relating to appearance."

Her mouth pulled up at one corner. "Yes, how very open-minded you are. You *do* realize it might be difficult to find a man over the age of fifty who does *not* wear glasses, do you not? To say nothing of all your other requirements. It seems oddly particular."

Not so odd if she realized what—or rather whom—spectacles had begun to bring to mind.

She folded the paper as it had been before and set it next to the teacup. "Well, I cannot promise your father will be pleased with your requirements, but given the fear he has of you proposing another *situation* to Arthur Fox, perhaps he will agree to it more readily than we think."

Chapter Twenty-Four

PHINEAS

I gathered a few books from my bedchamber and hurried in the direction of the library. I was a few minutes early for the time the viscount and I generally began the day, but that was not a mistake.

I had hardly known a moment's rest since the encounter with Lady Sarah four days ago. Between parish duties, planning lessons I thought would find success with Lord Danneville, and teaching those lessons, I was exhausted.

Sunday's sermon had gone tolerably well, despite the fact that I seemed conscious at every moment of precisely where Lady Sarah was sitting and whether or not she was looking at me. She was *not* looking at me. Not once during the service.

The Linton twins, however, had given me rapt attention and ready smiles for the duration of the service. Afterward, their parents had invited me to dine. In that moment, at least, I had thanked the powers that be that Mr. Daniel's health had declined enough that I might at any moment be obliged to give him his last rites.

My mood was lower than it had been in recent memory, too. In my more deluded moments, I rationalized this was a normal result of the pace I had been keeping and the lack of reading time I had. But I was too much a champion of truth to accept such an explanation for long. One did not *find* reading time; one brought it into existence by sheer force of will, even if it meant losing an entire night's sleep.

I opened the door gingerly, looking at the place Lady Sarah generally sat to read. It was empty, just as it had been for the past four days.

No longer could I persuade myself she had given up reading. No. Lady Sarah was avoiding me.

"She is out riding."

I whirled around and found Lord Danneville watching me stare at the empty space. In his arms, he held Mr. Vickers's cat, Chester, which had followed me home two days ago and been embraced heartily by the viscount.

"*Who* is out riding?" My question sounded pathetic and unconvincing, even to my own ears.

Lord Danneville gave me a look that was far too knowing for a child his age. "Sarah." He opened the library door and passed through. "She has gone out every morning this week."

"Oh," I said, hoping I struck the tone of a man receiving unsolicited information rather than one who was grasping onto precious knowledge.

He let the cat drop to the floor. "You must have made her very angry."

"I... I—"

"Whenever I see her now, she is writing furiously in that notebook of hers."

"It is what she uses to take notes as she reads." I should put a stop to the conversation—it was likely the viscount's method of delaying his lessons—but I was too weak, too hungry for any snippet of connection with Lady Sarah.

"So she says," he replied. "But there was not a book in sight the last few times I saw her with it, and when I tried to peer at it over her shoulder, she snapped it shut. And snapped at *me*. Can you not apologize?"

"Apologize for what?"

He crouched to pet the cat and shrugged. "Whatever you did to cause this lovers' quarrel."

My cheeks flamed. It was not the first time he had made a comment referencing the moment he had found us together by the lake. "Lord Danneville…"

"I would like you to become my brother, but if you intend to be stubborn, you will ruin everything."

My mouth had been open to speak, but at his comment, words escaped me. I was torn between embarrassment and how touching it was that he wanted me to become his brother. From someone as difficult as Lord Danneville, that was high praise indeed.

But it didn't change the fact that the idea was ridiculous.

"My lord…" I kneeled beside him and stroked the cat from head to tail. When I reached the end, hairs flitted into the air while others clung to my hand. I brushed them off and sighed, looking at the viscount. "I am afraid you have misunderstood things. Your sister and I have no quarrel. And there is not now, nor was there ever, any type of… understanding between us. I am honored to be your tutor and curate, but that is all I can be."

His forehead wrinkled with frown lines. I might have believed him as disappointed as I was to be told there was no prospect of Lady Sarah and me becoming more than we now were.

"Then how are we to practice *Ajax* if the two of you cannot even manage to be in the same room as one another?"

Ah. There it was. The real reason the viscount wished for a reconciliation between us. Our quarrel, as he called it, had been delaying *Ajax*.

I rose to my feet. "I think we may need to move forward without your sister. You and I can perform it together."

He stood, looking at me as though I belonged in Bedlam. "What, just the two of us? Certainly not! I shall talk to Sarah today and remind her of her promise."

I said nothing, for it was not my place to tell the viscount what to do. But the truth was, Lady Sarah had made no promise. She had no obligation whatsoever to spend time with me, and she had been so busy the past few days that the viscount had enjoyed more than a few hours on his own while I carried out parish duties and Lady Sarah went on visits and shopping expeditions with her mother.

Lady Bettencourt and Lady Sarah were both absent for dinner. Again. It had been thus for the past few nights, which had left me to take my dinner in my bedchamber. Tonight, however, Lord Bettencourt was present, and once Lord Danneville had left the table to prepare for bed, he cleared his throat.

"I received a letter from your brother-in-law, Russell, today," he said. "We are to expect him and his wife Saturday afternoon. They intend to stay until Sunday afternoon before continuing on to visit friends in Surrey."

This was not news to me, for I had the letter from Diana a few days ago. I had tried to persuade them against coming, but I might have saved myself the effort. Diana was a stubborn woman, and though she came under the guise of supporting me as I gave a sermon, I rather thought it was motivated just as much by a curiosity over my situation at Bettencourt Court.

"It is very kind of you to offer to receive them for the night, my lord."

"Not at all. It is my pleasure. In fact"—he took a sip of port—"if it weren't for the chaos that shall soon consume the house as we prepare for the ball, I would insist they stay longer."

My hand on my glass, I stilled. "Ball?"

"Yes. In a fortnight. I thought you might have heard talk of it amongst the servants. My daughter intends to choose a husband, and naturally, that means I must spend inordinate amounts of money."

I tried for a smile, but I felt sick inside.

"Vickers will be back by then," the earl continued, "and I have no doubt he will agree to ensure you are unoccupied that night."

The sickness in my stomach lifted momentarily, replaced by uncertainty and a bit of wonder. The earl wished for me to attend the ball? Was it to fill space, to even out numbers? Or— dare I think it?—did he consider me eligible enough to be included amongst those invited?

Not all the reason in the world could keep my heart from soaring at the thought.

He took another sip of port. "We haven't told George yet, which is what I wanted to discuss with you. I wish for you to keep him company and see he stays in bed. The last time we held a ball, he was quite upset at not being allowed to take part in the amusement. He got up to a great deal of mischief, and I wish to prevent a recurrence of that."

"Of course, my lord." My voice sounded strangled, but he seemed not to notice. Neither did he notice my heart, so recently hovering up near the windows, catapulting down and settling in a heap on the floor.

Chapter Twenty-Five

SARAH

S uppressing a sigh of exhaustion, I removed my bonnet and gloves, which Collins took from me. "Is Mr. Dono —" I stopped myself. "Lord Danneville in the library, Collins?"

"He is not, my lady. I believe they are in the kitchen gardens this afternoon."

I gave a nod and made my way for the library, ignoring my disappointment. It was irrational to feel such a thing, for the entire reason I had asked Collins their whereabouts had been so I could *avoid* seeing Mr. Donovan. I should be happy he was not nearby.

They had taken to studying in the library in the mornings and going outside during the afternoons. Each morning, I had to fight the urge to join them, so I had taken to riding. As for the afternoons and evenings, Mother and I had filled those with social engagements until I wanted to cry. I was accustomed to dinners and parties, but just now, I found myself entirely sapped of energy.

I entered the library, and my gaze went to the white cat

sitting in my place. It opened its lazy eyes and considered me for a moment.

I walked toward it. "You think you are very sly, don't you, sneaking into my place when I am not here? If it weren't for the coat of hair you leave in your wake, you might have fooled me." I stroked it a few times, and its eyes closed as it purred deeply. "Now go on with you. There are plenty of other places in this house for you to sleep." I shooed it, and it hopped down reluctantly.

Glancing around as though someone might be in the library without my knowledge, I picked up the decorative cushion sitting on the chair and ran my finger along the seam until I found what I was looking for: a hole. I had discovered it two days ago as I had been distractedly pulling at the tassels.

Very well. I had *made* the hole after tugging so much that one tassel had ripped off entirely. It had occurred to me I had just created the perfect hiding place, for no one else even sat on this chair—aside from the cat, of course—and who would think to look inside a pillow for something?

Slipping my fingers in the hole, I pulled my notebook out. Ever since I had taken to using it as a repository for the unwelcome thoughts I had about Mr. Donovan, I had been apprehensive one of the servants might come upon it while cleaning my room and read its contents.

Bumps skittered across my skin. I would burn the notebook as soon as I managed to rid myself of the intrusive thoughts I continued to have. Speaking of which…

I opened the pages and took out the pencil. I had sharpened it yesterday, for it had become quite dull with the amount of writing I had been doing.

Feeling eyes upon me, I found Chester staring, as though it had been watching me take the notebook from its hiding place and intended to watch me write every word.

"What?" I asked testily.

Ignoring the feline, I began documenting how, despite being physically absent, Mr. Donovan had crept into the dinner I had just attended with Father. I had thought of him when Father had introduced me to Mr. Heggs, a banker from Shropshire with brown hair—or had it been black? I could hardly remember. He hadn't hit his head against mine or dropped a stack of books on my feet. It was to his credit, of course, but it also made him entirely forgettable.

And with every gentleman I met, Mr. Donovan's words pressed themselves upon me, and I was left asking myself: would the man before me understand my ambitions? Would I make my mark upon the world by his side?

Confound him for putting such visions in my head when I was on the cusp of accepting that my life would not be out of the ordinary.

Confound him for looking at me through those spectacles with such sincerity and understanding.

Confound him for having lips I cared to know the feel and taste of.

And finally, confound him for instilling me with an appreciation of romance novels. To combat the desire to discuss them with him, I had decided to reread them.

But it merely made me miss him more, which in turn made me hate him for changing me into an irrational woman full of sensibility and far too many emotions. I was no better than Marianne Dashwood.

I stilled. Oh, heavens! Was I Catherine Morland?

I *was*. With my penchant for reading romances, it was only a matter of time until I began reading the gothic variety, seeing life entirely through that lens, just as she had.

A muted laugh from outside reached me, and I glanced through the window. George and Mr. Donovan were walking toward the house, both of them smiling widely.

Confound that smile. I wrote furiously, trusting that doing so would rid me of my current sensibilities, for I had felt much more mistress of myself after doing so the past few days.

I put the pencil into its place and slipped the notebook into the hole amidst the stuffing. Hurriedly setting it on the chair, I primped it, for it sagged where the notebook was.

The door opened, and I whipped around. Mr. Donovan and George stopped on the threshold, looking in at me. Had they seen me tinkering with the pillow? I couldn't have them suspecting anything.

"There you are," I said brightly, as though I hadn't just been cursing Mr. Donovan sixty seconds ago. He looked every bit as surprised to see me as I was to see him. He was too intelligent not to know I had been avoiding him.

"You've come to practice!" George said with excitement. He had been quite sour toward me whenever I had seen him this week, for each time I professed myself too busy to practice *Ajax*.

I should do the same now, but after seeing the expression on his face, I couldn't bear to disappoint him again. Perhaps, with my notebook's assistance, I could keep a minimal sort of friendship with Mr. Donovan. We lived in the same house, after all, and I could not avoid him forever.

More than likely, in my efforts to keep my distance from him, I had exaggerated his good points. A dose of reality was precisely what I needed. And fighting him with a stick sword couldn't hurt, either.

"Yes," I said, glancing at Mr. Donovan. "I have come to practice. But only for half an hour." Better not to test my limits too heavily too soon.

Mother and I spent the better part of the next morning going over the details of the upcoming ball with the housekeeper. Additional maids and footmen would need to be hired for the evening, and the housekeeper had left with an entire list of things which needed to be bought. I was already sick to death of the whole thing, and it wasn't for another sennight.

But Father insisted that, to attract wealth, one needed to display wealth. It was Mother who had said it first, in fact, but as usual, Father had restated the idea in his own words and had subsequently become quite fond of it.

Things between Father and me were still difficult, but he seemed to come around a bit each day.

There was no one in the library when I went there after finishing with Mother and the housekeeper. The solitude was just what I wished for. Solitude except for Chester, of course. I didn't complain at the feline's presence this time, for it was comforting to know that what lay hidden in the cushion was even better hidden with a cat distracting from it.

I slipped the pillow from behind the cat, and it gave me a darkling look before resettling and shutting its eyes again.

I knew at once something was amiss. The pillow was too light, too evenly weighted. Searching for the hole, I put my hand through and rummaged about amongst the stuffing. But it was futile; there was nothing there.

My heart raced as my mind calculated the possibilities. Had a servant cleaned the pillow on this of all days? I discarded the idea immediately, for it was still covered in far too much cat hair for that to be the case.

Was it George, then?

My eyes widened, and my stomach clenched. Good heavens, was it Mr. Donovan?

I stooped to Chester's level. "Who was it? You must have

seen it, for heaven knows you only leave this chair when I demand it. Tell me!"

The cat's eyes were wide and watchful now, but he gave no response, intent on keeping his secret.

I let out a sound of frustration and rose to my feet. I should have burned the dratted notebook. But I had not, and now all I could do was try to find out who had discovered it. With any luck, it would be one of the maids, for they couldn't read.

I rushed out of the library and nearly ran into Mother.

"My dear." She looked surprised, but pleased. "Your father just received a letter from Mr. Wilks. He will be present at the ball next week after all."

"Mr. Wilks?" Mother and I had discussed so many gentlemen over the past week that I could no longer remember who was who.

"The wine merchant. From Dover."

The wine merchant. He would undoubtedly have shipping connections, which meant the potential for *me* to have sailing connections, which meant the possibility of Athens.

"Ah," I said with a smile. "That is fortunate indeed."

"It is more than that, my dear. He meets every single one of your requirements, for he recently turned fifty, is obscenely rich, and he has a nine-year-old son."

I waited.

She chuckled softly, a glimmer of reluctant amusement in her eyes. "And no spectacles *that we are aware of*. Your father is very hopeful, my dear. He seems quite taken with Mr. Wilks."

I hardly heeded her words, for talk of spectacles only reminded me of my notebook, which was very much missing and a matter of serious concern.

Hughes approached. "My ladies, the carriage of Mr. and Mrs. Russell is just down the drive. They shall be here in a matter of two or three minutes."

"Thank you, Hughes," Mother said. "I will inform Lord Bettencourt myself."

He bowed, and both of them began to walk away.

"Hughes," I called to him. "Do you know if anyone cleaned the library today? I left something on the chair and cannot find it."

"It was Mary, my lady, but as she came downstairs complaining that the cat would not let her so much as approach the chair without hissing at her, I do not believe she would have found anything. If you told me what it was, I could ask amongst the servants."

"No need," I said, just as Mr. Donovan and George came in through the back door. The more I made of the notebook's loss, the more interested people would become, but inside my panic was growing. "It was nothing truly important." *Only the innermost thoughts and feelings and confessions I would die rather than have made known.*

Hughes bowed again and left.

George was naming off the classical poets and whether they were Greek or Roman, while Mr. Donovan listened intently, nodding with each correct classification. Both of them glanced up at me, and I scoured their expressions for any clue that would tell me whether they had read the humiliating contents of that dratted notebook.

George smiled. "Collins says we have visitors!" It was not the mischievous smile of a child who possessed something that did not belong to him.

"Indeed," I said, my gaze moving to Mr. Donovan. How was his expression always so very inscrutable? It was those accursed spectacles. If I were a believer in magic, I would have pointed to those as evidence of it.

The muffled crunching of gravel met our ears, and Mother and Father emerged from the study, beckoning us to follow them through the front door to greet the guests.

I was admittedly curious to meet Mr. and Mrs. Russell. The latter in particular, for Mr. Donovan's brother, Valentine, had not been anything like I had imagined. Would his sister be more similar? Part of me hoped they would both be quite wretched—and, ideally, full of information about Mr. Donovan that would help me see him in a less flattering light.

But overwhelming such curiosity was my need to know what had become of my notebook. George's apparent innocence could not be taken for granted. He must be questioned.

As we filed out of doors and onto the stone stairs, I hurried to keep pace with George, whose excitement kept him in the front of our group.

"Did you steal it?" I said in something between a hiss and a whisper, keeping a smile on my face. The traveling chaise had windows, and I could see the dim outline of its occupants.

"Steal what?" George asked, frowning.

"It should be a simple answer, George," I said through clenched, smiling teeth. "Or have you stolen so many things I must needs specify?"

"I did not steal anything!" he said so loudly that all my muscles tensed.

Mother looked at us questioningly just as Mr. Russell stepped down from the chaise, followed by his wife. Mr. Russell was a fine-looking man, tall in stature and dark in coloring but with light, piercing eyes and an easy—dare I say mischievous?—smile. His wife was his match in beauty, with hair a similar color to her brother's. She wore confidence the way Mr. Donovan wore spectacles. That is to say, it suited her very well.

"Welcome, Mr. and Mrs. Russell," Father said in his most genial voice. "How pleased we are to have you at Bettencourt Court."

George seemed genuinely put out by my accusation, and guilt niggled at me. I hated when he was upset with me.

"I am sorry," I leaned to whisper as Mother and Father

continued their conversation with the guests. "Forget I asked such a thing."

"I shall try," he said doubtfully.

Satisfied I had done the best I could do at present to smooth things over with him, I turned to greet Mr. and Mrs. Russell.

Despite my dearest wishes, they were both aggravatingly likable. In fact, I rather thought I would like to have Diana Russell as a friend. In addition to the confidence with which she carried herself, the way she spoke hinted at no small degree of intelligence. Based on the ease with which she conversed, she had received the lion's share of the social graces in her family.

I watched with interest—and a reluctant smile—as Mr. Donovan received his sister's hearty embrace. He seemed to be accustomed to it, for he laughed and kissed her on the cheek.

Our eyes met, and doubt suddenly assailed me. *Was* it he who had found my notebook?

My stomach twisted and churned at the thought. It was unbearable. And because of Mr. Donovan's confounded calmness of manner, I would never know unless I asked him.

Chapter Twenty-Six

PHINEAS

"Where is my niece?" I asked of Duke as we strolled along the wooded path that surrounded the lake. Diana, Lady Sarah, and Lord Danneville were up ahead, giving me plenty of opportunity to observe how well they were getting along.

"We considered bringing her," Duke said, "but Rebecca insisted we leave her with them."

I smiled slightly. "Valentine insisted Rebecca insist, you mean?"

Duke chuckled. "That is what we suspect, yes."

"Then I shall have words with *him* when next I see him. For depriving me of my niece."

"We weren't terribly difficult to convince, I admit, for I didn't imagine Charlotte's cooing and general rambunctiousness would be conducive to the atmosphere you are hoping for during your sermon."

I suppressed a sigh at the thought of tomorrow's service. "Oh, I would much rather the attention be on her than on me."

He glanced over. "How *has* your experience with the curacy been?"

I frowned as I thought on the last three weeks.

"Telling," Duke said, his observant eyes surveying me.

"I was thinking," I protested.

"And *I* was breathing. You need hardly announce such a thing, Phineas, for it is implied. Am I correct in my assumption you are not enjoying the curacy as you had hoped?"

"It is not that. Well, I suppose it *is*, in a way. I do not think I realized what precisely would be required of me as curate—or vicar. That is, I *knew* it, but I did not..." I pressed my lips together in frustration.

"You knew it, but you did not *know* it."

It was not the precise language I had been searching for, but it did convey what I meant. "Yes."

"The dreaded gap between knowledge and experience. And what of tutoring young Danneville?"

I gave a wry chuckle and watched as he tried to engage Diana in a stick-sword battle. Lady Sarah attempted to remonstrate with George, during which time Diana caught him unawares and stole his stick.

Both Lady Sarah and Diana laughed as George frantically searched off the path for a replacement. It was bittersweet to see the three of them enjoying themselves so well.

"In tutoring, too, the gap you speak of has been present. It has been quite challenging. And yet enjoyable somehow."

"How so?"

"The viscount is as opposite from me as you can imagine, Duke. I could not understand him at first. He seemed intent on disliking me. Covered my glasses in oil the first day of lessons."

Duke covered his mouth with a hand and cleared his throat. "Excuse me. How very frustrating for you."

"Not as frustrating as the flies he let loose in my bedchamber."

Duke's eyebrows shot up. "Flies?"

"Ten of them."

"And how did you manage *then*?"

I watched Lady Sarah, remembering how the viscount had accused her of being the one whose idea it was to capture the insects. She had confessed she had wanted to get rid of me. Apparently, that time had passed, but part of me preferred her outright antagonism to the polite avoidance I was now treated to.

"With the help of an obliging cat," I said, "which I used to teach Lord Danneville about the order of the natural world."

"Well done, Phineas. Very resourceful of you."

"Thank you. I think I have come to understand Danneville now. He is full of energy—so full he cannot sit to learn. At least not for long. He simply must *do*, but when he does, he learns both rapidly and willingly."

"And his sister?" Duke ducked under a low-hanging branch.

I whipped my head around. "What about her?"

"How do you get on with her?"

I struggled for words. "I... I... there is... she..."

Duke put a hand on my shoulder. "Say no more. It was inevitable you would feel such a way about her. Diana will be thrilled."

My brows drew together as I debated whether to inquire just how he thought I felt about her or to address the implied meaning in his comment. Since discussing emotions was never comfortable for me, I chose the latter. "You mean you sought this position for me knowing about Lady Sarah and intending for me to...?"

"I knew of her existence, yes. But the scheming you must acquit me of. That was all your sister. I was unaware of what she had in mind until later."

I shook my head, but it was as much at myself as at Diana. I might have known she would be up to something. She always was.

"She shan't rest until you are happily married, you know. She credits herself with both Theo's and Valentine's matches. Yours is the final challenge, and a lofty one at that."

I looked at Lady Sarah, whose arm was linked with Diana's, as though they were the oldest of friends instead of acquaintances of a mere thirty minutes. Who knew what mischief Di was up to at this very moment? What regrettable words she was saying to Lady Sarah?

If I truly thought Diana could make such an impossibility a reality, I might have begged her to remain at Bettencourt Court indefinitely. But not even someone as determined as Diana could make such a thing happen.

"Far too lofty," I said. "In what moment of madness did she think to match her awkward and unsuitable brother with the daughter of an earl?"

"I have tried to talk sense into her, believe me. But she will have none of it, and if she knows of your sentiments toward Lady Sa—"

"I have no such sentiments."

Duke cocked an eyebrow at me. "What, no sentiments at all?"

"None."

"I see. So the way you have been looking at her since the moment we arrived is merely a figment of my impressive imagination?"

I clasped my hands tightly behind my back. "Sentiment has no bearing on the situation, only cold, uncomfortable reality."

Duke's lips turned down at the corner. "Perhaps you are right. But even if Diana fails—"

"*When*. When she fails."

"—she will not hesitate to find another woman, Phineas. You must resign yourself, I'm afraid."

I heaved a sigh, thoroughly regretting Lord Bettencourt had ever extended an invitation to Diana and Duke.

Diana, Lord Danneville, and Lady Sarah had stopped on the path as Diana and the viscount skirmished with their stick-swords. My sister was amusing herself to no small degree, and Lady Sarah seemed to be enjoying it every bit as much, her lips stretched in the most genuine of smiles. One hand pressed against her stomach as though her laughter was so full and deep it needed to be contained. She was entirely and overwhelmingly enchanting.

Duke cleared his throat loudly, and I whipped my head around to look at him.

The edge of his mouth and one brow were raised. "I imagine the entire household is aware of your *lack of sentiments,* if that is the way you look at her."

I quickly turned my head away as we approached the others. "I haven't any idea what you mean."

"Then you are far less intelligent than we have all been giving you credit for."

Diana and the viscount clashed sticks one last time before Diana raised her sword victorious and Lord Danneville let out a curse.

"George!" Lady Sarah cried out in vexed mortification while Duke chuckled.

"You needn't worry on my account," Diana said.

"No indeed," Duke said, coming up to his wife and wrapping an arm about her waist. "She has the most unbecoming vocabulary of us all."

She smiled as though she had just been paid a high compliment. "That is only because Valentine is not here."

"Nor Rebecca," I said. "I have heard a surprising number of cant phrases from her lips. Though, I doubt Lady Sarah wishes Lord Danneville to take *any* of you as examples."

"Understandable," Diana said. "You are by far the best choice of an upstanding model from amongst us Donovans."

"The *only* choice for such a thing," Duke said in an undervoice loud enough for all to hear.

"Nay, then," Diana complained. "Theo is quite exemplary, though not nearly as fit for the role of tutor." Diana turned to Lady Sarah, who was listening to this exchange with a curious expression. "All my life, my lady, I have had an ambition to hear something shocking from both Theo's and Phin's lips. I have been sadly disappointed in their upstanding characters. But back to the matter at hand"—she addressed Lord Danneville—"if you wish for an easy victory, my husband is the proper choice, I think." She shot a sidelong, mischievous glance at her husband.

Duke threw his head back and let out a laugh. "I shall beat anyone who wishes to try me. In fact, I submit I could beat both you and Lord Danneville at the same time."

Diana raised her brows. "What do you say, my lord? Shall we let such an outrageously arrogant statement go unchallenged?"

The viscount raised his stick. "I would rather die a thousand deaths!"

Diana tapped her stick against his, while Duke hurriedly searched for one of his own. She glanced at me, then at Lady Sarah before crouching and whispering in Lord Danneville's ear.

I gave her a quizzical look as a smile stretched across the viscount's face. She meant mischief—that was clear as day—but what precisely she intended to do, I couldn't tell. Whatever it was, it had something to do with Lady Sarah and me, and that was enough to set my heart abuzz with nerves. I had seen Diana's machinations and the havoc they could wreak, and I had no desire for her to employ them here.

But before I could think how to prevent something, she and the viscount began to run. "You must catch us if you wish to beat us!" the viscount yelled.

And, as though his very honor was on the line, Duke swiped

up the nearest stick and chased after them, leaving Lady Sarah and me quite alone.

Mortified by my sister's heavy-handed tactics and wondering whether Lady Sarah recognized this attempt for what it was, I debated running after them for a moment before deciding against it. I was not well-versed in the finer points of social interaction, but I was quite certain that abandoning a woman in the forest would appear on any list of unacceptable choices. The best thing to do was, as always, approach the situation rationally.

"I suppose we should follow them," Lady Sarah said, her calm voice at odds with my heart.

She was being rational. Why couldn't I be?

I could. I *would*.

"Certainly." I took off my spectacles and began to clean them, and Lady Sarah shot me a sidelong glance—a glance that made me wonder if she recognized the gesture for what it was. What else did she perceive about me that I would rather keep hidden?

I could feel myself and my thoughts spiraling into dangerous territory, and I made a concerted effort to pull them to a safer place.

I am merely walking with the daughter of my employer.

There. That was not so out of the ordinary, was it?

I looked around for something else to focus my mind on, some bland observation to make to keep my thoughts in hand, but they crowded in on me like the surrounding trees. Perhaps if I treated my feelings as simple, observable, measurable phenomena, I could give them less power.

My heart is beating more quickly than usual, though it is still well within the limits to keep me alive.

My hands are trembling slightly, but—I made fists with both of them—*they still maintain near-perfect functionality.*

There. My heart began to calm a bit.

"Mr. Donovan," Lady Sarah said, her voice higher than usual, "did you happen to come upon my notebook in the library yesterday? Or perhaps this morning?"

"Your notebook?" I frowned, trying to remember whether I had noticed it there, but the only time I had seen it was when Lady Sarah had been using it. If it had been sitting in the library unattended, I would have been tempted to read it, particularly after what Lord Danneville had said. "No, I have not seen it."

She looked at me in a way that told me she wasn't entirely certain she believed me. Did she think I had taken it?

"It has gone missing?" I asked, sincerely troubled at the thought she might suspect me of underhanded behavior.

"Yes, I'm afraid so."

"I'm sorry to hear that, my lady. How frustrating it must be to have all of your carefully taken notes suddenly gone. Would you like me to help you search for it?"

"No!" She said it so quickly, with such alarm. Clearing her throat, she relaxed her shoulders. "That is, I thank you for the kind offer, but there is no need."

"Of course. Only let me know if I can be of service somehow. Though, I have no doubt everything you have written is safe in your mind. It is inevitable, with a mind as strong as yours."

Why was she regarding me with such… such… *dismay*?

She pulled her gaze away. "Is George very out of sorts?"

"About postponing the play, you mean? He is, but we shall manage."

"I am certain you will. I hate to disappoint him, but there simply isn't time for it before the ball."

Ah, yes. The ball where she was expected to choose a husband. Where *I* would entertain her brother to ensure he didn't sneak glasses of champagne as he had admitted to doing on the last occasion.

Well, better to be playing the nanny than to torture myself

watching gentlemen vie for Lady Sarah's hand. The mere thought made my stomach tighten.

"You mean to say that playing the part of Menelaus does *not*, in fact, comprise part of the ball preparations?"

She laughed, and the sound loosened something in my chest, bringing the feeling of ease I had cherished between us. It was a bittersweet feeling, though, for this ball would necessarily bring that to an end, and I hated the thought. Even more, however, I hated the thought that she might marry someone who did not understand what a treasure they had in her.

"Unfortunately not," she said. "Father wishes me to be practicing at the pianoforte and reviewing the steps of the dances. I fear playacting and stick-sword fighting are not among the accomplishments valued by gentlemen these days."

"Not *some* gentlemen, at least," I said softly.

She glanced at me, and I held her gaze. "I hope there will be someone in attendance who is able to appreciate all of you, my lady, from your keen mind to your skill at stick-sword battles."

She swallowed, her wide, blue eyes intent on me. I offered my best attempt at a smile just as the path turned and the others came into view.

Duke and Lord Danneville were fighting while Diana looked on, a smile on her face. Her gaze flitted to us, though, and I shot her a look to convey that I knew precisely what she had done. I couldn't be angry with her for it, though. Not when it had given me more time with Lady Sarah.

Lord Danneville lunged at Duke, who stumbled theatrically backward into his wife's arms. The viscount cried out in victory, while Diana attempted to clap while holding her husband from under the arms.

"Fighting Agamemnon and Menelaus will be the easiest thing in the world after *that*," the viscount said with breathless excitement.

"I have no doubt," I said. "The time has come for a lesson in the library, though, my lord."

There was a tense moment as his face showed signs of the inward battle he was fighting, wavering between resisting the change in activity and accepting it. Lady Sarah and I shared a glance as we waited to see which would win out.

Finally, Lord Danneville heaved a sigh and dropped his stick dejectedly.

Together, he and I made our way out of the woods and toward the house, while the others lagged behind. I glanced behind us to ensure they were out of earshot.

"It seems you and my sister are thick as thieves, my lord," I said.

He smiled but said nothing, which was unusual for him— and confirmed my suspicions.

"What were you whispering about together?"

"Oh, nothing," he said with far too much nonchalance.

"Hmm. How precisely *does* one whisper about nothing?"

He grinned conspiratorially. "Well, it wasn't *nothing*… but I shan't tell you what she said."

"I rather think I can guess what it was."

"How?"

"Because I know my sister."

He glanced up at me curiously. "You *truly* think you know what she said?"

I nodded.

"What was it, then?"

"I think," I said slowly, "that it was something about racing ahead with her and Mr. Russell."

The way he smiled was more than enough to let me know I was correct. "She wanted to leave you and my sister behind together."

We passed out of the trees and onto the lawns leading to the house. "I see. And did she explain why?"

The mischievous smile reappeared. "She wanted you and Sarah to have time alone."

I sighed. "My sister fancies herself a matchmaker, my lord, but you mustn't heed her, for she is quite mistaken in this instance."

"She is not, for Sarah *does* fancy you."

"My lord...?"

"She *does*."

I wanted to ask him how he could say something with such confidence, but that was quite beside the point.

"I *know* she does because that is what she has been writing in that little notebook of hers."

I whipped my head toward him as we reached the front door. "What?"

He nodded authoritatively as we stopped just shy of it. "It is all about you."

I gave a little scoffing laugh at the unexpected burst of imagination from the viscount. What precisely had Diana said to him? What nonsense had she filled his brain with in such a short time?

"It is!" Lord Danneville protested. "I will show you."

My mind buzzed with questions, and I stuttered as I tried to choose which one to verbalize. "You... you... what did...?" I blew a breath through my nose. "Did *you* take her notebook?"

"I *found* it. And I will give it back. *After* you read it."

"My lord," I said, shaking at the thought of being able to read Lady Sarah's inner thoughts—and ones allegedly about *me*. What I wouldn't give... "I cannot read it."

"You *can*, though. Her handwriting is quite good. She never mentions you by name, but it is quite obvious you are the one she is referring to. There is one page where she says—"

I put my hand up. "Please, my lord. No more. It is quite inappropriate to read someone's private musings, whatever the subject."

"Or whomever."

I pinched my lips together. "You must return it to her. Without delay."

His brows pulled together. "And what if I don't?"

"Then I shall be honor-bound to tell her you have it in your possession."

His expression grew dark and frowning. "That is not very sporting of you, Mr. Donovan."

"It would not be very sporting of me to keep what I know from her. Promise me you will return it."

He let out a huffing breath. "Very well. But I don't see why you shouldn't know what she has written. Surely it is not proper of *her* to be writing such things about you in secret."

What things? And in what way were they not proper? My mind burned with the questions, willing me to ask them, to explore the possible answers. But I could not. If I showed even a shred of interest, the viscount wouldn't hesitate to answer my questions.

I couldn't do that to Lady Sarah, as much as I wanted to.

Chapter Twenty-Seven

SARAH

The morning was cool and gray, and a shallow mist hung over the lawns as I looked through the window and pulled on my gloves. Mr. Donovan and George were walking through the fog in the direction of the church.

Mr. Donovan's positive influence on George knew no bounds, for normally, he had to be poked and prodded out of the door each Sunday. Once there, he was restless and prone to mischief. Now, though, not only would he be there well before the service, he was holding a few of Mr. Donovan's books in his arms. Among them would certainly be the book of sermons I had recently seen him poring over in the evenings when I passed by the library. Of course, it wasn't strictly necessary for me to pass the library when I went from the drawing room to my own bedchamber, but who could resist a glance into a room full of books when given the opportunity?

Dinner last night had been an interesting affair. The Russells were some of the most agreeable guests I could remember having at Bettencourt Court, and Mr. Donovan was more than usually talkative in their presence. It was perhaps fortunate for me that he was called away midway through the meal and did not return until the rest of us had retired to bed, for I found him entirely too enthralling. Neither had I been able to resist engaging with him more than once on the topics introduced.

The muted voices of Mr. and Mrs. Russell making their way down the corridor and toward the stairs met me, and I slipped on my bonnet, not bothering with the ribbons, for I had offered to accompany them on their stroll to the church.

Mrs. Russell turned as she heard my footsteps on the stairs behind them. "Ah, Lady Sarah. I am relieved to see you. I have no doubt if we attempted to make the walk on our own, we would find ourselves in a bog or some such thing."

"I very much doubt that," I said as we reached the bottom. "But as I am selfishly wishing to make the journey with you, I shall claim the path is winding and difficult to follow."

"And we shan't hesitate to believe you," Mr. Russell said, offering his arm to his wife with the little admiring glint in his eye I had noted every time he looked at her.

In fact, watching them together stirred feelings in me I wasn't entirely sure what to make of. I had never seen a couple like them. There was a mixture of playfulness and competition between them I wondered at. Neither of them hesitated to correct the other. It was a level of parity hitherto unobserved by me, and it inspired a hint of jealousy.

Perhaps more than a hint.

"I understand you have a daughter," I said as we walked through the lifting mists.

Mrs. Russell nodded. "Though when we return, we may well find Charlotte has renounced us in favor of Uncle Valentine and Aunt Rebecca."

"She certainly has the personality for it," her husband murmured.

Mrs. Russell smiled mischievously. "Charlotte and I are a great trial to him, for both of us are terribly contrary and stubborn."

I glanced at Mr. Russell to see what he made of this and found him smiling in amusement, that same adoring sparkle in his eye. "My wife insists on making people believe I would prefer shrinking violets, even though she knows very well it is not true."

She smiled saucily. "I am merely waiting for him to realize the mistake he made in marrying me."

He frowned and shook his head. "Such an admission would be far too humiliating."

"Oh, you needn't worry for me, my love. I am not easily humiliated."

"Quite true. But I meant it would be humiliating for *me*. After all, I have built a reputation upon being right." He let out a resigned sigh, though the corner of his mouth twitched slightly. "I suppose there is nothing for it but to make the best of things."

His wife smiled. "How very distressing a prospect." After a moment, she looked at me. "Mind you choose your husband wisely, my lady."

"I am endeavoring to do so," I said, thinking of the list. The notebook was still missing, and its mysterious disappearance had me looking askance at everyone at Bettencourt Court, despite having questioned all the servants individually. *Someone* must have it in their possession, but who? The question haunted me.

Although we were well in advance of the hour, there was a line of people waiting to enter the church, where Mr. Donovan stood greeting them.

"What an impressive parish," Mr. Russell said, seeming to note the same thing.

"Never more impressive than since the arrival of your brother-in-law," I said as nonchalantly as possible. "People are quite taken with the new curate."

"Poor Phin," his sister said with amusement. "He looks quite uncomfortable."

It was true. He kept fiddling with his spectacles and shifting his feet.

Mrs. Russell tilted her head as she regarded him, then looked at her husband with a slight pull to her brows. "I am not convinced he will be happy as vicar, Duke."

"Nor I," he said.

"It seems a great waste of his intellect."

Mr. Russell failed to suppress a smile. "Forgive my wife, Lady Sarah. She has a tendency to say heretical and sacrilegious things. One of our first encounters was in church, where she informed me with nary a blush that her thoughts about me were not appropriate enough to be expressed in such a venue."

She pinched her lips together and shot me a look. "By which I meant—and well he knew it—that my only words for him were insulting."

"So you say," he said as we came to the back of the line.

Mrs. Russell tilted her body from one side to the other, peering ahead. "Are we granted any special familial privilege, or must we wait in this interminable line with everyone else?"

I would have been glad for an opportunity to circumvent an individual greeting with Mr. Donovan—particularly in the presence of his family—for my heart seemed to beat more fiercely with every step we took nearer him. But wait we did.

He was shaking hands with each congregant who passed, and never had the prospect of such an uninteresting exchange seemed so full of significance. When our turn finally came, Mr. Donovan looked at us as though we were his greatest relief. His sister kissed him on the cheek, his brother-in-law shook hands with him with a few words of encouragement, and then it was my turn.

I put out my hand just as Mr. Donovan slipped his behind his back to join the other one, leaving me with a very empty, hovering hand. Embarrassed, I dropped it, clasping it with the other just as Mr. Donovan put out his hand again to shake mine.

Not wanting to repeat the process while the Russells and those behind us in the line—including the Lintons—looked on, I merely smiled and gave a slight nod of my head, though inside my thoughts were fluttering around like a flock of pheasants after a ringing gunshot. Why had he not given me his hand? Was he angry with me?

Oh, heavens. Was it my notebook? Had he read it, and now he was trying to ensure I understood there was not, and could never be, anything between us?

Mr. Donovan clasped his hands tightly in front of him so his knuckles turned white. "Pleased to have you in attendance, Lady Sarah."

I forced a smile. "Likewise. That is, I am pleased to *be* in attendance, not pleased that you are in attendance. Though I *am* pleased you are in attendance." Heart thudding as quickly as the words spilling out of my mouth, I glanced at the Lintons behind me, waiting for their turn, their brows slightly raised. "I am pleased you are in attendance," I continued, "because the service could not proceed *without* you. *That* would be a miracle indeed." Though my body seemed partial to the idea of vomiting, I chose to laugh instead. It was a nervous one, as though I hadn't spent years of my life learning how to avoid making the fool of myself I had just made.

"Just so," Mrs. Russell said calmly, threading her arm through mine. "And as the Bible instructs us not to seek for signs and miracles, we are quite content to listen to you."

She didn't need to pull me along, for I was eager to enter the church. The only miracle *I* hoped for was the last two minutes to be struck from the memories of all present. I might as well have read my notebook from the lectern. Certainly I owed Father an apology for all the money he had spent ensuring I was trained properly, for a mere handshake—or the lack of one, rather—had sent all of it out of the window.

I took in a deep breath to calm myself, and my eyes widened at the sight of George climbing the stairs to the lectern. I excused myself to the Russells, meaning to keep my brother from whatever mischief he had in mind, but I checked mid-step, for he was merely placing Mr. Donovan's books on the stand.

I had become so accustomed to expect devilry from him that I had immediately thought the worst of his kindness. Shame on me.

He straightened the books so they were just so, then looked up. As his gaze fell upon me, he stilled. Had I become so quick to censure him that he felt he could not even do a good deed without a stern look from me? I smiled reassuringly, and he turned, taking the steps down to the stone floor and making his way to our family's box.

I joined, sitting in the place beside him and nudging him with my arm. "That was very kind of you."

He smiled mechanically.

The pews filled and Mother, Father, and the Russells joined us as conversation buzzed. Finally, Mr. Donovan made his way to the lectern. Once he was in place, he looked out over the congregation. There were more people today than the week prior, and there had been more people *then* than the Sunday before *that*. I wondered if greeting people at the door was preferable to him to overseeing the service and giving the sermon. I felt a stirring of nerves on his behalf and nearly walked up and removed his spectacles for him.

His sister had said she was not convinced he would be happy in the church. Did he have other dreams and aspirations? I shared her opinion that his intellect would be wasted in the church. Or perhaps not wasted, but at least less fruitful than in another venture.

After cleaning his spectacles and clearing his throat more

than once, Mr. Donovan opened the book of sermons, his gaze scouring the congregation again as though he could hardly fathom how many people were in attendance.

He looked down, opened his mouth, then clamped it shut. Frowning, he picked something up.

I stilled, my heart ceasing to beat. Lying open in his hands, Mr. Donovan held my notebook. And he was reading it. In front of the entire parish.

He had lied to me. He *had* taken the notebook.

My entire body erupted with the heat of embarrassment and anger.

But no. That couldn't be true. The man I was watching seemed every bit as surprised as I was, as evidenced by the way he snapped the notebook shut with such force it fell to the floor. When he emerged from picking it up, he set it beneath the sermon book, his face the color of a beet as his gaze flicked to me.

And then I remembered… George had carried Mr. Donovan's books to the church. George had set the books on the lectern. George had looked strangely guilty when he had found me watching him. George had hardly reacted when I had praised him for helping Mr. Donovan.

He had taken the notebook and slipped it into the sermon book.

My jaw clenching and stomach sick, I looked over at my brother beside me. He had shifted away so there were two feet between us—an admission of guilt if one had been required. He studiously avoided my gaze, studying the Book of Common Prayer with a diligence that would have inspired the Archbishop of Canterbury himself.

My fingers itched to box his ears, but instead I grabbed the fabric of my skirts and turned my focus from him. Mrs. Russell looked at me and then her brother with a curious light in her eyes. Devil take the Donovans! Perceptiveness seemed to be a family trait.

Mr. Donovan cleared his throat and began the service. Soon, he was reading a passage from Luke chapter 7 about the woman who anointed the feet of Jesus with costly oil. I had heard Mr. Donovan read many times before, but today his reading was halting, his face still retaining a bit of its color as he stumbled over words every now and then. It was quite unlike him.

Good heavens. What had he read in my notebook? I wasn't certain I even wished to know.

"It may easily be comprehended," he read, "how great must once have been the passions over the heart of this Sarah." His eyes widened. "Sinner. Over this sinner." There was a pause, and when he spoke again, his voice had a strangled quality to it. "And what grace now operateth within her."

I could feel a few gazes on me, including Father's, but calling on every bit of training I had received over the years, I kept my expression calm and undisturbed. After all, who was to say he hadn't meant Sarah Daniel? I glanced at her and was annoyed to find her looking at Mr. Donovan with far too much hope in her eyes, as though she was having the same thought.

The sermon continued, and slowly Mr. Donovan gained confidence while the words went through one of my ears and immediately out of the other.

What did it all mean? I wished to know what Mr. Donovan was thinking, to see his face for any hint of his thoughts or feelings, but he kept his gaze firmly on the book. Too firmly.

He seemed to have selected the longest possible sermon, and by the time the service finished, I was tempted to bolt like an unbroken stallion. But I needed my notebook.

As soon as the final words were said, George stood. I grabbed the bottom hem of his coat to keep him from going anywhere. Standing, I pulled him toward me, waiting until the others had left the pew before speaking.

"You will retrieve my notebook immediately," I said, smiling through clenched teeth for the benefit of anyone who might be watching.

"I won't."

"So much for our pinky promises, then?"

His brows pulled together. I was not the only one who would experience the ill-effects of an end to our allyship.

"Is this the revenge you promised me?" I continued. "A few minutes of pain in your eye for my humiliation?"

"He deserved to know how you feel about him. Besides, I *like* him."

"Well, you may put aside whatever nonsense you have in that head of yours, for there is nothing between us."

"That is not what I witnessed by the lake."

"Go retrieve my notebook," I said slowly, my voice shaking as much from discomfiture as from frustration.

He held my gaze for a moment in a battle of stubborn wills until he finally huffed and turned.

I didn't wish to watch the interaction, so I left the box and found Mrs. Russell awaiting me. My composure was in tatters, and the smile she gave me was a sympathetic one. How much did she know or guess?

"Duke wishes to speak with your mother and father on the walk back, so I thought I would ask you to keep me company again."

"Of course," I said, relaxing a bit at her easy manner. "It would be my pleasure."

We made our way out of the church and soon found ourselves on the path toward Bettencourt Court. To my relief, she kept the conversation on the upcoming ball, giving no indication that anything out of the ordinary had happened at church.

"It sounds as though it shall be the most talked of event in Kent," she said after we had discussed the plans for the evening's entertainment. "And everyone there for *you*."

I couldn't help a sigh. "I would much rather take refuge in the library."

She laughed. "You would undoubtedly find Phineas there, though the viscount tells me the two of them shall be spending the evening together."

The mere mention of her brother had my heart skittering, but there was no indication she had ulterior motives in mentioning him.

"Yes, it is very kind of him, for George inevitably causes trouble when he is unsupervised."

"Your brother and I share that trait, I think. But Phineas will ensure he does nothing to ruin the evening."

The thought of Mr. Donovan upstairs acting as a nanny to George when there was such entertainment to be had downstairs struck me as unfortunate. But Mr. Donovan was not the type to seek out social situations, so perhaps this was as he preferred it. Part of me wished I could join them upstairs. The conversation would certainly be more entertaining.

"If I may ask, my lady, how has Phineas seemed to you since his arrival? His feelings can be difficult to decipher."

I nearly snorted at the understatement. "Indeed. I imagine you are a much better judge of that, but I *think* he is content here." Despite my initial efforts to make him quite the opposite.

"And his work with Lord Danneville? Has it been satisfactory?"

"It has. George has made a great deal of progress under his tutelage. I admit, I was not encouraged at first, for I did not think a man who reads romance novels a fitting tutor."

"A man who reads romance novels?"

I glanced over at her and the bemused expression she wore. Was she unaware of her brother's reading preferences? "Yes. He was quite staunch in defense of them when I confronted him, though, which came as quite a surprise to me."

"I should think so." Mrs. Russell's confusion only heightened. "Do you mean to tell me you believe my brother Phineas to be a great reader and defender of romance novels?"

"I not only believe it, Mrs. Russell, I *know* it."

She blinked. "I do not wish to cast doubt upon what you are saying, of course, but I hope you will forgive me if I find it nearly impossible to credit. Phineas has long held the lowest opinions of such works. He has taken no pains to hide that fact."

"Well, it appears he underwent a change of opinion without your awareness. Perhaps it occurred while he was at Cambridge." It seemed doubtful, I had to admit.

She smiled, her eyes twinkling. "I assure you his attitudes toward romance novels were very much intact as recently as the day he left to Bettencourt Court, for he was gifted a set upon his departure by my sister-in-law, Rebecca, and his ingratitude was the subject of discussion at dinner that evening."

I frowned. "And yet, just days after he arrived, I discovered him reading such a book. When I remarked upon it, he staunchly defended it, going so far as to call my own commitment to the pursuit of truth into question when I stated I made it a rule *not* to read novels."

Diana laughed through a hand. "This is diverting, indeed. To hear of something so contrary to everything I know of my brother!"

I laughed halfheartedly, torn between perplexity and the impulse to share in her amusement. According to his sister, Mr. Donovan had *not* been a reader of romance novels, and yet he had not only led me to believe such a thing—he had managed to make *me* into one as well.

It was beyond anything. And I would certainly not let it pass undiscussed.

Chapter Twenty-Eight

PHINEAS

As if my debacle of a sermon had not been enough, I was obliged to attend to the line of people who came to speak with me once it was—mercifully—over. At the end of that line was Lord Danneville. I was under no illusion that the appearance of Lady Sarah's notebook in the pages of the sermon book had been a coincidence, and it put me quite out of charity with him.

I had only read two sentences before realizing what was before me, but that had been enough to tell me things I never should have known. For instance, that Lady Sarah found the color of my eyes a difficult shade of blue to describe, or that she had been wishing for my company at the ball she had attended last week.

I didn't know what to say to Lord Danneville. I simultaneously wished to throttle him and to thank him profusely. I could do neither, so I remained silent as he held my gaze.

"Now you know," he said, though I could see a hint of wariness in his eyes. "I am here to retrieve the notebook and return it as promised."

I opened my mouth only to clamp it shut again. When I had

made him swear to return it to her, I had not meant he should do so only *after* causing mischief with it. But he knew that very well.

Without a word, I scaled the stairs to the lectern, retrieved the book, and returned to his side without allowing myself even a glance at it. It was just a collection of papers with pencil markings on them. It didn't mean anything. It *couldn't* mean anything.

I handed it to the viscount without a word, and after a moment, he turned on his heel and left. Lady Sarah had left some time ago, and I wouldn't be surprised if she avoided me entirely now.

My duties at the church and among the parish did not truly require my attendance through the afternoon. I saw to them with painstaking meticulousness, though, folding the vestments twice, reorganizing the record books, stopping by the vicarage to see to Chester despite knowing very well he was still at Bettencourt Court, and even paying a visit to Mrs. Bamford, who immediately asked after my wife. Apparently, her memory was not so terrible that she had forgotten that untruth.

But I could not stay away from Bettencourt Court forever. Neither did I truly wish to. Diana and Duke were there, after all, and they would be leaving soon. That was enough to bring me back.

Their belongings were already being transferred to the traveling chaise when I arrived at the courtyard. I hurried up the stairs with a pinch of guilt in my chest for neglecting my family out of cowardice.

I knocked softly on the door of the bedchamber Diana had slept in, and she opened it swiftly.

"There you are," she said with a smile. "We thought you might never return."

"Parish duties," I said with a grimace.

She raised a brow but said nothing. "Part of me wishes we

could take you with us, but I think you are quite happy here. Aren't you?"

Happy. What a strange question to answer. *Was* I happy at Bettencourt Court?

I was, and I wasn't. I enjoyed tutoring Lord Danneville, frustrating and difficult as it could sometimes be. I was happy in Lady Sarah's presence, but I *shouldn't* be, and that inevitably made me *unhappy*. And as for my duties as a curate... I sighed. I wanted to enjoy them more than I was, but they taxed me greatly.

Diana grasped me by the shoulders and looked me in the eye. "There is hope yet, Phin."

Duke stepped out from the dressing room, fiddling with his cravat, and the conversation moved to talk of their imminent journey and then to the necessary farewells.

"Lord Bettencourt has extended an invitation for us to return," Diana said. "Perhaps we shall bring Theo and Elena with us."

"Have you heard from them?" I asked.

"Provided the weather remains decent, they should be in port by the end of the month," Duke said.

"They want to be home in plenty of time for Elena's confinement," Diana added in a tone that told me she was proud to be the conveyer of such information.

I was thrilled at the prospect of welcoming Theo and Elena home, joyous at the thought of them welcoming their first child. But somewhere deep inside, there was a bit of sadness, too.

I was being left behind.

I t was tempting to find a reason to excuse myself from dinner, but I refrained, for I had no wish to give heed to the more cowardly parts of my nature. Just as importantly, though, I wished to see Lady Sarah.

I was becoming incapable of passing an entire day without some sort of interaction between us. The days when I had gone without a conversation with her, however small it might be, had felt like interminable failures in some strange way. Whenever I read an intriguing passage of Dryden, I itched to go in search of her and ask her opinion on it.

Tonight was different, though. Something had happened today, and I didn't know what it meant for the friendship that had once existed between us. But my curiosity was overpowering my embarrassment and reluctance; I had to know.

Lord Danneville sat directly across from me at the dinner table. His unwonted quiet during the meal made me wonder if I had been too harsh on him with my earlier silence. Or perhaps his reserve was a result of guilt. Had he not given the notebook to his sister?

Good gracious. Did she think I still had it? No wonder every time she looked at me it was with a spark in her eye. Something told me there would be a confrontation between us in the near future. A day like today could not be ignored.

I pulled at my cravat, unsure if I was more afraid or impatient.

T he library was dark but for the light of the candle illuminating the book before me. It flickered threateningly, reminding me it had but little life left, and I had a short time in which to complete my preparations for tomorrow's lessons.

I had only been there a matter of minutes when the door creaked as it opened, and Lady Sarah walked in, shutting the door behind her.

I stood, my heart racing, for I knew why she was here.

She was calm, her posture poised, as always, but there was an intensity in her eyes and a flare to her nostrils that told me her presence was no coincidence.

"You lied to me, Mr. Donovan."

I put my hands out and stepped toward her to defend myself, but my foot caught on the chair, and I stumbled forward.

Lady Sarah's hand grasped my own, helping me regain my balance.

"Thank you," I said softly as our hands parted. I met her gaze, willing her to believe me. "I assure you I did not lie to you, my lady. I did *not* take your notebook, and the moment I discovered it was in Lord Danneville's possession, I made him promise he would return it to you. I had no notion what he intended to do with it. That is, I knew he wanted me to read it, but of course I refused. I did not read any of it."

She lifted her chin. "That is not entirely true, is it?"

I paused, understanding her reference to the portion I had read at church.

"Whatever you read of my *study notes*, Mr. Donovan"—she held my gaze more intently than ever, her voice softer than usual—"it will be for the best if you endeavor to put it out of your mind."

I swallowed, meeting her gaze and trying to decipher what precisely I was seeing. A hint of regret, perhaps? But quiet as they were and much as they cut me to hear, her words were quite clear. Whatever she felt for me, it was unwelcome, and she didn't wish for me to know it. "Of course."

I took a step toward her. "I would never betray your confidences, my lady. I hold you in far too high a regard. I hope you will consider me a trusted friend, one who will support you in whatever will bring you most happiness."

"Whatever will bring me most happiness..." she repeated, her eyes scouring my face in a way that stole my breath entirely.

The candle flickered, casting the room in dark momentarily, and Lady Sarah sucked in a breath, straightening. "That is not the lie I came to speak with you about."

"Oh." I frowned. "I assure you I have not lied to you, my lady."

"Your sister claims differently."

My heart dropped. What mischief had Diana been about before leaving? Had she told Lady Sarah of my true feelings for her?

"You convinced me you were a reader of romance novels, Mr. Donovan, when the truth is you thought every bit as ill of them as I did."

I blinked, taken off guard.

She took a step toward me, almost threatening, though there was something in her eyes that told me she was not truly angry. "You made me feel as though my aversion to them was a flaw rather than something to be admired."

I held my ground, my skin prickling at the narrowing distance between us. "And what would you have done, my lady, if I had *not* made such a defense of them?"

She stopped, regarding me thoughtfully. "I would have had Father dismiss you."

I gave a nod. "Precisely. And I *am* a reader of romance novels now."

A little smile tugged at the corner of her lips. "As am I, thanks to you."

"Do you regret it?"

Her lips twisted to the side. "I do not. But I read them with the understanding you would discuss them with me. All of them."

"And I assure you, I am quite willing to do so."

"Very good, for I have a great deal to say."

I inclined my head, my heart racing foolishly at the prospect of another discussion, at more time with her. "Which I am anxious to hear."

"Only so you may vex me by countering every comment I make."

I chuckled. "I have no wish to vex you, my lady. I merely enjoy discussing things together, which prompts me, at times, to play the devil's advocate."

"Then you may play that part tomorrow afternoon while we discuss *Emma*."

"Gladly, if you feel you truly have the time for it. I know you are occupied with ball preparations."

"I am. But I have had hardly a moment to devote to reading, which puts me quite out of humor. I will endeavor to see to all my duties tomorrow morning in order to keep myself at liberty in the afternoon."

I gave a nod, though a thought occurred to me, making me frown slightly.

"What is it?"

"Only I think your brother will be quite unhappy if he finds you and I discussing books but not taking the time to practice *Ajax*."

She sighed. "You are undoubtedly right. Though, I rather think he deserves to be unhappy after the mischief he has made."

"Perhaps so. But as I will be the one most affected by his sulking, I hope you will consider humoring him."

She shook her head. "Yet another vexatious comment. But I will oblige on your behalf."

I bowed, pushing my spectacles back up, for they insisted upon slipping whenever I did so. "I am grateful to you, my lady."

Agreeing to spend the afternoon with her was unwise, and for a man who prided himself on making rational decisions, I was looking forward to it with an alarming amount of anticipation.

When I left my bedchamber the next morning, there were two stacks of books waiting for me outside of my door. Atop one pile were the volumes of *Emma,* and I picked up the first one, eagerly opening the cover.

To my delight, there was a note there, just as I had hoped there might be.

Devil's Advocate,

I thought you might wish to have these to study in preparation for our approaching discussion. I have plenty to say on the matter, shocking as that will undoubtedly be to you, and I expect your counterarguments to be fully developed and convincing.

Yours, etc.,

Lady Sarah Danneville

I looked at that word *yours* again and again, wishing it was more than a mere formality and knowing how idiotic it was to entertain such thoughts.

Chapter Twenty-Nine

SARAH

"Perhaps the two of you should practice more while I fetch my knife to sharpen my sword." George's expression was calculated to inspire us with the innocence of his suggestion. But I wasn't fooled. This was not the first time since we had begun practicing *Ajax* half an hour ago he had made a blatant attempt to throw his tutor and me together.

We were standing on the lawn behind the house—our usual practicing place—and I glanced at Mr. Donovan. His eyes were on George, the slight curve to his mouth informing me he, too, recognized the suggestion for what it was.

"For your sister's and my safety, I would prefer you did not sharpen your sword, my lord," Mr. Donovan said, adjusting his spectacles. "And as we have only five minutes until your father expects you in the courtyard, I think we should utilize our time wisely by reading through the next scene."

George and Father were making a journey into town. I had no doubt George would find a way to broach the subject of Harrow while they did so. I could only hope Father would be sensible enough to realize how unwise it would be to send

George to Harrow given the progress George was making under the direction of Mr. Donovan.

George sighed but acquiesced. It never ceased to amaze me how Mr. Donovan managed to disappoint him or refuse him what he wanted without making him fly into a rage. Of course, things would be quite different if he were at Harrow, surrounded by dozens of his peers to impress. But it was progress, all the same.

Collins came to fetch George a few minutes later, leaving Mr. Donovan and me alone, stick-swords in hand.

"Are you still at liberty to have our discussion, my lady?"

More than once, I had nearly asked him to dispense with the formality. But I had resisted, realizing the protection it afforded. It was already too easy to forget the difference in station between Mr. Donovan and myself.

"I am not only able, I insist upon it. Perhaps we can walk around the lake?"

He nodded, picking up his coat from the ground—shed during the practicing of the play—then put out a hand toward me.

The day was warmer than usual, making me wish I had thought to wear a dress with shorter sleeves. Mr. Donovan refrained from putting his coat back on, letting it drape over his arm instead. The edge of a brace peeped out from the edge of his blue waistcoat, threatening to slip over his shoulder. I resisted the urge to shift it into its proper place, for it teased me, making me think of how Mr. Donovan would look without a waistcoat or—

"So, then. Emma." He cut into my thoughts quite providentially—and rudely.

"Yes, Emma."

"What do you make of Emma, my lady?"

I laughed. "Not so fast, Mr. Donovan. If I give my opinion first, you shall immediately take on the opposing one, and I shall never know what you *truly* think. So, you tell *me*. What do *you* make of Emma?"

"Well, that depends. *Emma* the book or Emma the woman?"

"Let us start with the book."

He smoothed the coat over his arm, his brow pursed in thought. "I found it the most amusing of the authoress's works. It had all her usual wit, of course, but a much more naïve heroine than we see in her other works, saving *Northanger Abbey*."

"Naïve in what way?"

"In her understanding of both herself and others, I think, for she claims to know her own mind only to discover she has been quite wrong—in all things, in fact."

"I agree with that assessment. However, I did not find it the most amusing among the works, for, from quite early on, I found it impossible to understand Emma or to agree with her, which led me to become frustrated with her at every turn."

"How do you mean?"

"She says in the beginning that she has everything she requires: status, wealth, independence. She tells Harriet that the only thing that could induce her to marry would be love."

"And what perplexes you about that?"

I shrugged. "That love, of all things, would be the thing to change her mind, to make her wish to change her situation."

"You find love an unworthy reason to pursue matrimony?"

"I have merely observed that people tend not to make the wisest or most reasonable decisions when they are guided by emotion." I glanced over at the pensive expression he wore. "Come, now, Mr. Donovan. I await your vexatious counterargument. Do not fail me now."

He smiled slightly. "I *shall* fail you, for I quite understand what you mean. I have felt that way myself. All my life, I have sought to follow truth and reason for fear of precisely what you say. It has only been recently that I have begun to consider whether there is any merit to an alternative approach to life."

My breathing quickened. "What do you mean?"

He stopped, looking out over the lake. "One by one, I have watched my siblings marry. One by one, they have gone against reason in doing so. One by one, they have fallen in love. And yet each of them are… well, they are happier than ever."

I shouldn't have asked, but I couldn't help myself. "And you?"

His eyes scoured my face. "What *of* me?"

"Do you intend to follow their examples?"

I held my breath, wishing I knew what he saw when he looked at me.

Finally, he looked away. "I cannot say. I had assumed I would never marry, for I saw no reason to do so. But I must admit my devotion to reason alone has wavered of late."

Of late. Did he mean since his arrival at Bettencourt Court? Was it too much to hope I was part of the wavering?

"I have begun to suspect that it is… insufficient. There is a part of me that, more and more, refuses to be filled by the things that used to fill me." He smiled wryly. "Do you despise me for admitting as much?"

I swallowed, shaking my head. "I am not so different from you. Part of me is afraid that Emma Woodhouse, Elizabeth Bennet, Marianne Dashwood, and Anne Elliot are right, and years from now, I shall find myself wondering what my life might have been like. Emma was fortunate enough to realize her mistake before it was too late; what if I do not? That fear—the fear of regret—has pestered me. And yet I am afraid of losing myself, of being consumed."

He nodded, and I knew—I *knew* he understood me. He understood me in a way no one else did.

Perhaps that was why I missed him so when he left to join the Lintons for dinner later that evening. And during his absence, I felt the first glimmers of sympathy with Emma. I wondered if what I felt knowing that Mr. Donovan was being fawned over by the Lintons was what Emma had felt when she discovered Harriet was not in love with Frank Churchill but with Mr. Knightley.

"Sarah."

I blinked and found Father, Mother, and George looking at me, their hands poised at the sides of their dinner plates.

Mother smiled indulgently at my absent-mindedness. "Your father was just saying that Mr. Wilks shall be here Wednesday. He will be joined by his son. He felt it would be beneficial for you to meet Richard."

"His son," I said blankly.

"Yes," Father said. "It seemed quite a sensible request to me, for it is not just a husband you will be gaining if you marry."

I could find nothing to respond. Of course, I had been the one to give the stipulation that any husband of mine would already have an heir. What I had failed to truly consider was that, as a result, I would immediately become a mother of sorts.

"This way," Father continued, "you will have time to become acquainted outside of the ball, which will necessarily require you to divide your time amongst the guests. If all goes well, we will be able to send a notice to family first thing Monday morning."

"My dear?" Mother said, looking at me with concern. "What is it?"

"It is only that… well, it seems as though everything is quite arranged already."

"Hardly," Father said significantly. "There is still the matter of ensuring a good impression with Mr. Wilks. And with his son, too, for I gather he values him too dearly to marry anyone the boy dislikes. We have arranged everything in as advantageous a way as possible, Sarah, but the result of it all will be upon *your* shoulders. I trust you will do everything in your power to ensure our efforts do not come to naught, for I have gone to great pains to find someone who complies with your *requirements*"—he looked at me darkly—"and I expect you to hold to your end of things now that I have secured this opportunity."

A sick feeling settled in my stomach, but I nodded. Everything Father was saying was reasonable. "Of course. But why hold the ball at all, then?"

"We can hardly cancel at this stage. I did not expect Wilks to require so little encouragement to entertain the prospect of a match between you, for I have it on good authority he was being courted by Lord Bascombe in hopes of a match with *his* daughter. Besides, this way, if you botch things with him and he chooses her, there will be other avenues to pursue."

Mother laid a hand over Father's. "What your father means is that we wish for you to be able to clearly see the options before you. The ball will provide such an opportunity."

"And George"—Father settled his stern gaze upon him—"I expect *you* will give young Richard a warm welcome."

"Yes, Father."

I hardly heard the discussion that followed. All I could think was that, if things went according to Father's wishes, I would be engaged in less than a week.

The sentiments, the fears I had expressed to Mr. Donovan earlier reared their heads. I found myself facing Ovid's Hydra, who grew three new heads for every one I managed to cut off as my anxieties multiplied.

In the drawing room, the pages of the book I held were left unturned as my foot tapped rhythmically on the floor. Next to me sat my notebook—that dreaded notebook which held my most intrusive and encompassing thoughts.

Mother was dozing in the chair nearest the empty fire grate. She was exhausted, and little wonder. She had been working tirelessly to ensure the success of the ball. Father had warned us he would not be joining us, as he had correspondence to ensure everything was in order for settlement discussions with Mr. Wilks.

I shifted in my seat, another wave of malaise washing over me, then glanced at the tall case clock across the room. Ten o'clock.

Mr. Donovan was still gone, despite his assurances that he had informed the Lintons he could not remain with them long after dinner. What was keeping him? Perhaps he was beginning to admire one—or both—of the twins. He *had* said his resolve not to marry had weakened of late. What if it was one of the Lintons who had inspired it? But the way he looked at me…

A few minutes later, the crunch of carriage wheels on the drive met my ears. Mr. Donovan had returned.

The sound roused Mother, and she shifted, covering a yawn. After a quick glance at the clock, she rose and found her way to me, smiling sleepily. "Still reading?"

I nodded, though I hadn't read a single word.

"Goodnight, my dear." She leaned down and kissed my hair, then left me to myself.

I listened for the sound of the front door opening, imagining Mr. Donovan entering, pulling off his hat and gloves. Would he go immediately to his bedchamber?

No. He would go to the library. It was where he always retreated after a social engagement. For him, just as for me, it was a refuge. He had become a fixture there, and the room had come to feel almost empty without him. He belonged there every bit as much as the books.

And just as each one of those books, Mr. Donovan was a new world, begging to be explored and understood. And if I refused to do so, I feared I would forever wonder what I might have discovered if I had dared to open him and read his pages.

I could not face the future without knowing what I was rejecting.

Chapter Thirty

PHINEAS

I stepped into the dim library and inhaled, letting the familiar smell settle within me. Again and again, I breathed in, and slowly but surely, my muscles relaxed. There was, as usual, but one candle lit. It was the same one from last night, nearer than ever to guttering. Beside it, one of the servants had placed a new, unused candle to be lit at need.

Chester stretched on the chair Lady Sarah usually occupied. He hopped down and came over to me, brushing against my legs and leaving the expected trail of white hair behind. I had become fond of the cat, a fact which unsettled me. Would I become like Mr. Vickers with time, so lonely and strange that even my tea could not persuade a furry friend to remain with me? And all the while, my Cambridge peers would become professors and tutors, or fellows in the Royal Society.

Dinner with the Linton family had been even less pleasurable than I had anticipated. After my discussion with Lady Sarah, I had promised myself I would do everything in my power to leave thoughts of her behind and to consider the young Linton women fairly. If companionship was what I sought, why could I not find it with one of them? They were kind young women, if a little silly, and they came from a good family. They certainly seemed to hold an interest in me.

But despite all they had to recommend them, I couldn't banish Lady Sarah from my thoughts. After such a long time of priding myself on my reason and intellect, I had to admit I was far less in control of myself than I had previously supposed.

I was in control of nothing, in fact. Like Emma, everything I had thought I understood was turning out to be wrong. My hopes for a career in the church seemed to be materializing, but now that the goal was within reach, I was no longer certain it was what I wished for.

What I *wanted*—and what simultaneously terrified me—was to tell Lady Sarah how I truly felt. Perhaps it was the result of reading so many novels about men who declared their feelings to the women they loved. Whatever it was, keeping what I felt inside of me was beginning to feel unbearable.

I went over to the stack of novels in the corner and picked up the top one: *Persuasion*. I turned the pages until I came near the end and found the letter Captain Wentworth had written. I read over it, envying his eloquence and, even more, the reaction it had elicited. Anne had run to him eagerly.

But that was the difficulty, wasn't it? For every declaration like Wentworth's and every reaction like Anne's, there was a Mr. Collins and an Elizabeth, or a Mr. Elton and an Emma. There was more rejection in those novels than there was success. Perhaps most discouraging of all was how easily I found myself represented in those rejected men of the cloth. Worse, I was not even a vicar. I was but a lowly curate.

No matter how much I might wish for it, I was not a Darcy or a Wentworth or a Knightley. I was Phineas Donovan. Third son. Curate. Tutor. My choice of a companion seemed to be Chester or a wife I could bear with, but who would never inspire in me the things Lady Sarah inspired in me.

I looked at *Persuasion* again and sighed at the sight of those words: *I am half agony, half hope.*

What I would give to feel justified in even *half* hope.

I whipped my head around at the squeaking of the door. Lady Sarah stepped inside and shut the door behind her, her bright eyes settling on me. She was dressed for dinner, her cream-colored gown cut low across her chest, her fingers clasped underneath, fiddling distractedly.

I scoured her face for any indication of the purpose of her visit, for it was clear she had expected to find me here.

"I heard the carriage," she explained, answering my unasked question.

I nodded, still unsure what to make of this late and intentional encounter or the look in her eye.

"How was dinner?"

"Long." I let out an uneasy laugh, for this sort of polite conversation made me nervous in even the most trivial of situations. And this did not feel trivial. "They were very kind," I amended.

She smiled slightly, but it lacked something. "I am not surprised to hear either of those things. They all admire you greatly."

"They hardly know me."

"Perhaps not, but they would do so even if they knew you better."

I shut the book I held, needing a reason to look away from her. What was I to do with such praise? "You flatter me, my lady."

"Have you ever known me to be guilty of such a thing?"

I glanced at her and the wry smile she wore. "No."

"I have been thinking on our conversation," she said, taking measured footsteps toward me. All the while, her fingers fidgeted nervously, making my heart beat faster and inspiring me with the wish to cover them with my own hands.

I cleared my throat, trying not to pay attention to the way the distance between us was decreasing. "Which conversation, my lady?"

Still, she came toward me. Just when I thought I would be obliged to step into the bookshelves to avoid a collision, she stopped. "I do not want to live with regret, to wonder what might have been. I want to *feel*." Her eyes explored my face for a moment, settling upon my lips. Slowly, hesitantly, she reached out a hand. "For once," she whispered as her finger touched my bottom lip, "I want to feel."

I shut my eyes as the tingle of her touch spread, emanating like a wave, defying everything I knew as it grew in strength until it permeated me entirely, body and mind.

She was closer than ever, her body pressing the book I held against me. She let her fingers fall from my lips, and they tingled with the memory of her touch until I opened my eyes to assure myself I had not been dreaming.

But she was there, looking at me in a way that made my legs quiver and my body burn.

"I have fought it mightily, Phineas. I have done everything I can to rid myself of this desire for you, but rather than purging me of what I feel, every word I have written in that dreadful notebook has only solidified it."

Her words, so unbelievable and welcome, struck me dumb.

"Tell me I did not misunderstand our conversation, that I am not wrong to hope you were speaking of me." She shut her eyes in frustration, took in a breath, then met my gaze again. "Tell me what *you* want, Phineas."

I shifted the book, freeing me to draw nearer so her skirts sat against my leg. When I spoke, I hardly recognized my voice. "Surely you know…"

"Say it," she breathed, her eyes closing. Her blonde hair glinted in the flickering candlelight, her lashes pressed against the top of her cheeks, and the sight filled me with suffocating emotion and need.

Trembling, I guided my hand to her cheek. Its warmth and softness urged my eyes closed again, begging to be experienced through touch alone. "I want *you*, Sarah," I whispered. "Mind, body, and soul."

I sought and found her lips, easily, naturally, as though they had been waiting to be united. Her hands slipped inside my coat, undoing the buttons of my waistcoat, pressing against my chest, then grasping my braces. With them, she pulled me closer, and I dropped the book that separated us, letting it clatter to the floor. Wentworth had given his confession by letter; I would offer mine with my lips and hands. Words were insufficient. I needed to hold Sarah, to know her by experience.

And suddenly I understood. I knew why, for centuries, poets and playwrights had attempted to capture the essence of love. Theirs had been an impossible task, doomed to fail before it ever began. No words, however fitting, however carefully chosen, could describe the experience of kissing Sarah Danneville, of holding her and feeling her come undone in my arms.

She deepened the kiss, leaning into me, and I stumbled backward to keep my balance, my back knocking into the bookshelves. A few books tumbled off onto my shoulders and to the floor.

She pulled away, breaking free from my grasp and stepping backward. Blinking and breathing quickly, she rubbed her lips together. The room was dark, the candle extinguished. Only the light from the entryway trickled in to lessen the oppressiveness of the darkness. She took another step back and another, her wide eyes fixed upon me.

They dropped to my open coat and waistcoat, then to the books scattered on the floor around me. She brought her palms up in front of her, regarding them as they trembled, just as mine did. My body was still ablaze, my breath refusing to slow.

She shook her head and took another step back.

"Sarah," I pleaded, for I saw it in her eyes: the enormity of what she had done. What *we* had done. "I should not have... I did not mean—"

"You did nothing wrong," she said, putting a hand to her stomach. "It was just..." She put a hand to her lips, shutting her eyes for a moment. Her eyes opened, and she fixed her gaze upon me. "It is too much. I cannot forsake reason."

I nodded, my throat thick. Her meaning was clear: to choose me would be to go against reason. And she was right. I had nothing to offer her.

"I understand, my lady. You may count on me to support you in what you feel is best for you. As a friend." The words tore my heart.

She let out a quivering breath, then nodded. And with one more glance at me, she was gone.

And I was alone again, surrounded by disarray—the books at my feet and the thoughts and feelings within me.

Chapter Thirty-One

SARAH

"They seem to be getting on quite well, don't they?" Mr. Wilks said, his eyes on George and Richard, who were throwing paper darts on the lawn. Phineas was not far off, holding a basket of the remaining ones.

"They do," I said, watching with mixed feelings. Richard was a year younger than George, but he was a confident little fellow. I could easily see the two of them getting up to mischief together, despite the fact that it had only been a day since the Wilkses' arrival. And while Richard had taken to George quite rapidly, I could not say the same for how he had responded to me. He was civil, but my smiles and kindness had been met with an impressive stoicism. I wasn't deterred, though. George could be the same way.

Mr. Wilks was the same height as I was, which allowed me the veriest glimpse of the balding spot on the crown of his head. It was to be expected, of course. I had wished for a man old enough to be widowed and have an heir.

George threw a dart, and it sailed well past the others. He raised his fists in triumph while Phineas clapped. I suppressed a sigh at the sight of that smile. Phineas had been as good as his word, treating me with friendly civility since our encounter in the library.

It was maddening, for whenever I saw him, I wished he would pull me into the nearest room and demand I stop being reasonable. Then he would kiss me until I forgot who I was or that I was meant to be entertaining Mr. Wilks in a way that would lead to a proposal.

But Phineas never pulled me in to the nearest room. He never made me forget Mr. Wilks. In fact, it had been his idea for George and Richard to throw paper darts. I was certain he had done so to give Mr. Wilks and me uninterrupted time together, for Mr. Wilks preferred to have Richard in his sight as much as possible. Richard seemed to prefer the same, for he had balked when his father had stated we would be watching from a distance. Mr. Wilks had been on the verge of giving in when Phineas and George had intervened and successfully distracted Richard.

I had no desire to marry Mr. Wilks. Which was precisely why I *should* marry him. I would be perfectly mistress of myself. I would never be consumed as I had been in the library. It was something to rejoice in.

But I was not rejoicing. "Have you any interest in sailing, Mr. Wilks?"

"Oh, yes. In fact, I have three ships of my own."

"I was *not* aware of that," I said, my interest piqued. "And where have you gone?"

He chuckled. "That is quite a list! But most recently? To the West Indies. I could have sent my man of business in my stead, but Richard most particularly wished to go—he has quite an adventurous spirit, you know, and I thought it good for him to learn the business."

"Very wise of you. Have you had any dealings in the Mediterranean? In Corinth or Athens or Rome, say?" I held my breath.

"Once or twice, yes." He clasped his hands, grinning as his

son sent a dart flying near George's. "You have some interest there?"

"I am a student of Latin and Greek. I have an ambition to see the sights."

"Hm. Well, there is always good wine to be had from Rome, you know, and I rather think Richard would enjoy a visit."

I smiled, feeling the first glimmers of hope that, even if I could not have *everything* my heart desired, I might be able to achieve my wish to see the ancient world.

"Father!" Richard called out. "Come fly one yourself!"

Phineas sent me an apologetic look, as if to say, *I tried.*

Mr. Wilks smiled indulgently. "Shall we, my lady? I should like to try my skill at these darts."

I followed willingly, eager to be agreeable in exchange for *his* agreeable response to my ambition.

Despite being decades older than the rest of us, Mr. Wilks was skilled enough at throwing darts. And while my own gaze strayed to Phineas more than I would have liked, Phineas did not seem to suffer from the same impulse.

He was kind to Mr. Wilks and engaged him in polite conversation, making a number of remarks in praise of Richard, which naturally endeared him to the boy's father.

And I was left to wonder whether, with enough time, I would be able to look at Phineas without thinking of that kiss—and whether I would be glad or disappointed if I managed to forget it. It had been difficult enough to refrain from admiring him without first-hand experience of his person; now it was impossible. If I hadn't known him better, I might have thought the removal of his coat for the dart-throwing calculated to take my mind to the moment I had unbuttoned his waistcoat.

My cheeks warmed at the very thought.

What had I been thinking to allow myself that moment of weakness? And, more importantly, had I ruined myself forever as a result? Would I always crave the feeling again?

I had been right to stop it, though. I had felt the very thing I had always feared—the utter willingness to be swallowed up in another person. In that moment, I had no regard for anything but the expression of my increasingly powerful feelings toward Phineas.

Mr. Wilks threw a dart, and it sailed a matter of ten feet before dropping to the ground. I stared at it. Mr. Wilks was a reasonable choice. He was the sort of man Father expected me to marry. I would be comfortable, reasonably independent, my ambitions within reach.

"My lady?"

I found Phineas watching me, holding the basket. His gaze dropped to my hands, which held a dart. I must have picked up the one on the ground without thinking. He was waiting for me to give it to him.

Behind him, Mr. Wilks, Richard, and George were walking toward Bettencourt Court.

"The boys expressed a desire to eat something, and Mr. Wilks professed himself hungry as well."

"Oh," I said, setting the dart in the basket.

We turned to walk in the direction of the house.

"He seems a very good man," Phineas said.

I clasped my hands behind my back to keep them in order. "Yes, he does."

"And Richard is a very bright child."

"Indeed."

He cleared his throat, and silence ensued as we reached the front door. He opened it, and our gazes met.

"I hope you will be very happy with him, my lady. You deserve to be."

Chapter Thirty-Two
PHINEAS

Bettencourt Court was abuzz with activity. The guests had begun arriving half an hour ago, and, with Lord Bettencourt's permission, I had agreed that Lord Danneville and Richard could observe the comings and goings of the guests. Unlike the entry hall, the top of the staircase where we stood was bathed in darkness. I leaned against the wall, my arms folded across my chest as I supervised.

"The sourest face I ever saw!" Lord Danneville said between a shout and a whisper as a man shrugged out of his coat and handed it to one of the hired footmen. The boys had been commenting upon—or rather insulting—each arrival. I had been doing my best to temper their enthusiasm for abusing the guests, but this activity was preferable to the others they had discussed engaging in during the ball. So long as they kept their voices down, it was harmless enough.

Richard sniggered, a hand over his mouth, and both of them ducked when the sound-bearing qualities of the room carried their laughter to the sour-faced—an unfortunately accurate descriptor—gentleman, who looked around to locate the origin of it. Like most of the unattached male guests, he seemed to be nearly twice Sarah's age.

Unsuccessful in finding the source of the laughter, the man turned to the footman, who indicated to him where he could find the ballroom.

"Take care or you shall be called out," I said. "Or, more probably, *I* shall."

"Surely you are not afraid of *him*."

I was not afraid of what he could do to me physically. My fear was for the pain my heart would sustain when Sarah—Lady Sarah—inevitably chose one of the arriving guests.

"That is Captain Charlton," Lord Danneville said of the tall, thin man who had just come through the door. "*He* grows uglier every year."

My protests were but half-hearted. I was doing my best to be happy for Sarah, but it was becoming more and more difficult as I watched the arrival of each attendee and tried not to ask myself why I had been so unfortunate to be born into my particular circumstances.

And then I would inevitably wonder if my father had been right all along. Perhaps I would have seemed a prospect worth considering to Lord Bettencourt if I had remained in the Navy and followed the example of Theo, climbing through the ranks to become a captain rather than the lowly tutor and curate I was. Then it might have been me rather than Captain Charlton handing my hat and coat to the footman. Hopefully, I would not be growing uglier every year, though.

There was a lull in the arrival of guests, and the two boys turned from their task in boredom.

"Well," said the viscount, "it is just as I expected. You are a far better choice than any of them, Mr. Donovan. Stuffy, old chuffs, the lot of them."

Feeling my neck and face fill with color, I glanced at Richard, whose father was just such a stuffy, old chuff, and stuttered out a protest. "Really, my lord…"

"You needn't worry about Richard here." He nudged him with an elbow. "He doesn't want his father to marry Sarah any more than you and I do."

I opened my mouth to protest yet again. Need he make it sound as though I was so actively against it?

"I am closer to her age than he is!" Richard said. Yelled, rather. The boy seemed to have no concept of what it meant to speak softly. "Besides, I don't *want* a new mother."

"See?" Lord Danneville crowed.

"Be that as it may," I said slowly, "it is not for us to decide these things."

The viscount's eyebrows pulled together, his good humor evaporating. "Why do you not at least *try*? It is as if you do not even *want* to marry my sister. Or perhaps you do not want to be my brother." The anger in his voice was audible, but so was the hurt.

Resisting the urge to glance at Richard to see what he made of this exchange, I kneeled before Lord Danneville and put my hands on his shoulders. "There is nothing I would like more, I assure you. But it is not meant to be."

"Wait," Richard said slowly. "*You* want to marry Lady Sarah?"

I thought I might choke on the awkwardness of the question. I rose to a stand. "I… that is…"

"She *loves* him," the viscount said.

"My lord," I pleaded.

"She *does*," he persisted. "I have read her journal, and I have seen them together. Kissing, even, in the library!"

My eyes widened as my heart plummeted into my stomach. Lord Danneville had witnessed what had happened?

"I couldn't sleep," he explained, "so I came downstairs to fetch a book, but…" His eyes widened significantly.

Richard stared at me, surprise etched on his face.

"I beg you will forget Lord Danneville's words," I said. "My feelings for Lady Sarah matter not a whit. There is no thought between either of us of a future. There is no chance of such a thing."

"If you would only show some courage, there *would* be!" the viscount said loudly enough that I glanced at the front door. Mercifully, it was still closed and the footmen in conversation with one another.

"I think we should move upstairs," I hurried to say. "What do you say to a game of backgammon?"

Both boys snorted away such a suggestion with disgust.

"Very well," I said, racking my brains for a way to change the subject and find a different activity. It was difficult to appeal to boys of the age and personality of my charges, for the things they enjoyed were not the things *I* enjoyed. But over the course of the last few weeks, I had learned to find the common ground between my interests and the viscount's. Perhaps I could do so tonight as well. "Come, then. We will do something more... exciting."

Both looked at me warily.

"I promise you shall enjoy it," I said as the front door opened again.

They looked at one another as if silently conferring, then nodded curtly.

My promise required me to lead the boys to my bedchamber, where I rummaged through my trunk until I found what I was looking for.

When we reached the door that led to the roof of Betten-court Court, however, it was locked. I chewed my lip for a moment. I had no desire to disrupt the housekeeper, Mrs. Lloyd, on a night such as this.

"Father keeps the spare keys in the top drawer in his study," Lord Danneville said. "I shall go fetch them."

I stopped him, holding him by the arm.

Guilt shone on his face. He was eager for any reason to go downstairs, and well I knew it. I slipped into the nearest bedchamber and pulled the bell. When the housekeeper arrived minutes later, she was breathless and none-so-pleased, but she agreed to unlock the door.

Armed with a map and two candles, the three of us did our best to locate the individual stars in the night's mercifully clear skies. To my relief, both boys seemed to enjoy themselves. Most importantly, the conversation remained in safe avenues, never returning to its earlier path.

When it came time for the boys to retire, I was exhausted and struggling to maintain a pleasant humor. When the boys asked to bring Richard's mattress into the viscount's room, I agreed willingly enough just to avoid the inevitable struggle if I refused.

Slumping onto the floor outside of Lord Danneville's door, I took off my spectacles and rubbed my eyes. The sounds of the boys' whispers reached me, but within a quarter of an hour, the talking dissipated and ended altogether.

The sound of music permeated the corridors of the house, a reminder of what was happening while I monitored the boys. Sarah would be dancing and conversing with all the eligible men present, while they all admired her—rightly so—and did everything in their power to show themselves the best candidate for a husband. How I envied them that.

I rested my head against the wall, leaving my spectacles on the floor to give my ears and nose the rest they craved after so long with the wiry rims resting upon them. And there I stayed as the minutes ticked by, as a reel changed to a cotillion and then to a quadrille. When I finally replaced my spectacles to look at my pocket watch, it was nigh on midnight. The boys had been safely in their beds for nearly two hours, and my muscles were begging me to move.

Taking care not to cause too much noise, I rose to my feet

and pressed my ear to the door, listening for any sign of life within. There was none, though, and I breathed a sigh of relief, backing away.

Exhausted as I was, I knew I would find no rest in my bed. I would toss and turn, just as I had every night since Sarah had come to the library. My mind needed refuge, and there was but one place it could find it.

Chapter Thirty-Three

SARAH

"Would you prefer a different beverage, my lady?" Mr. Wilks watched me with a hint of concern.

I glanced at the drink he had procured for me, hardly remembering taking it from him. "No, thank you. I am merely catching my breath."

It was the first dance I had sat out tonight, and every bit of me wished to sit out the remainder of them. Mr. Wilks alone had taken note of my declining energy, for which I was grateful. He was a good man, as Phineas had said, and unlike some of the men present, who looked at me as though I was some sort of prize to be hunted and won, his attentiveness was more genuine.

Perhaps that was because he was more secure in his suit than the others. He had more reason to hope for success, for none of the others in attendance had been asked to stay nearly a week at Bettencourt Court.

"Do you enjoy balls and parties, my lady?"

I took a sip from my drink before answering with a rueful smile. "Not as much as I should. I prefer a quiet night in the library amongst the pages of a book." Not for the first time tonight, my mind wandered to that room. Was Phineas there, as his sister had said he would be? Wherever he was, I envied him.

"Or a voyage to Rome or Athens?" Mr. Wilks suggested. He wore a dark green satin coat and buckled shoes, proclaiming his age every bit as effectively as his head of balding gray hair. But the truth was, in my new, high-waisted gown, *I* was the one who stood out amongst the attendees. My parents had heeded my wishes, inviting staid gentlemen of advancing age.

"Yes," I said. "I would certainly prefer that."

"Then you should have it."

I studied him, waiting for him to explain his meaning.

"Without wishing to display an unseemly forwardness, my lady, I see no reason we could not manage such a thing. Part of the honeymoon, even. I could go about the business of arranging favorable terms with the local merchants while you wander about, exploring the city and the ruins as you please before we sail to the next port."

I held his gaze, my mind a whir. Mr. Wilks was offering me everything I wanted: Rome, Athens, Corinth, Corfu, Rhodes. And, not least of all, the independence to explore them at my leisure while he did the things that interested *him*. It was better than I could have hoped for.

Why, then, did I feel so aggravatingly empty as I considered the prospect?

Why, when I looked at Mr. Wilks' kind face, did I wish to replace it with a pair of blue eyes, wiry spectacles, and hair the color of burnt sugar?

All evening, I had been courted and attended to by men anxious to please me. I was to choose from amongst them, preferably the one standing beside me, the one who had the means to provide me the best possible situation in marriage.

But all I could feel was a swirling sickness at the thought of marrying any one of them, including the thoughtful Mr. Wilks. I felt akin to none of them.

It all felt so suffocating.

I gave my drink to the passing hired footman as the dizziness set in. "Would you excuse me, Mr. Wilks? I must see to something. I shall only be a moment."

"Of course," he said, looking more concerned than ever.

I offered him the best reassuring smile I could manage and made my way toward the door that led into the entry hall. It would be empty, for all the footmen were busy taking trays around or hurrying to the kitchens to refill them.

My breath was coming quickly, and I put a hand to my chest, as though it would calm the beating of my heart and my rapid breathing. Shutting the door behind me, I leaned against the wall and tried to suck in deep, slow breaths, focusing my gaze on the pattern of the rug that lined the floor.

A movement in the corner of my eye caught my notice, and I stilled.

"Richard?"

He was standing a dozen feet away, in the middle of the entry hall. He was dressed for sleep, his wide, guilty eyes on me.

Pushing off the wall, I hurried over to him. "Is everything well?"

He nodded quickly, his eyes darting to the drawing room door as though what he feared was within. His father, perhaps.

"What are you doing? You should be in bed." I smiled slightly to soften my words. I didn't wish for him to think I was already trying to act like his mother. But it had to be nearing midnight. He should have been asleep hours ago.

"I... I wanted a glass of milk, but I didn't wish to disturb the servants—they are all so occupied."

I nodded. "And where is Lord Danneville?"

He hesitated. "He is in the kitchens, for he was hungry, too. Please don't tell my father, my lady."

"I shan't. And what of Phine"—I cleared my throat—"and what of Mr. Donovan?"

"He is in the library, I believe. He has been quite blue all evening." There was a pause. "I believe he went there hoping he would have the opportunity to speak with you."

My heart constricted. Phineas was out of sorts. He needed me.

It was my fault, for I had as good as thrown myself at him, begging him to kiss me. And then I had bid him to forget it as though that was even possible. Not for me, at least.

These past few days, he had appeared to be well, had given no indication he was hurt. But it seemed he had merely been hiding it well.

"Go upstairs, Richard," I said, my eyes flitting to the library doors. "I shall have milk and something to eat sent up for you."

"Yes, my lady."

I went in search of one of the servants, instructing them to have George return to his room and to take up the milk and some bread and butter.

Once the maid had gone to see to my orders, I glanced toward the library doors. I needed a respite from the ball, and it would be remiss of me not to ensure Phineas was well. Without him, it was quite possible George and Richard would have poured ink in the punch bowl or something equally mischievous.

I walked over to the library door and paused. The door was barely ajar, and I nudged it enough that I could see within. Phineas was seated, a book open before him. His elbow rested on top of the desk, his hand supporting his head so it was impossible for me to see his face.

An ache pulsed in my heart—a tangible need for him. Even just his friendship.

Gently, I pushed the door open.

He dropped his hand and glanced over, pressing his glasses farther up the bridge of his nose.

He blinked swiftly and rose from his seat. He wore no satins or buckled shoes. His coat was draped over the back of the chair, his waistcoat unbuttoned, and his cravat loosened. The familiarity of it sent a flutter through me.

The orchestra struck up a new song, and his gaze flicked behind me. "What are you doing here, my lady?"

I lifted my shoulders. "Seeking refuge."

He said nothing, his eyes on me as though he was trying to understand my intentions. He looked so serious and somber. I craved a smile from him, to see the way his cheeks pushed his spectacles up, the way his eyes gleamed.

"Perhaps you should come join the entertainment," I said. "Dance and make merry."

"A ball like that is no place for me, my lady. There is good reason I was not invited. I belong *here*."

I walked toward him. Now that I was here, now that I could see him, all I wanted was to be near him. Friendship with Phineas would never be enough. "And what if I belong here, too? What if that is all *I* wish for? To be here."

His throat bobbed as I approached. "Then I will leave you to enjoy the library in peace." He bowed his head and brushed past me.

I grasped his hand, and he stopped, turning his head to look at me, then at my hand holding his.

I relished the feel of it, wishing my gloves away so I could feel his skin on mine. "Richard said you were out of sorts."

He smiled ruefully. "And after I took such pains not to appear so." He suddenly frowned. "When did he tell you I was out of sorts?"

I gestured behind me. "Just now. He came downstairs for a glass of milk, and I caught him as I was taking a respite in the entry hall. When I asked him where you were, he told me you were here and had wished to speak with me."

His frown deepened.

"What is it? I do not blame you for his coming down, Phineas—"

He shook his head. "I did not tell him I wished to speak with you." He looked me in the eye intently. "Sarah, I must tell you. Richard does not wish for a match between—"

The library door opened, and Father appeared there, Mr. Wilks and Richard behind him.

Chapter Thirty-Four

PHINEAS

I t took me a moment to realize what was happening—and how it must appear to our audience. I pulled my hand from Sarah's grasp, clasping it with the other one behind me. We were on dangerous ground; that much was evident from the way Lord Bettencourt looked.

His eyes flitted between the two of us, his brow furrowing and darkening like a storm cloud. "What is the meaning of this?"

The silence was deafening, the sound of the strings playing in the ballroom at odds with the palpable tension in the room.

"Mr. Wilks here came to express his concern over you, Sarah —at the manner of your departure from the ballroom and the fact that you had not yet returned. We came in search of you and, only thanks to Richard, discover you *here*, of all places." His eyes shifted to me as if to say, *and with* him, *of all people*.

Richard shifted so he was concealed almost entirely by his father. This was his doing, and I knew precisely why he had done it. He hoped a bit of scandal would prevent the marriage between Sarah and his father.

I opened my mouth to speak, but the earl put up a hand to

stop me, his gaze on his daughter. "You will return to the ball-room immediately, Sarah." His voice and jowls shook with the effort to maintain control of himself. "You have guests who took precious time out of their evening to attend this ball. Mr. Wilks, if you will accompany her, please."

Mr. Wilks was frowning, but he nodded. "Go to bed, Richard," he said softly.

Sarah stayed where she was, her nostrils flaring and her eyes on her father, until she heeded him and strode over to Mr. Wilks.

The earl watched her as she accepted Mr. Wilks's arm, then his gaze moved to me. His jaw hardened. "I will speak with you tomorrow, Donovan. I have other pressing matters to see to this evening."

"Yes, my lord."

And with one final, simmering look, he turned on his heel and was gone.

I was Wickham.

That was the conclusion I came to during the hours of tossing and turning in my bed.

Like Darcy's father, Lord Bettencourt had been generous with me, welcoming me into his home, giving me the opportunity to function as curate in the parish, allowing me to tutor his heir, and inviting me to dine with the family.

And how had I repaid him? With scandal.

I could have prevented it if I had been more disciplined, if I had done what I knew to be right. I had let too much familiarity grow between Lady Sarah and myself—a familiarity I had no right to.

It was but seven o'clock in the morning when Collins came to my bedchamber to inform me Lord Bettencourt wished to see me in his study. I descended the stairs with a surprising amount of calm. I must have expended all my anxieties over the course of the night. Now was the time to accept my fate, to reap what I had sown. Perhaps, below my disappointment in myself, there was even a bit of relief I would not be obliged to become like Mr. Vickers.

Lord Bettencourt was seated behind his desk, a letter in hand, which he looked up from at my entrance. He appeared tired and irritable, and it was no wonder. I didn't imagine he would have retired until the early hours of the morning.

Setting the letter down, he motioned for me to have a seat.

I obeyed, remaining quiet as he let the silence tick on for a few moments.

"I cannot think you are aware, Donovan," he finally said, "that, for years now, I have been trying to persuade my daughter to marry. It has taken a great deal of work to ensure she has not allowed her obsession with reading and learning to overtake the development of the accomplishments expected of the daughter of an earl. She has had no interest in marriage, so you can imagine my delight when she conveyed to her mother and myself that she had undergone a change of sentiment and was ready to look for a suitable husband."

I said nothing, for what was there to say? Evidently, a reply was not expected of me, though, for Lord Bettencourt continued.

"I agreed to hold a ball so that she might choose from amongst the sort of men she had expressed an interest in. I went to great lengths in order to secure an acceptance from Mr. Wilks to my invitation. Only imagine my joy when I received word he intended not only to come to the ball but had agreed to stay at Bettencourt Court, along with his son. I thought, *this will do very nicely.* Just as I had lost hope of things ever falling into place, they did so better than I could have anticipated. Until last night."

His eyes bored into me, and I dared not respond.

"You have put me in a delicate and difficult position, Donovan. After our conversation, I will have to face Mr. Wilks—my daughter will have to face him. There is undoubtedly talk amongst the servants, which means it is only a matter of time until word of last night's occurrences becomes next week's dinner party gossip. And if Mr. Wilks leaves Bettencourt Court without having made an offer of marriage to my daughter, the damage to her reputation will be even greater."

His words stung my conscience, convicting me. My own reputation was of little account, for I was hardly known. Society was much more forgiving of men, too. But for Sarah... for her family...

I took in a breath, seeing what was required of me—what would most help Sarah.

"The blame is mine, my lord," I said. "I overstepped the bounds of propriety, and I accept full fault for doing so. Your daughter is innocent of wrongdoing. Her name should not be sullied by my mistakes. I will attest to this in the presence of Mr. Wilks to ensure he understands."

Lord Bettencourt searched my face, his knit brow taking on a more thoughtful tone. He steepled his hands, tapping his pointer fingers together. "I had great hopes for you, Donovan. I have been pleased with the work you have done with my son. And I had intended to offer you the vicaracy once Vickers leaves." His lips turned into a more pronounced frown. "You must understand that neither of those things will be possible now."

I nodded, swallowing.

"I must protect my family, and I have a responsibility to the parish, as well."

"I understand, my lord."

He let out a sigh, grimacing in a way that told me there was a measure of sympathy amid his frustration and anger.

"I will let Collins know to await your instruction for the carriage to be brought around."

All I could manage was yet another nod, for my stomach swam and my mind was blank.

I was leaving Bettencourt Court. It wouldn't take me long to gather my things. Within the next hour or two, I would watch the house, the family, and Sarah fade into the distance—into memory.

I let out a puff of air, looking around the bedchamber for any sign of what I might be forgetting.

I walked to the trunk of books sitting near the door. Beside it sat a pile of books I hadn't managed to fit inside it. I took stock of the array of books, trying to determine whether there was a better way to arrange them to fit the few that remained or whether I would simply have to keep them with me in the chaise.

Either way, that decision was the last one I needed to make. Otherwise, I was ready—ready to leave. I would make my way to Duke and Diana at Birchleigh Hall, for the thought of going to my father was not a palatable one. It would be difficult enough to face Duke after the trouble he had gone to securing the position for me.

I pulled the cord to summon one of the servants, then kneeled by the trunk. My eye caught on one of the titles: *Sense and Sensibility*. It was the first book Sarah and I had discussed together—the beginning, in a way, to our friendship.

I pulled it from amongst its fellows and opened the front cover. The note Sarah had written was still there, and it brought a sad smile to my face.

There was that word again at the end, just before her name. *Yours*. I had experienced a few precious moments tasting what it would be like to be hers. I would spend the remainder of my life thinking back on them. Every time I read these books, I would think of Sarah, for good books must certainly be read again and again.

I glanced at the stack of novels beside the trunk and frowned.

There was a quick knock on the door, followed by its opening. Lord Danneville stood in the doorway, his gaze going to me, then the two trunks. "You cannot leave!"

I sighed and rose to my feet, simultaneously glad to have the opportunity to say goodbye to the viscount and regretting it.

"It wasn't me, Mr. Donovan, I swear," he said with wide, sincere eyes. "When Richard told me what he intended, I told him not to do it, for I knew it would only cause you harm. And, like a fool, I believed him when he agreed not to." His brow furrowed, the hurt of betrayal written on his face. "But he waited until I was asleep."

Smiling ruefully, I put a hand on his shoulder. "You mustn't blame yourself, my lord. You couldn't have known. And the fault does not lie with Richard. I have not acted wisely. It is for the best that I leave, though I will miss you greatly."

His head shook from side to side, his eyes filling with tears so that my heart felt like it might break, physically impossible as I knew such a thing to be.

I pulled him close to me, swallowing my emotion as best I could.

A throat cleared.

"The chaise is ready, sir," Collins said from the doorway. Beside him was Hughes, looking sober.

I released Lord Danneville and nodded. "The trunk by the bed is ready to go down. I can help you carry this one in just a moment."

The two of them stepped into the bedchamber and walked over to the trunk full of my clothing. It was by far the lighter of the trunks, and they lifted it without much trouble. It was the books that would break their backs.

I waited until they had left the room to address the viscount again. "I am sorry we shan't be able to perform *Ajax*, my lord. But I hope you will continue to study, for you have a strong mind."

"I do not," he said.

"You do. You have a mind meant for more than mere learning, though. You are meant to *do*, and that is a strength I envy in you." I put out my hand.

He sighed and shook it. "I haven't given up yet, sir."

I tried for a smile, realizing it would be futile to argue with him on this point. In time, he would accept the way things were —the way things had to be.

Chapter Thirty-Five

SARAH

If the ball had felt long before Father discovered me in the library with Phineas, it had been interminable afterward. My disappearance coinciding with that of Father and Mr. Wilks had occasioned some talk, demonstrated by the whispering comments and curious glances we received.

Mr. Wilks took up the challenge quite admirably, acting as though nothing had happened. Indeed, I wondered if it hadn't bothered him in the least. It was not as though he was in love with me.

But at the end of the night, once the crowds had dispersed, and it came time for us to bid one another goodnight, there had been a little frown on his brow and a hint of preoccupation in his tone.

Part of me wondered if George was as much to blame as Richard for the appearance of Father and Mr. Wilks at the library. He had made it quite clear he wished for a match between Phineas and me. But in my heart, I knew it didn't truly matter. It was my fault. I was a wretch, for Mr. Wilks did not deserve to be unhappy at my hands, and neither did Phineas.

It was nearly two when I retired to my bed, but sleep eluded me far beyond that. I was woken by my maid in the morning—a rare occurrence.

"Forgive me, my lady," she apologized, "but the earl wishes to see you in his study as soon as you are dressed."

I sighed and nodded, and together, we saw to the task. I had hoped to seek out Phineas first this morning, but I had overslept as a result of the late night, and I doubted Father would appreciate my delaying our meeting to seek out the tutor. In any case, it would be preferable for me to smooth Father's feathers before he spoke to Phineas. If I was not already too late...

Father was waiting for me outside of his study. As expected, he looked anything but pleased when his gaze landed upon me. He strode over to meet me.

"Father," I began.

He held up a hand to stop me. "I have no wish to hear explanations or excuses, Sarah. I have been patient with you thus far, but that patience has run thin. In fact, it is entirely expired. I have agreed to and abided by even the most ridiculous of your requirements, and for you to repay me as you have is outside of enough. There is but one thing required of you now: to hold up your end of the bargain. Mr. Wilks is in the study. Despite the compliment he paid you by coming to stay, you have done your best to humiliate him, and it is time for you to repair your error, to act honorably toward him."

I swallowed as the words convicted me. "And what of Mr. Donovan? Does he not deserve that I act honorably toward *him?*"

"Mr. Donovan is no longer in this house. He took responsibility for what happened—though, you can be certain I am not foolish enough to believe you entirely innocent, Sarah. He paved the way for you to salvage this match. Do not let that go to waste." He walked toward the door and, before I could respond, opened it.

I stood frozen in place, trying to comprehend what Father

had said. Phineas was gone. Gone where? Did this mean he would not replace Mr. Vickers?

He had taken full responsibility for what had happened, and in doing so, he had lost his livelihood.

Father cleared his throat, and I blinked, taking stock of Mr. Wilks, who stood in the study, waiting for me. There was nothing for it but to swallow the lump in my throat, ignore the nausea roiling in my stomach, and speak with him.

I stepped into the room, Mr. Wilks's eyes searching my face with uncertainty. Guilt niggled at me. Had I truly humiliated him? What *was* my obligation to him?

Father closed the door behind me, and there was silence for a moment as we observed one another.

"Mr. Wilks," I said, "I must ask your forgiveness for what you witnessed last night."

"There is no need, my lady. Your father has explained everything."

I had no response. What precisely had Father said? That Phineas had been entirely at fault? It was a lie—a terrible lie.

Mr. Wilks took two steps toward me. "Even if he had not, though, I know you do not seek a love match, my lady. And neither do I. My desire to come to know you better, to see whether a marriage between us is what suits us both, is still intact. I have three more days at Bettencourt Court, and I hope that, during that time, we can come to know one another better. What do you say?" There was such sincerity in his eyes.

I was torn in two, a woman of entirely different minds. Father had been right when he had said that, in finding Mr. Wilks, he had adhered to my every requirement, ridiculous as they might have been. In truth, he was more than I had asked for, for kindness had not featured on my list of requirements, and yet Mr. Wilks *was* kind.

And yet, my reluctance remained.

But he was not offering marriage to me yet. He was merely

asking I give things a chance. For three more days. It was an eminently reasonable request, and Phineas had sacrificed himself to enable such a thing.

I tried for a smile and nodded even as my heart wandered to Phineas, wondering where he was and what would become of him.

Chapter Thirty-Six

PHINEAS

BIRCHLEIGH HALL

I finished cleaning the lenses of my spectacles, then rubbed at my eyes. It wasn't necessary, for it wasn't my vision causing me problems. My mind refused to settle long enough for me to focus on the words before me.

The things occupying my mind were various: what I was to do with myself now that my future prospects were no more, whether wisdom and practicality dictated I should seek another position in the church despite the change my desires had undergone, and, more than anything else, whether the feelings consuming me would ever give way. Would I ever read without wishing to discuss things with Sarah? Would I ever enter a library without remembering the most sublime moments of my life?

The muffled sounds of commotion met my ears, and mere seconds later, the door opened.

Diana's eyes were bright. "They are here!" She came over and shut the book. "Take a respite from your wallowing to come greet them."

"I am not wallowing," I said as she pulled me up.

She shot me a look that told me she didn't believe me for a second. Then she wrapped her arm around mine. "I do not blame you, Phin. Indeed, I have been wallowing a bit, too, to be quite honest. I became quite attached to the idea of you and Lady Sarah."

We stopped at the top of the staircase and looked below, where trunks were being stacked by the servants. Nearby stood a woman in a gray pelisse and a straw bonnet. A mane of long, wavy brown hair emerged from underneath, reaching nearly to her hips.

A man walked up beside her, wrapping his arm about her waist and doffing his hat to kiss her.

The image was bittersweet at its most potent, for I was over-joyed to see Theo after so long, to see my brother so happy. But he had something I now craved as powerfully as food: love.

"Theo!" Diana called out, pulling me down the stairs so all my concentration was needed to prevent tripping.

The next few minutes were a whirlwind of embraces and introductions. Both Theo and Elena were suntanned and tired from their voyage. Elena's stomach was beginning to round, attesting to the fact that she was in the family way.

Duke soon descended with Charlotte in his arms, rosy-cheeked and rubbing her eyes from her afternoon nap. Her orneriness and lack of enthusiasm at the arrival of her aunt and uncle elicited a much-needed dose of laughter from me.

By dinner that evening, Valentine and Rebecca had joined the welcoming party, and we were being regaled with tales from the seas and stories of India and other places the rest of us had never seen.

Talk turned to life at home in England, and Diana took on the task of giving a synopsis of all that had occurred in their most recent absence.

"All of this has been quite exciting for us," she said at the end, "but naturally, we cannot compare with squalls and elephants and that sort of thing."

Elena smiled and looked to me. "And what of you, Phineas? We didna expect ta find ye here. I thought Theo said ye were livin' away?"

Diana sent a sympathetic grimace, and I cleared my throat. "I was. But I was... dismissed two days ago."

I glanced at Duke, trying once again to gauge his feelings on the topic of my dismissal from Bettencourt Court. He had been so calm and unruffled when I had arrived on their doorstep, but I couldn't help wondering how he truly felt. Had I ruined his relationship with Lord Bettencourt?

"Can you believe our own Phineas has been making scandals in your absence?" Diana asked teasingly. "I suppose now that Valentine has reformed, and Duke has made me respectable, *someone* had to take on the task."

Duke shot his wife a look. "I would tell you to ignore her, Elena, but as you and Theo know her very well, I will resist doing so."

"And yet you somehow managed to say it all the same," Diana shot back without malice. "The truth, if you wish to know it, is that Lord Bettencourt's daughter fell in love with Phineas, and the result was his dismissal."

"Diana," I said softly, partially because it pained me to hear her say such a thing, partially to prevent the further spread of gossip. I had been trying to convince myself I had done what was best for Sarah in leaving. She had never wanted love, after all. Neither had I.

I wanted it now, though.

"I am sorry, Phin," Theo said with a frown. "It is certainly their loss. What shall you do now?"

"I cannot yet say with any certainty. I am still considering the church, of course, but it is difficult to find a living, as you know. I have written to Cambridge to see about the option of a fellowship or, failing that, whatever position they might see fit to offer me. I also sent a letter to the father of one of my Cambridge friends. He is a fellow in the Royal Society and carries out a number of experiments I would gladly assist with, so I sent him something I wrote about Bernoulli's Principle." I shrugged, trying not to think too much on the overwhelming uncertainty of the future. "Only time will tell."

"What would ye do if ye had yer choice?" Elena asked.

I would marry Sarah Danneville. That was not what she was asking, though. "Research of some sort. But beggars cannot be choosers, as they say."

And I was certainly a beggar.

Chapter Thirty-Seven

SARAH

With each passing day, it was made more and more clear that Mr. Wilks was an admirable, decent man. We could converse on a variety of topics, and I had learned a great deal about his business interests. While he was careful with his money, he did not seem at all the sort of man to rule his wife with an iron fist. In short, he was precisely the sort of man I should want to marry.

But I *didn't* want to marry him, and three days hadn't changed that. A hundred of them could not.

How was I to convey such a thing to him, though? And how would I convey it to Father?

Those were the questions plaguing my mind as I dressed for the day, knowing with Mr. Wilks's departure this afternoon, it was an issue that could not be deferred any longer.

Meanwhile, George had been avoiding me, sulking in his bedchamber or taking refuge—of all things—in the library. I, on the other hand, took pains to avoid the room, for it seemed empty without Phineas. Even Chester seemed not to care for it, for he had disappeared entirely. I could only assume he had returned to the vicarage.

George and Richard seemed to have had some sort of falling out, for they spent none of their time together, and Richard insisted on accompanying his father and me on our walks and excursions. He made it quite evident on such outings that I had made no progress in his esteem.

I dismissed my maid, staying seated in front of my mirror. As the door shut, I met my own gaze in the glass and took in a deep breath. I knew what I needed to do, but having the courage to do it was another thing entirely.

I found Mr. Wilks outside with his son, playing at shuttlecock and battledore. He seemed to recognize with a glance that I had sought him out to have *the discussion,* for he told Richard to go inside and wash up.

"I will follow in just a few minutes," he said as Richard looked between the two of us warily.

I smiled, hoping it would communicate he had nothing to worry about from me, but my efforts were wasted, as he merely turned away with a frown.

"I rather think I know why you have come, my lady." Mr. Wilks took my hand, and suddenly I worried he was quite *wrong* about why I had come. "You do not wish to marry me, after all, do you?"

I let out a shaky laugh, and he squeezed my hand. "I have known it, I think, all along."

I grimaced. "I am very sorry, Mr. Wilks. I never meant to waste your time, and I certainly did not mean to embarrass you. I have merely been..."

"Confused?" he offered. "In love?"

I opened my mouth wordlessly, for I hadn't decided whether I would tell him the particular reason I didn't feel I could marry him.

He smiled knowingly and let my hand go. "I know the look of love, my lady, for I have worn it myself."

I turned my gaze away, still unaccustomed to the idea that I might wear my heart on my sleeve like Marianne Dashwood.

"I loved my wife dearly," he continued, "and I would never wish to deprive someone of that experience."

I sent him a look of gratitude. He was an inarguably good and kind man, and he deserved happiness for himself. "What of you, then?"

"You needn't worry for me, my lady." He smiled a bit impishly. "There is never a want of families looking for a man of my means."

"Shall you marry for love again?" He had spoken so highly of it, I could only assume he would wish to experience it again, but perhaps one only loved in such a way once.

"In truth, I am not sure I shall marry at all. At least, not yet." He glanced toward the house as though his mind was there. "I thought Richard would welcome a mother figure, but I suspect I have misjudged him. I do not think he wishes for me to marry again."

"He is very fond of you."

He smiled appreciatively. "He is."

"He is *not*, however, fond of me."

He chuckled. "It has nothing to do with you, my lady, and everything to do with not wishing to share me. But I thank you for your kindness toward him." He grew more serious, meeting my eye. "I must apologize on his behalf. His behavior the night of the ball was... inexcusable. And I am terribly sorry for it. He confessed to me this morning that it was entirely his idea to urge Mr. Donovan into the library—and then to see that you were found there together."

I raised my brows, remembering how Richard had been there, shrinking behind his father. I hadn't thought much of it at the time, but now...

"I imagine it was not his idea alone, Mr. Wilks."

He shook his head. "Lord Danneville had no part in it. He

was asleep the entire time and had, in fact, tried to persuade Richard against doing anything to interfere in our courtship."

I stared at Mr. Wilks, letting his words sink in and settle. George had tried to prevent what had happened. That was something, indeed.

"In any case," Mr. Wilks continued, "I apologize again—profusely—on his behalf. Though, in the end, perhaps everything will be as it should be."

"Perhaps so," I said, well aware the next thing I needed to do was to tell Father the unwelcome news.

The meeting with Mr. Wilks had gone far better than anticipated; I was not fool enough to hope for the same with Father.

Perhaps it was cowardly of me, but before making my way to Father's study to tell him the last thing he wished to hear, I went first to the library. George was there, folding darts with a pile of crumpled, discarded paper at his feet. The sight of it sent a wave of nostalgia over me.

He looked up at my entrance, then returned his eyes to his work.

"Where is Richard?" I asked, walking toward him slowly.

He shrugged.

I stopped, watching his precise folds and the way he used a coin to sharpen the edges.

"George?"

"What?"

"I know it wasn't your fault."

He stopped mid-fold, remaining silent.

"Richard admitted to his father you had nothing to do with what happened—that you tried to convince him not to do anything."

He remained silent, and I crouched beside him, looking into

his face. "I am sorry for thinking you played any role in it. I am very proud of you, George."

His jaw shifted, but he didn't meet my gaze.

"And," I said, taking in a breath, "if you truly wish to go to Harrow, I shall try to help convince Father."

His head whipped around, his eyes bright with disbelief.

I smiled ruefully. "Though, after what I am about to tell him, you might have a better chance if I stay out of it entirely."

"What are you about to tell him?"

"That Mr. Wilks and I have decided we do not suit."

His eyes searched mine, and in them, I thought I saw a glint of hope—a specific hope I dared not feed in myself.

I put out my pinky finger, and he smiled before linking his own with it.

When I stepped before Father's study minutes later, I took a moment to prepare myself.

I was not meant to have such a luxury, though, for the door opened.

Mr. Wilks stepped out, closing the door behind him, then turning to smile at me. "I have informed the earl of our decision, my lady."

I stared, speechless.

"I do not think there is any need for you to talk to him just now." He wrinkled his nose and spoke in a low voice. "Better to give him a bit of time."

I nodded absently, and he smiled. "I hope you and Mr. Donovan shall be very happy together, my lady. You certainly have a friend in me." Then he bowed and walked away.

Uncertain what to do now that the worst part had been done *for* me, I made my way to my bedchamber. There was a maid at my door, a stack of books in her arms.

She turned at my approach. "There you are, my lady. I was just cleaning Mr. Donovan's bedchamber—I should have done so before now, but with the ball, there has been a great deal to do."

I tried not to fixate on the books as my curiosity demanded. "Of course, I quite understand."

She smiled gratefully. "I found these there, and a paper with your name on top."

Heart beating at a gallop, I took them from her arms. "Thank you. You may go."

She nodded, curtsied, and left.

Supporting the books as best as I could with one arm, I opened the door and slipped inside, a lump in my throat. All the books were there, with *Pride and Prejudice* sitting at the top of the pile.

Stomach aflutter, I opened the cover, and disappointment spread through me. There was nothing there—no note in Phineas's handwriting.

I had been hoping for... what? A goodbye? Some lingering evidence of his affection?

But perhaps the books themselves were precisely that.

I walked toward the table next to my bed and set down the stack, stepping back and looking at them there. I frowned at *Pride and Prejudice*, noting a place near the end of the book where the pages didn't lie flat.

Picking it up and sitting on my bed, I let the book fall open to the pages in question.

My heart skipped at the sight of the small, folded piece of paper there and my name, written in Phineas's steady script. The folded edge was sharp and precise, much like George's had been in the library.

Fingers trembling, I opened it and let my gaze fly over its contents.

My lady,
I beg you will accept these as a friendly—and apologetic—

parting gift. I never meant to harm you. May you find a friend with whom you can discuss *Mansfield Park* and *Northanger Abbey*, and may you enjoy those conversations as much as I enjoyed ours.

Your servant, as ever,

Phineas Donovan

P.S. Lord Danneville showed great courage in standing up to Richard Wilks. He may yet prove a good fit for Harrow.

I kept my eyes on the note far longer than required, for they were stinging.

There was no declaration of love, of course, but how could I have expected something like that of him under the circumstances?

I folded the letter and set it in its place, my eyes catching the underlined words on the page. It was the beginning of Chapter 60.

Elizabeth's spirits soon rising to playfulness again, she wanted Mr. Darcy to account for his having ever fallen in love with her. "How could you begin?" said she. "I can comprehend your going on charmingly, when you had once made a beginning; but what could set you off in the first place?"

"I cannot fix on the hour, or the spot, or the look, or the words, which laid the foundation. It is too long ago. I was in the middle before I knew that I had begun."

My throat caught even as my lips pulled into a smile. *This* was Phineas's declaration of love.

A soft knock sounded on the door, and Mother stepped inside.

She and I had barely talked since the night of the ball. She had said nothing to me on the topic of Phineas *or* Mr. Wilks, acting as though nothing had happened. And I... I hadn't had the heart to broach the subject, for I wasn't certain I wanted to hear what she thought of me and my behavior.

But she was here now.

"I spoke with your father," she explained.

I stiffened slightly, wondering if she was coming to censure me.

She walked over, her gaze flitting momentarily to the book in my hand before returning to my face. She took a seat beside me on the bed.

"I am sorry, Mama," I said.

"Sorry for what?"

I looked at the note and ran a finger along the edge. "For disappointing you and Father."

"Oh, my dear," she said, twirling one of my curls around her finger. "Your father will need time to accept this change, of course, but for my part, I am quite pleased."

I brought my head up, thoroughly confused.

She smiled. It was soft and knowing. "I watched the friendship between you and Mr. Donovan grow with great but entirely secret hopes in my breast. I have wanted nothing more than for you to experience the happiness of love."

I blinked, uncertain if I was hearing correctly. Mother had been *hoping* for an attachment between Phineas and me? Between George's tutor and me? "Why did you not say something?"

She raised a brow. "How would you have reacted if I had?"

I bit my lip.

"You needed to learn for yourself the value of love. To choose it for yourself." She reached for the book in my hand, and I allowed her to take it. She closed it and turned it so she could read the title. "This is one of my favorites, you know. I was quite pleased when I discovered Mr. Donovan to be a reader of novels."

"You knew?" It seemed Mother had been keeping any number of secrets.

"George told me. He went snooping in Mr. Donovan's room one day and discovered the set."

I chuckled, shaking my head. "I might have guessed as much."

We both smiled for a moment, then I turned to her, mine fading. "And Father?"

She laid a hand on mine and squeezed it. "Leave him to me." She paused, her brow furrowing. "I know you think little of me at times, Sarah, but I am not without influence."

"You recognize it, then? The way he takes your ideas as though they were his own?"

"Recognize it? I quite count upon it."

I stared at her. "How can you bear it? Or stay silent?"

"In the instances where it matters, I do *not* stay silent. But neither do I choose to humiliate your father by saying something in company. These are the things we discuss between us." She smoothed the sleeve of my dress. "You and I are very much alike, my dear, but in this area, our similarities cease. You wish to be recognized for your wit, your ideas. I love and admire that about you, and you *should* be recognized for it. But public recognition is no longer something *I* wish for. I left the Bluestockings for a reason. The excitement of being known for my intellect was thrilling at first, but it was short-lived. I have come to prefer a quiet, undisturbed life." She smiled. "I am content with how things are."

I let out a long sigh and rested my head on her shoulder.

"Now," she said, pulling me nearer and laying her head on mine, "let us decide how to make you into Lady Sarah Donovan."

Chapter Thirty-Eight

PHINEAS

Being surrounded by my siblings for the past few days had been a simultaneous mercy and affliction. The differences between us—and they were numerous—seemed to have softened and become less important with the passage of time, smoothing the rougher corners separating us and dampening any conflict.

But the fact remained that Theo, Valentine, and Diana all retired at night to be with their spouses. When we sat in the drawing room after dinner, they flocked to one another. And despite all the laughter and general conviviality of the reunion we were having, for me, something was missing. Some*one* was missing.

Days after my letter to Cambridge, I received a response informing me that, at present, they were not at liberty to offer me a position. My inquiries into any potential parish positions had been similarly unfruitful, and a slowly building, simmering panic was beginning to set in. I could not trespass on Duke and Diana's kindness forever. Valentine had generously offered for me to come stay in their home whenever it suited me, but that was of necessity but a temporary answer. Soon Rebecca would enter her confinement, and I would only be an added burden.

It had been nearly a week since my departure from Bettencourt Court when Theo came into the library during my studies.

"May I?" He held a letter in his hand.

I smiled. "This is not my library, Theo. You have as much right to be here as I."

He chuckled and stepped inside, closing the door behind him. "I suppose you are right. But libraries have always felt like *your* domain. What are you studying?"

I shut the book I held, as though Theo would be able to tell immediately that my reading was as much sentimental as it was studious. "Sophocles."

"Ah," he said. "You were ever a lover of the Greek playwrights and poets."

It was true, of course, but *Ajax* had never been a favorite until Sarah.

He rested on the edge of the desk, looking at the letter in his hands. "I have a proposition for you, Phin."

I readjusted my spectacles, looking at him with as much interest as I could muster while inside I was feeling a measure of resignedness. If Theo offered for me to come stay with him and Elena, my beggardom would be complete. I was officially the charity case of the family.

"I have received a request to captain a voyage."

I kept my eyes on him, wondering if perhaps he would ask me to stay at home with Elena while he left. There were still a few months before her confinement, but perhaps this would be a long voyage. Though, after seeing them interact, it didn't seem at all like Theo to leave his wife at such a time. But I was hardly an expert on love.

"It is far less notice than I am usually given, but after talking with Elena, we have agreed that the trip is short enough—and lucrative enough—to merit serious consideration. We will still return in plenty of time for her confinement."

I nodded, not knowing what else was expected of me.

"I know you have never been terribly fond of sailing, Phin, but with such short notice, I am in dire need of men to accompany me. Given the situation you find yourself in, I wondered if you would consider joining me. I would pay you well for your troubles, for it is no small thing to have someone I trust by my side."

My heart sank. For so long, I had waited for my opportunity to leave the Navy, to put sailing behind me and pursue my own interests. Theo was asking me to return to it, and even if his intentions were kind and good, it couldn't help but drive home what a failure I had become.

"The commission is to Turkey—Athens, specifically. We would be in port for a fortnight—perhaps more."

"Athens?" A bit of my reluctance dissipated, and Theo smiled.

"I thought that might do the trick. In fact, I am counting on it. I assure you, I will give you the freedom to do as you wish during our time in port, provided you are there to help with the loading and unloading of cargo."

I tried to picture how it would be to walk the streets of Athens, to walk where Aristotle had walked, to climb the Acropolis, to see Hadrian's Library and study the poets in that ancient city. Perhaps, by my return, enough time would have passed, enough reflection could have been done, and enough connections made to pave a way for my future.

"When do you set sail?" I asked.

Theo clenched his teeth together. "We hope to leave within the week."

My brows shot up. *Very* short notice."

"Yes. I'm afraid the need is pressing. The sooner we can

leave and return, the less likely we are to have rough seas, for the season is changing. It is a time-sensitive opportunity, too. With most Mediterranean vessels returning to port for the autumn and winter, Athenian merchants are eager to sell off their goods at a lower price. And then, of course, there is the matter of returning before Elena's time draws too near."

I nodded, understanding his reasoning.

And while I wanted to see Athens, I knew a reluctance to leave. Perhaps it was some hope that I would receive news of Sarah. If so, it was certainly foolish, for the only news I would receive was of her engagement or marriage.

That was a point in favor of going with Theo. It would be better to be far away when the inevitable occurred. Hopefully, the pain of knowing what was occurring back at home would be mitigated by seeing what I had only read about. Nevermind that I would be living out Sarah's dream. She would find a way to achieve it. I had no doubt of that.

I let out a breath, setting my jaw. "I will come with you—if you truly wish for me."

Theo's mouth broke into a smile, and he clapped a hand on my shoulder. "Good man, Phin. I promise to be a reasonable captain. You may even bring your books aboard."

I smiled, for it was no small thing for him to allow it. Every bit of spare space would be needed for cargo.

If I was going to sail again, doing so with Theo would undoubtedly be the most pleasant experience possible.

"Taking your entire library, are you?"

I looked up from my trunk of books and pushed the spectacles higher on the bridge of my nose. Valentine rested a shoulder against the door frame, watching me with an odd glint in his eyes.

I chuckled. "If you think I can fit my entire collection of books into a trunk this size, you are sadly deceived."

"You are certainly traveling a number of books lighter than when I last helped you carry this trunk. Perhaps by the time you return from Athens, Rebecca will have forgiven you for leaving her novels at Bettencourt."

I raised a brow. "Rebecca shall forgive me? Or *you* shall?"

He inspected a spot on the wall. "I haven't any idea what you mean, brother."

I chuckled and looked down at the assortment of books, hoping the position of my head would conceal the way the reference to the novels—and to my leaving them with Sarah—affected me.

I would never know whether she had read my note—or comprehend why I had placed it precisely where I had. Perhaps she would never open the books again.

Other than those novels, though, I had chosen many of the same books that had traveled with me to Bettencourt Court. Of course, there was simply no prospect of me reading even the half of the books in this trunk during my journey, but evidently, I had become an optimist at some point, for I couldn't convince myself to leave any of them behind. It was surprising how often I felt guilt for neglecting an inanimate object like a book.

"Well," Valentine said, "perhaps you should make a bit more space in that trunk in case there are any other books you wish to take with you."

I glanced at him to ask him to explain his cryptic remark, but he was already gone.

I shook my head and sighed, for it was very like Valentine. Turning back to my trunk, I looked over its contents once again, wondering if perhaps he *was* right. Was I forgetting some critical piece of literature? Or did he mean I should make space for anything I wished to bring *home* from Athens? That was a valid point.

"I think you have neglected a few of the more important works."

I stilled, staring at my books, knowing that voice and, more importantly, knowing it was impossible for me to be hearing it. Silent, I blinked once. Twice. I reached for my spectacles.

"You needn't clean them."

Unable to bear it any longer, I turned to look.

Sarah smiled, her arms full of books. "May I?"

I couldn't seem to find my voice, but I nodded, still unconvinced what I was seeing was real.

But it *was* Sarah, from the glint of her blonde hair to the soft blue pelisse that brought out the color of her eyes so magnificently. And that hint of a smile…

She moved to set the books down, and I hurried to push myself up so that I could assist her.

Supporting the books in the crook of an arm, she used her other hand to stop me, and I lowered myself to the floor.

"Your history of helping me carry books is not encouraging," she said as she set them next to the trunk.

I laughed—a strange, choked sound, for my mind and heart were still unsure what to make of her presence. "You brought them back."

On the surface, my words might seem like a statement of the obvious, but there was a great deal hidden within them. For instance, the fact that she had come all this way quite unnecessarily. And then, too, that I had never *expected* her to return them; they had been a gift.

"I did." She smiled as though she was quite aware that what I had said was woefully deficient in comparison to what I had meant. "Do you mean to stay down there all day? Will you not shake hands with me?"

My mouth broke into a smile at the reference to *Sense and Sensibility*, and I rose to my feet. My mind was beginning to catch up to what was happening, making sense of things as well as it could, but there were plenty of gaps—things that had been neither proven nor disproven. It offered enough space for hope. Far *too* much space for it, in fact.

All I knew for certain was that Sarah was here and she had brought the books I had left. Beyond that, I could make no factual statements regarding her presence.

"You didn't need to bring them all this way," I said.

"What sort of reader would I be if I failed to return the books I had borrowed? People have been hunted down for less."

"But you did *not* borrow them," I pointed out, eager to find any holes in her logic—a result of that pesky hope I was trying to stifle. "I *gave* them to you."

"Yes, but according to your brother Valentine, they were not yours to give."

I could hardly counter that. Rebecca had never explicitly said she was giving rather than lending them to me. It was my fault for assuming the former.

"But you could not have known that," I argued. I was beginning to sound desperate. Perhaps because I was. I wanted her reasons for coming to be stronger than returning a few books. "What shall you do now?" Even to my own ears, my voice sounded painfully hopeful.

She lifted her shoulders. "Return home, I suppose."

"Oh." I swallowed. "Yes, of course." Was there a glint of mischief in her eyes?

She held my gaze, and I was nearly certain I saw it there. "Unless..."

"Unless?" I repeated, feeling the lift that word provided under the wings of my hope.

"There was one thing I had hoped you might help me with."

"Anything." I said it before I could stop myself. She smiled, and I cleared my throat. "That is, I am at your disposal, my lady."

"*Entirely* at my disposal?"

I swallowed and managed a nod.

"That is well, for it is a scientific question."

My skittering pulse thudded to a stop. "A scientific question…?"

She nodded. "When you taught George how to fly a paper dart, repeating the exercise was a vital part of the experiment, was it not?"

I blinked, casting my mind away from the intriguing routes it had been traveling and back to the afternoon I had spent throwing darts with Lord Danneville and, later, Sarah. "Yes. It was important to ensure that a previous flight by each dart was not simply a matter of fortune—a favorable wind or a bad throw. It demonstrated a pattern."

"A pattern." She took a step toward me. "That is precisely what I hope to establish."

"What sort of pattern?" I tried to keep my voice measured, but there was nothing measured about what was happening inside of me.

Her eyes scoured my face, running over my eyes, my cheeks, down to my lips. "A pattern of connection."

It was becoming impossible not to let my thoughts and feelings gallop down the road they had been insisting on following since she had appeared in the doorway.

Her hand went to my cravat, fiddling with it for a moment before shifting under my waistcoat and curling around the brace there. "It is a vital thing to establish, I think. A question needing to be explored."

The way my body responded to her touch, the way my mind craved her thoughts and my gaze lived for her smile—all of it told me and had been telling me for some time that a pattern of connection certainly existed, at least on my end.

But who was I to deprive her of the opportunity to explore the question for herself?

"I could never forgive myself if I stood in the way of the truth," I murmured, wrapping my hand around her waist.

She moved in closer, and her body pressed against mine, her lips brushing my cheek. "I did not come to return your books, Phineas," she whispered into my ear, sending a waterfall of chills down my neck and back. "I came for this."

Closing my eyes, I pulled away, but only enough that my mouth could find hers. Whatever answer Sarah received from this experiment, I would ensure she knew precisely where I stood and how I felt. Our lips melded together, our hands gripped and pulled, moving and exploring, testing and proving, until every doubt was laid to rest and every question provided with a resounding answer. Never had I treated testing a hypothesis with more dedication—or more bias, for I knew precisely what result I wished for, and I used every means available to me to ensure she received the same result.

When our mouths finally broke apart, we might as well have run from Bettencourt Court to Birchleigh Hall. Her head nestled into my neck, her chest rising and falling against mine.

"What are your findings?" she asked softly, breathlessly. "Have we established a pattern?"

I shut my eyes, breathing in the smell of her, then shook my head. "No."

The hand caressing my back stilled, and she pulled away to look at me, a hint of uncertainty in her eyes.

"Two times might be thought mere luck," I said. "We had better try again."

She bit her lip, trying to suppress a smile. And then she was kissing me again and I her, pressing against every limit of the hypothesis to ensure its soundness.

"What about now?" she finally asked. "A secure pattern?"

I shook my head again, and her aggravated expression made me laugh.

"It is true, though. Every time I kiss you is a unique experience." I caressed her cheek with my hand. "I feel new things, think new things. If there is any pattern, it is the consistent desire I have to repeat the experience."

She smiled and pulled me into an embrace. "Drat you for scaring me, Phineas."

I laughed softly in her ear and pressed my hands into her back to bring her closer. "And now that we have seen to the scientific question, will you explain to me what precisely we are doing—what *you* are doing here?"

"I had *hoped* you would ask me to marry you."

I shut my eyes, reveling in those words. "And your father?"

"Perhaps you could ask him yourself?"

I pulled back, looking at her to see if she was in earnest. "I betrayed him, Sarah. And I've just done so again."

She shook her head, touching her finger to the bit of hair dropping onto my forehead. "He likes you, Phineas. He merely needed time to accustom himself to the idea of... us. Mother has been vital in making that process happen more swiftly."

"And what does he say to your coming here?"

She smiled. "He was the one who accompanied me."

My eyes widened. Lord Bettencourt was here, knowing full well I wished to marry his daughter? "You are certain he will say yes?"

She laughed, tracing the rim of my spectacles. "I *am*. I have a notion Mother convinced him I might make another attempt to follow in Lady Hester Stanhope's footsteps. He finds you a much more palatable option."

"Well, *that* is not saying much, is it? But, Sarah, there is something I must tell you."

"What?"

I indicated my trunk. "It is being packed for a voyage with Theo. We are to leave the day after tomorrow."

There was no change in her expression, no hint of disappointment. Indeed, her smile only grew. "And I am coming with you."

"You are?"

She nodded, obviously pleased with herself.

"But... but how? How did you even *know* of the journey?"

She raised a brow.

"Diana," I said, and her smile was confirmation enough. I chuckled. "She is the answer to every such question."

"She and, in this case, Mr. Wilks. Did you know they were acquainted? She saw him at some dinner or other and together they concocted the idea for your brother Theo to captain Mr. Wilks's ship."

My brows shot up. Mr. Wilks, suitor of Sarah's, had commissioned Theo to charter his ship to Athens? The last I had known, Mr. Wilks meant to propose to Sarah. Now he was aiding and abetting *our* union?

She wrapped her arms around me. "It will be our own *Odyssey*."

"You hate *The Odyssey*."

"I hated *you*. Or rather, I wanted to hate you. In some ways, I still *do* hate you—for being so entirely and completely easy to love."

I couldn't help a laugh, while inside I was still reeling from this sudden good fortune. Surely, I did not deserve to be this happy. I could not even fathom it. "So, we are to make the journey together and marry when we return?"

"If you refuse to go downstairs and ask Father for permission, I suppose that is our only option! But I think you will find he holds the necessary license for us to marry before the ship leaves port—*if* you wish for that. Phineas! Where are you going?"

"To ask your father permission to marry you!" I called back to her.

Her hurried footsteps sounded, approaching quickly, and

with a grin that would split my face any second, I stopped, taking her hand in mine and pulling her in for a kiss at the top of the stairs.

Chapter Thirty-Nine

SARAH

It was not an ordinary wedding for an earl's daughter, for the small ceremony, performed by Mr. Vickers, was followed by something unique: a spontaneous performance of *Ajax*.

It was not, perhaps, the truest to the original play, for Sophocles' Athena and Odysseus had not, according to my memory, held hands or sneaked kisses when they thought no one was watching. Neither had Agamemnon or Menelaus—played by an exceedingly reluctant Valentine and a zealous Diana, respectively—struggled to remember their lines in the original.

But the audience, made up of Father, Mother, Admiral Donovan, Rebecca, Theo, and Elena, seemed not to mind. Indeed, they laughed at the mishaps, and they cheered mightily for George as he put heart, soul, and sharpened stick-sword into portraying Ajax. His performance included an impressive death scene in the fifth episode, only slightly marred by his returning to life enough to whisper corrections of the lines that followed.

The audience also pretended not to notice when Phineas and I missed entrances because we were too busy threading our fingers together or speaking of the future before us.

Tomorrow, we would set sail for Athens. We would walk those ancient streets together. We would study the poets side by side amidst the ruins of the places they had roamed.

I would not become Lady Sarah Danneville, unmarried woman of intellect, exerting power and influence at home and abroad. Instead, I would be Lady Sarah Donovan, married woman of intellect, exerting power and influence at home and abroad at the side of her husband, fellow seeker of truth.

And that was far, far better.

PHINEAS

BLACKWICK HALL, OCTOBER 1819

When all was said and done, only two carriages were required to make the journey from Dover to my childhood home, Blackwick Hall. Both carried multiple trunks strapped to the top and passengers within. Theo and Elena's carriage led the way, while Sarah and I followed closely behind.

Sarah's face was tanned, just as mine was—a combination of all the days at sea and the time we had spent exploring Athens in the heat. In Kent, however, the weather was gray and chilly, the clouds on the horizon portending rain. It was a welcome change.

Sarah peered through the carriage window, her hand clasped in mine and resting on my lap. "What a welcome we are to receive. Is that Valentine?" She leaned closer, squinting. "And Duke?"

She moved for me to see, and, sure enough, both were

standing on the steps of Blackwick, conversing as servants emerged from the house and formed a line.

The carriages slowed and finally stopped, the doors opening to allow us to descend. I put out a hand to assist Sarah down, smiling at Valentine and Duke.

Valentine wasn't looking at me, though. He was staring at the carriages, eyes wide with horror.

"Good heavens, Phin. We sent you off with two trunks. I remember quite vividly, for my back retains the effects of carrying one of them. Please tell me those"—he nodded at the ones strapped atop the last two carriages—"are not full of books."

"I will gladly tell you they are not," I replied, "for it is the truth. One of them still contains our clothing. But the rest of them *do* contain books."

"And they almost sank my ship," Theo joked.

"Nay, I reckon that was *my* fault," Elena said, a hand on her round stomach as she smiled. "At the rate this bairn is growin', we'll have another set of hands to carry Sarah and Phineas's trunks sooner than we think."

"Then there is no need of me here." Valentine turned on his heel toward the house, but Duke caught him by the arm.

"Not so fast," Duke said. "We agreed to bear this burden together."

"Books are a blessing, not a burden," Sarah chastised with a smile.

"Easy for *you* to say when you won't be the one carrying them," Valentine murmured as he rolled up his sleeves.

"It is not Phineas's fault," she said, "for they are *my* books."

I squeezed her hand. "Sarah discovered a few yet-untranslated works which she will be taking on the task of translating."

"As well as some for which the current translations are entirely unsatisfactory. Where are Diana and Rebecca?"

Duke looked at Valentine, eyebrows raised expectantly.

Valentine scrubbed a hand over his jaw, but the smile beneath couldn't be hidden. "Diana is attending to Rebecca inside. She gave birth to our baby girl a week ago."

The rest of us were struck momentarily speechless. And then Valentine was swarmed with embraces and congratulations.

"Rebecca is impatient to see you," Valentine said once he could breathe, "for in your absence, she managed to convince Duke and Diana to read her precious romances."

"It is true," Duke admitted. "The pressure was immense, and we too weak." He squared Theo and Elena with a significant gaze. "Beware, for you are her next targets. She is determined to hold family discussions, modeled after the ones Phin and Lady Sarah engaged in." He said it with an accusing glance at the two of us.

"What a lovely idea," Sarah said.

"Thrilling," Valentine said with heavy sarcasm.

"I take it ye dinna like them," Elena said.

"He pretends not to," Duke said, grasping Valentine by the shoulder. "But the fact that his daughter is named after Elizabeth Bennet should tell you what you need to know of his true feelings."

"There is no *pretending* necessary," Valentine said, wriggling from his hold. "And as for Elizabeth, it is a very sensible name and was even before *Pride and Prejudice*, as our former queen could tell you."

Sarah and I shared amused glances, and she winked at me before speaking. "It is a lovely name, certainly. As for these discussions, perhaps we could start with one focused upon whether Edmund Bertram is the most admirable of the author's heroes."

"Edmund Bertram?" Valentine spat. "That dimwitted little —" He stopped, evidently remembering himself and his declared dislike for the books. "That is, it hardly matters to me what subject you choose. Are we going to carry these trunks or not?"

Sarah helped Elena inside while the rest of us assisted the servants in carrying the trunks. I forbore telling Valentine that, when Sarah and I left in two weeks for Lord Bettencourt's smaller estate in Cambridgeshire, there would be an additional trunk. I could hardly leave behind the rest of my books at Blackwick, after all.

Once we were inside, Diana scurried down the stairs to greet us, full of her usual energy.

"Rebecca and the baby wish to see you as soon as possible, but you must absolutely change and clean up first." She shot us a look. "You will hardly recognize Father, Phin. He has become the most suffocatingly doting grandfather imaginable. If you attempt to even draw *near* to the baby in your dirt, he will have a fit. And as for Charlotte, well, you need only look at how full of toys the nursery is to see how he has been spoiling *her*. I am quite eager to return home, if truth be told. He is with Rebecca and the baby even now, so I cannot stay with you, for I mustn't leave her with him too long. Oh! This came for you a fortnight ago." She handed me a letter. "And this one for *you* three days ago." She handed another to Sarah. "Though I am quite agog with curiosity, I imagine you wish to read them in privacy, so I shall leave you be. For now." With a little smile, she left us in the entry hall.

"Mine is from George." Sarah grimaced. "His penmanship is atrocious—worse than it used to be, even."

I chuckled. "I think the mark of a man extends a *bit* further than his penmanship, my love."

"Happily for *you*."

I blinked, sincerely surprised and the smallest bit offended. I had always taken pride in my handwriting. "You disapprove of my penmanship?"

"No," she said with an impish look as she broke the seal on her letter. "If you must know, it was one of the things that first drew me to you." Her eyes ran over the contents of George's epistle. She smiled indulgently. "His new tutor cannot compare to you. No surprises there. He is more anxious than ever to go to Harrow. He apologizes for not properly appreciating either of us." She lowered the letter, looking up at me intently.

"What is it?"

"I have been thinking." I tugged gently on one of her golden curls. "I know, my love. You always are."

She chuckled softly. "I have been thinking of opening a school. Just a small one—small enough that we can tailor things to each student—each girl—just as you did with George." She looked at me, a hint of anxiety in her eyes. "I want to teach them more than accomplishments. In fact, I rather think I will have to employ someone to take on that task, for I should find it terribly boring. But I wish to teach them physics and philosophy, Greek and French. It would be unconventional, of course, and Father might dislike it at first, but… well, what do *you* think?"

I let my eyes roam over her face, overwhelmed for the thousandth time that I had the pleasure of calling this woman my wife. "I think," I said, taking her free hand in mine, "you will have the entire county begging you to take their daughters. I cannot imagine anyone better to take up such a project."

Her eyes bright with joy, she pulled me to her, pressing her lips to mine. She pulled away somewhat abruptly. "How selfish I am being! What of your letter?"

"What letter?" I hid it behind my back and went in for another kiss. She obliged, then reached behind my back, stealing it from me.

She broke the seal, then handed it to me.

"I like when you are selfish," I said, holding her eyes and taking it reluctantly. I unfolded it and let my eyes run over the words. "It is from your father." My heart stilled while my eyes read and reread the next sentences. "He has recommended me for an appointment as Regius Professor of Greek at Cambridge.

He says I should expect to shortly receive a letter from the Prince Regent." I glanced at Sarah, utterly shocked.

She smiled widely and took the letter, running her eyes over the words. "A deserving recommendation, my love. It puts me in quite a good humor with Father." She adjusted my spectacles. "And now, am I permitted to be selfish for a moment again, *Professor* Donovan?"

I answered without words, my wife in my arms, my family nearby, and my joy full.

THE END

Goodwill for the Gentleman (Belles of Christmas Book 2)

The Christmas Foundling (Belles of Christmas: Frost Fair Book 5)

The Highwayman's Letter (Sons of Somerset Book 5)

Of Lands High and Low

A Seaside Summer (Timeless Regency Collection)

The Road through Rushbury (Seasons of Change Book 1)

Eleanor: A Regency Romance

Acknowledgments

Every book is a labor of love, but this one has been a greater labor than most. That is true for not just me but my family and the friends who have closely supported me through the task of writing about two early 19th century intellectuals–a daunting task.

My husband supports me in every possible way, and I love him dearly for it. His support for me has been as thorough and genuine as Phineas's for Sarah. He's a true gem.

My kids typed–very slowly–some of the words in this book as they've begun to take greater interest in my work. I generously ascribe any typos to their "help."

To my critique group—Kasey, Jess, Deborah—you are my people, and your friendship is the best part of this gig by far!

To my beta readers—Mom, Heidi, Brooke, Kelsy, Heather, Michelle—thank you for reading the embarrassing first version of this and for making it better than it ever would have been without your careful eyes and feedback.

Thank you to my editor, Cassie Mae, for her efforts to make the book shine!

Thank you to Nancy Mayer for her astoundingly deep research and knowledge of the era.

Thank you to my Review Team for your help and cheer-leading in this rollercoaster of a business.

And thank you, finally and most importantly, to God, for blessing me with everything I have.

About the Author

Whitney Award-winning Martha Keyes was born, raised, and educated in Utah—a home she loves dearly but also dearly loves to escape to travel the world. She received a BA in French Studies and a Master of Public Health, both from Brigham Young University.

Her route to becoming an author has been full of twists and turns, but she's finally settled into something she loves. Research, daydreaming, and snacking have become full-time jobs, and she couldn't be happier about it. When she isn't writing, she is honing her photography skills, looking for travel deals, and spending time with her family. She is currently traveling the world full time with her husband and twin boys.

Printed in Great Britain
by Amazon

40402034R00179